KT-513-276

JAMES PATTERSON

THE HOUSE NEXT DOOR

WITH SUSAN DiLALLO, MAX DiLALLO
AND BRENDAN DuBOIS

CENTURY

1 3 5 7 9 10 8 6 4 2

Century
20 Vauxhall Bridge Road
London SW1V 2SA

Century is part of the Penguin Random House group of companies
whose address can be found at global.penguinrandomhouse.com.

Penguin
Random House
UK

The Witnesses first published as ebook by BookShots Digital in 2016
This edition published by Century in 2019

www.penguin.co.uk

A CIP catalogue record for this book is available from the British Library.

ISBN 9781529123906
ISBN 9781529123913 (trade paperback edition)

Printed and bound in Great Britain by Clays Ltd, Elcograf S.p.A.

Penguin Random House is committed to a sustainable future
for our business, our readers and our planet. This book is made from
Forest Stewardship Council® certified paper.

CONTENTS

THE HOUSE NEXT DOOR

JAMES PATTERSON

with SUSAN DiLALLO

PROLOGUE

"HURRY," I HEARD SOMEONE say. "He's losing a lot of blood."

Blood?

Stunned, I sat there for I don't know how long, listening to the whir of police sirens. Vaguely aware of flashing lights and a flurry of voices around me.

"Ma'am, can you hear me?" one of the voices asks. I squint and look up. It's a policeman, his face close to mine. He looks concerned. "Are you okay?"

I open my mouth to say something, but nothing comes out. I nod my head yes.

"Do you remember what happened?" the cop asks.

Do I? I'm not sure.

I remember being afraid. Very afraid. A scream. A crash. The screech of metal. And then—

Something is trickling down the front of my face. I taste blood. I lift my hand to brush it away, and a sharp pain rips across my elbow. I look down. A bump the size and color of a plum is throbbing there.

The cop calls out to an EMT guy. "She's conscious. But her arm looks kinda banged up."

Suddenly there is a commotion next to me. They have cracked open the door on the driver's side to get to the driver. More flashing lights. Another ambulance. More voices.

"Come look at this," someone says, and the cop crosses to the driver's side. They have lifted the driver out and put him on a gurney. Blood has seeped across his neck, down his shirt.

"He hit his head on the wheel?"

"That's what I thought, at first," says the EMT guy. "But look."

"Jesus," says the cop. "Is that . . . ?"

"Right," says the other man. "A bullet hole."

Suddenly, everything changes.

"Ma'am," the cop says, "I need you to step away from the car."

Cradling my arm, he helps me onto a gurney. As they wheel me over to an ambulance, I hear the crunch of broken glass. Then I see the second car, on its side, just to the left of mine. Half on, half off the road. The whole front side of it is smashed in. And slumped over the steering wheel . . .

I know that car. I know that driver! Slowly, bits and pieces of memories start to come back. A pop. A flash of light. And then it hits me: the horror of what I've done.

The two men I love—bruised, bleeding, dying—maybe dead?

And, dear God, *it's all my fault* . . .

CHAPTER 1

Six months earlier

YOU WANT TO KNOW the whole story? Let me start from the day when everything began to fall apart.

Just an ordinary school morning.

Joey is scrambling to finish his homework. Caroline is still asleep. Ben can't find his oboe. And my husband and I are arguing.

"This whole oboe thing is ridiculous," Ned says, gesturing with a piece of seven-grain toast. "The kid hates the oboe. He doesn't practice from one week to the next. And why he needs an oboe tutor..."

"So he can keep up with the other fourth-graders," I call out from the bottom of the hall closet, on my knees, searching.

"You're kidding, right?" Ned yells. But I know what he means. I've heard the school orchestra play. Even on a good day, it makes your teeth hurt.

Ben stands there, Pop-Tart in hand, watching as I push aside various snow boots.

"Would it kill you to help me look?" I say.

"Me? Why do I have to help?"

From the kitchen Ned shouts, "Because it's your damn oboe. You're the one who lost it."

"I left it right here on the hall table," Ben says. "Donna must've put it somewhere."

Donna is the cleaning lady who shows up on Mondays, cleans her little heart out, and for the next six days is systematically blamed for everything that's lost or broken. Poor Donna has had more things pinned on her than our local supermarket bulletin board.

I get up off my knees. Ned is standing next to me, still fuming. I know I have a choice: *Let It Go,* as Maggie, our couples therapist, has suggested, or *Push Back Gently.*

"Look. He's finally learning to play the scales properly," I say. Gently.

"And for that I pay seventy-five dollars a week?"

"Seventy-five dollars," I add, still in my gentlest voice, "is about *half* what you paid for the tie you're wearing. Which, incidentally, seems to have a small butter stain on it."

"What? Oh, for God's sake." Ned checks his reflection in our hall mirror. "I just got this tie. It's an Armani. Here," he says, carefully unknotting it from around his neck and draping it on the hall-closet doorknob. "Drop this at the dry cleaners, will you?"

He bolts up the stairs, two at a time, in search of another tie—then reappears and kisses me good-bye. His lips miss my cheek entirely. I wait to see if he notices that

I have chopped three inches off my hair since yesterday, and I've gone from Deep Chestnut to Honey Brown. He doesn't.

"Be home late again," he says, checking his reflection one last time in the hall mirror. "Asshole client meeting that doesn't start till six." Then he grabs his car keys and leaves.

We soon find the oboe, of course.

In the one place I'm never allowed to look.

CHAPTER 2

WELCOME TO BEN'S BEDROOM.

I am a Navy SEAL, cautiously making my way through enemy territory. I step carefully to avoid minefields.

No. Wait.

I am actually your basic forty-four-year-old suburban mom, cautiously making my way through piles of clothing scattered on the floor. It all needs washing, but I am under strict orders never to pick up anything I find lying there. This, as a result of accidentally laundering various dollar bills, student IDs, and cell phones left in pockets that I forgot to check.

A foot from Ben's trundle bed, I spot the corner of something leathery and brown peeking out from under an Imagine Dragons T-shirt. Sure enough, it's the oboe case. I lift it up, shake off some Cheez Doodle dust, and carry it downstairs.

Ben frowns and says, "Dad said I didn't have to go."

"He said no such thing. Now go get your backpack.

And where are your brother and sister? Joey! Caroline! It's eight twenty-five."

Caroline comes down the stairs, a vision of long blond hair and denim, holding her sixth-grade science project: a mock-up of the Mount St. Helens volcano, molded out of Play-Doh. She's only eleven. But with her blond curls and deep blue eyes, someday soon she's going to break some hearts.

Joey, age sixteen, appears on the top landing—high tops untied, hair gelled and standing straight up so that he resembles a hedgehog. He gallops down the stairs.

"Careful!" I say, as he zips past Caroline. "And would it kill you to carry that for your sister?"

"No! He'll tip it!" she says, hoisting the volcano high above her head.

"Fine. Whatever. Can we *just get going*?"

Then the usual mad scramble—lunch bags grabbed, jackets pulled from hooks, protein bars shoved into pockets, the three of them pushing through the front door and arguing over who gets the front seat. Another morning gotten through. I take out my keys and am about to lock up.

And that's when the phone rings.

CHAPTER 3

"**MAYBE THEY'RE CALLING TO** say it's a snow day," Ben says.

"In September?" I ask. But he has a point. When the phone rings that early in the morning, it's generally someone from the school phone chain with news of a weather day, an early closing, or—these days—a bomb threat.

I go back and answer it.

"Hello," says a male voice. "Is this Laura Sherman?" The voice is warm and friendly—two things I have no time for.

"Sorry. We're on the do-not-call list," I say.

I am about to hang up, when the voice gets more insistent.

"Laura, wait! Please. My name is Vince Kelso."

"Look, if you're running for office . . ."

"I'm your new neighbor. At thirty-seven Maple."

Thirty-seven Maple. The house next door. A total eyesore. The house had been vacant for quite a while. We were hoping someone would buy it and tear it down. But my friend Darcy, whose house is on the other side, said people moved in last week. She went over with brownies and rang the bell. No one answered. She left the brownies and a note asking them to call if they needed anything.

She never heard from them.

"My gosh. I owe you an apology," I say. "I've been meaning to stop by and bring over a plant or something and..."

"No problem," he says. "But I was wondering if I could ask a favor."

"Sure. I mean, I guess. Look, Mr. Kelso..."

"*Vince,*" he says. "Please. Call me Vince."

"*Vince.* I don't mean to be rude, but my kids are waiting in the car."

I look out the window to see if this is true. It is. Joey is in the front seat of our dusty Volvo wagon, practicing his best Justin Bieber pout in the rearview mirror. Ben and Caroline are in the back, arguing. As I watch, Ben hits Caroline over the head with his lunch bag. The bag breaks.

"I don't know a soul here. I was wondering if you could pick my son Vinny up after school today and take him to soccer practice."

"Today? Gee," I say, letting my eyes wander to our lawn. The grass needs cutting, and the garbagemen have left our big plastic garbage bins sprawled in the gutter. "Today's a little tough. See, Thursday's my busiest day. First there's my daughter's dance class. Then I have to get my son across town for his oboe lesson and..."

"I would never be asking," he continues "but my wife is suddenly quite ill. They had to take her away..."

"Oh. Gosh..."

"And you're my last hope."

"Me?"

I hear him take a deep breath. Then he says, quietly, "Honey, I'm all alone here...and I could really use a friend."

"Of course," I say.

"Swell," he says. Swell? Where is this guy from? The 1950s?

"I heard you were an angel," he says, sweetly. "I guess they were right."

Who's "they"? I want to ask. Certainly no one in my immediate family.

But he has already hung up.

CHAPTER 4

I LOCK THE FRONT door behind me and walk to my Volvo wagon. As I get closer to the car, I see Ben's peanut butter and jelly sandwich glued to the rear seat.

"Ben hit me with his lunch," Caroline says.

"It was her fault," Ben says. "She started it. She wouldn't move her stupid feet."

"Shut up," Caroline says.

"Hey! We don't use words like that," I say, pulling out of the driveway.

"Yes, we do," Joey says. "All the time."

"Well—we shouldn't," I say. So much for today's lesson in parenting. We drive past the post office, the Stop & Shop, the dry cleaners (*damn—I left Ned's tie hanging on the doorknob*). We drop Joey off at the high school. They are still arguing about whose foot belongs where.

But I'm lost in thought, wondering about the weird phone call.

"What do you guys know about Vinny Kelso?" I ask as we make a left onto the street that leads to the school.

"He's new," says Ben.

"Keep going. What's he like?"

"Nobody likes him."

"And why is that?" I ask. The crossing guard in a shiny yellow vest holds up a hand to let a bunch of students cross.

"He's a nerd. He reads all the time."

"Well, shame on him," I say. "How does he expect to make friends, with an attitude like that? No wonder everybody hates him. But I bet you've been kind to him. Right, Ben? Taken him under your wing. Shown him the ropes." I keep my eyes on the road, but I'm sure Ben is squirming in the back.

"Well...I heard his mother got sick," Ben says, desperate to change the subject.

"Really?"

"Yeah. Casey in my class said she heard two teachers talking."

"That must be pretty scary for Vinny. For all of them." Suddenly, my heart goes out to the Kelsos. New in town. Family emergency. No one to turn to.

"Why are you asking about him?" Ben asks.

"We're going to do his dad a favor today. We're driving Vinny to soccer."

"Oh, Ma. Please, no!" Ben says. A look of horror crosses his face. I get it: an unpopular, possibly uncool kid will be sitting next to him in our car. If anybody sees...Ben's a goner.

We are almost at the school parking lot. I swing the car

around and let them off in one mad rush of coats and science projects and lunch bags. The car gets very quiet all of a sudden. Then Ben, standing on the curb, taps on the window.

"Don't expect me to pay for your lunch," I say. "That's what you get for hitting your sister with a sandwich."

"No. I was just thinking: why did they ask us?"

"They didn't ask us. They asked *me*."

"Why didn't they ask Darcy? She lives next door to them, too."

"I dunno. Maybe they didn't like her brownies."

He shrugs and runs up the steps just as the bell rings. The heavy metal door slams behind him.

As I drive off, though, I realize the kid's got a point. Darcy left them a note, with her phone number on it.

So: why me?

CHAPTER 5

WHEN I GO BACK home to pick up Ned's tie, the dust balls meet me at the door. I know they've missed me, because they follow me from room to room. To kill time, I vacuum the whole house. Then I write a few checks. Then I empty the dishwasher.

I can put it off no longer. I've got to deal with Harry.

Harry, the *H* of H & M Cleaners, is standing behind the counter as I walk through the door. As always, he's frowning. He is a short, stubby man with deep lines in his face from intense scowling. Harry wears granny glasses that are always speckled with dirt.

"Hello," I say, pulling the butter-stained tie out of my bag.

"You'll have it Tuesday," he answers, curling the tie around his hand and dropping it on the counter. That's Harry's way of saying *Hello. Nice to see you again. How's the family?* Harry and my son Joey must be enrolled in the same charm school.

Harry punches a few numbers into his computer, prints a receipt, and peels it in half. I get the pink half.

"Can I have it tomorrow?"

"You want it tomorrow, you should have brought it in yesterday."

"But it only got stained *today*."

Harry shrugs. "So what do you want me to do?"

"I want you to have it tomorrow. Look," I say. Then I point to a huge faded sign that has been hanging there since 1967. "It says IN BY TEN, OUT BY THREE."

"Look yourself," he says. "It's ten fifteen."

"But today's only *Thursday*. What if I brought it in *tomorrow* before ten? Would I have it tomorrow by three?"

Harry shrugs. "I can't promise anything. Tomorrow is the weekend."

I get back in the car and slam the door. I'm annoyed at Harry, but just as annoyed at Ned, who insists I go to H & M Cleaners. I don't understand a lot of things Ned insists on. Mouthwashes that burn. Sitting in the first row of a movie theater. Then again, when we were dating and I accidentally got pregnant with Joey, another guy might've walked. But Ned insisted on marrying me. You've got to love a guy like that.

And I do. Most of the time.

Once Joey was born, Ned insisted we move to the suburbs. Overnight, I kissed my half-assed acting career good-bye. Okay. So my life isn't quite Shangri-la. But I can't complain (although I do, all the time, in couples therapy). I have a lot of laughs with the kids. Ned is a pretty good father. Life could be a lot worse.

And when I read all these stories about husbands who cheat and lie and put their family in harm's way—I know Ned would never do anything like that.

CHAPTER 6

"WELCOME TO BEST BUY, sir," the young salesman in the red T-shirt says, smiling as he greets the customer at the door. "Can I help you find something?"

"No thanks," Vince Kelso tells him, waving him off with his hand. He heads deeper into the store, toward the cell phone aisle.

Soon another salesman approaches—this one bald, with a bad case of acne.

"Just looking," Vince tells him. Vince wanders around until he sees exactly what he's looking for: a young salesgirl. She has long red hair and is standing by a cash register.

"I wonder if you could help me," he asks her.

"Sure, sir," she says. As he expected, she is sweet and perky—perhaps a trainee, determined to make a good impression.

"So many cell phones. What's an old guy like me to do?" he says. He shrugs helplessly and looks at the plastic name tag on the young girl's shirt. "Amber," he adds.

Amber looks him over. He doesn't seem that old—way younger than her father. She thinks he was probably cute as a teenager.

She gestures to the aisle behind them and begins the sales pitch they taught her in orientation. "Okay. So, a lot depends on how you're going to use it. So, like, if you surf the internet, or do a lot of texting…"

"Now, honey," he says, looking right into her eyes, leaning in so he's a lot closer to her. "Do I look like a guy who texts a lot?"

She blushes a little. It's sweet.

"No, sir—all I meant was…"

"Actually, I'm looking for one of those prepaid ones."

Her face lights up. "Oh. Like a disposable? Sure. Those are at the end, over there. They're pretty popular. The contract fees are much less, and you can…"

But he's already shaking his head.

"I'm a pretty simple guy, Amber. Don't even need a contract. I just want something I can use and then toss."

"Oh!" Amber says. "So, like, a burner. Here's the one most people go with." She reaches for a black phone in a blister pack, hanging on a hook.

"I'll tell you how good a saleswoman you are," he says. "I'm gonna take six of 'em." He pulls five more off the rack.

"Awesome," she says, all smiles. It's her biggest sale of the day. Maybe even her biggest sale ever. Vince turns one over, to see the price. He reaches into his pocket and pulls out a wallet. He peels off four fifty-dollar bills.

"I knew I could count on you, Amber," he says. "Why, I bet, if I come back here in ten years, you're gonna be running the place. Am I right?"

"Oh, I don't know about that," she says. She looks away shyly.

"One last thing," he says as he pockets the change. "I don't know this brand. Where do I find the phone number?"

"It's right inside," Amber says, cracking open one of the blister cases with the cash register key. "Let me show you." She pulls out an instruction manual. "Oh, look—you got a good one. 914-809-1414."

"914-809-1414. I like that," Vince says. "Easy to remember. Well, you take care now," he adds. "And remember what I said. Don't let me down."

"No, sir," she replies, smiling. "Have a nice day."

He winks, puts the phones and the instruction manual in his briefcase, and leaves without taking the receipt.

CHAPTER 7

THE TIME: 2:30 P.M., outside Copain Woods School. And it's starting. A snake pit of road rage as the SUVs line up, each driven by an impatient mom or dad, jockeying for position. I like to think of myself as an A-team player at this.

The minutes pass. Suddenly it's three o'clock. A bell rings. Doors open. Out spills a gaggle of students, grades one through eight. They scatter in all directions in search of a familiar car. Horns honk. Drivers shout names. Caroline spots me quickly and waves. Ben appears behind her. I pull closer to the curb and they both jump in.

"Where's Vinny?" I ask. My eyes search the crowd. Down at the end is a face I've never seen before. A boy leaning against the building. The kid wears a reddish-brown shirt the same color as the bricks.

"That's him," Ben says, pointing. Then he scoots down in his seat so none of the other middle school kids can see him. I pull closer to Vincent Kelso Junior and roll down the window.

"You must be Vinny," I say. "I'm Mrs. Sherman. Hop in."

Vinny walks slowly. Behind me, the honking grows louder.

"A little faster," I say sweetly. He has some trouble opening the door. *A nice kid,* I think. *But not too swift.*

"Perhaps you two can help?" I say. Ben, still crouched down out of sight, groans. He opens the door handle with his foot. Vinny slides in and fastens his seat belt.

I begin to pull out of the Circle of Doom. Once we're safely away from the school, Ben sits up straight.

"So how do you like Copain Woods?" I ask Vinny.

"It's okay, I guess," he says. I turn around and look at him. He's a little guy, a few inches smaller than Ben. He has thick brown hair and a nose the size of a small turnip. Cute kid.

"What's your favorite subject?" I ask.

"They're all okay." He shrugs and looks out the window.

"But I bet you really like soccer."

"I kind of did. In my old school."

"And where was that?" I ask. Suddenly, he looks frightened.

"I don't know. Pretty far from here."

"Oh," I say.

We pull up in front of the high school to pick up Joey. He's standing at the curb, checking something on his cell phone. He looks up and gives me his usual warm greeting.

"Did you bring my racquet?"

"It's in the back," I say.

"Where are my ballet shoes?" asks Caroline.

"On the floor in front with me. Next to the backup sneakers, water, snacks, and oboe. Am I missing anything?"

"Yeah," Ben says. "Mr. Wellman says I have to bring a pencil."

"Don't you have one? I bought you a few hundred before school started."

"All the erasers are chewed," he says with a shrug.

"He can have one of mine," says Caroline. She opens her backpack. Her pencils, like everything else about her, are perfect: impeccably sharpened and lined up like wooden soldiers in her Fancy Nancy pencil case.

"I don't want yours. Yours have cooties."

She gives him a dirty look. All three boys begin laughing as I gun the car around and head for the tennis court.

I pull into the Roger Raymond Recreation Center, a low, white cement building surrounded by willow trees. Joey jumps out and gets his racquet from the back.

"Next stop, soccer field."

Caroline makes a face. "But, Mom . . ."

"You can be a little late to ballet," I say. "Vinny needs to get there on time."

She stews quietly as I turn the car around and head back.

We drop Vinny at the playing field. The minute he's out of the car, Ben leans forward and grabs my seat.

"Why are you so nice to him?"

"His father is paying me a lot of money."

"Really?" he asks.

"No. *Jeez*. To think I gave up a promising career in theater for a chance to mold young minds, and this is how they turn out. Don't you remember the story of the Good Samaritan?"

"I thought that was just for muggings."

"You're hopeless. It's for anybody who's in trouble, who needs a helping hand. And that little boy..."

"He's in trouble?" Caroline asks.

"Well, I'm not sure. But...something's not right."

"Who cares," Ben says. He crosses his arms and sulks silently as I make my way through the afternoon to ballet and to oboe. After the drop-offs, I sit in my car and check my emails (*$350K in life insurance for as little as $153 a month!...Storm windows, 50% off!...5 Things You Should Watch Before They Expire From Netflix*). Then I head back to tennis, back to ballet, back to oboe, and back to soccer.

Vinny is waiting out in front, covered in mud from the knees down. He's got a big smile on his face.

"We won!" he yells. He jumps into the car and smears mud all over my upholstery. "Seven–zip."

And I shift into drive for the final leg of my Thursday journey.

We're going to Vinny's house.

CHAPTER 8

THIRTY-SEVEN MAPLE LANE. The house next door. A small gray house with a bay window.

Vinny jumps out with a quick wave and a polite "thank you." I park in my driveway and decide I'll walk over and introduce myself.

Two small ironstone flowerpots flank the front door. Each one holds a miniature pine tree that's turning brown. As I get close, I realize everything about the house is turning brown. Several gray clapboards are rotting on the corners. I am about to ring the bell when the door opens.

Vincent Kelso Senior is standing in front of me, smiling. He is wearing jeans, a light brown cashmere sweater the same color as his hair, and tasseled loafers.

He's in his mid- to late forties. Great smile. Great teeth.

"Laura," he says. He takes my hand and holds it briefly between both of his. His whole face relaxes. *Not a bad-looking face,* I think. And for a split second, I sense that he might be thinking the very same thing about me.

He keeps his sky-blue eyes locked on mine, except for one brief moment when they dart to the area where he thinks my breasts might be. But of course, they are so hidden under layers of sweatshirts and turtlenecks, he isn't even close.

"Thanks for doing this," he says. "I owe you, big-time."

"Glad I could help. You've got enough on your mind," I say. He looks confused.

"Your wife...?" I add.

"Oh, right," he says. "That sure made moving more complicated. Not knowing the town at all. Or where things are."

"I could put together a list for you," I say. "Local merchants. Plumbers. That sort of thing." *The sooner the better,* I think, as I let my eyes wander to the hallway behind him. Paint is peeling from the walls, and there is a huge brown water spot creeping across the ceiling.

"Oh, I couldn't ask you to go to that trouble."

"No trouble, really. It would give me something to do."

"Ah. A little bored out here, are we?"

"Is it that obvious?" I say.

"Let me guess," he says. "Like the comedian says: You feel like the whole world is a tuxedo. And you're a pair of brown shoes."

I laugh. "Exactly."

"Well, if you don't mind doing that list... I sure would appreciate it. Any local people I can trust. Or people to avoid."

"Harry at H & M Cleaners, for one," I say. "He's sort of

rude and abrasive. I just had a bit of a run-in with him myself."

"I'm sorry to hear that," he says, frowning. "A nice woman like you…"

"Yeah. Well. On the list of life's problems…"

I let the end of my sentence linger in the air.

"Vinny's a great kid," I say. "He really seemed to enjoy himself today."

"I'm glad," he says.

"And Coach Mike is always welcoming to new team members."

"I'll have to remember to thank him. What's his last name?"

"Janowicz," I say. "I'll add his contact info to the list."

"This is so kind of you," he says. "I sure got lucky to find an angel like you."

Angel. That's only the second time I've ever been called that. The first was him, this morning, on the phone.

He stares at me for a moment. He smiles.

"I've got to go," I say too quickly. "Gotta start dinner for the kids. I've got three. Ben's in the fourth grade. Joey's a junior in high school. And my daughter, Caroline. That's her out there now."

I point. Caroline is standing in front of our house, chatting with a neighbor who's walking her dog.

"She's lovely," Vince says. "I can see where she gets it from. What was the name of that dry cleaner again?"

"Harry. But don't tell him I sent you."

"Never," he says with great solemnity. He holds his

hand up as if he is about to swear on a Bible. I say good-bye. Then he closes the door and I stand there, not moving at all. It's after six, and getting dark, but everything seems a little brighter than when I first rang the doorbell.

CHAPTER 9

FRIDAY MORNING I WAKE up at six forty-five, stumble downstairs in my bathrobe, get out the mayo, and open two cans of tuna to fix sandwiches for the kids. Ned is already up and dressed and making impatient faces at the Nespresso machine. It's casual Friday, which means Ned has scrapped his usual Brioni suit for some J. Crew khakis and a J. Crew shirt. Tall, lanky, his thinning blond hair still swooping across his eyes, he looks the way he always does: handsome, but perpetually annoyed.

"Do you think Caroline looks like me?" I ask him.

"Don't be silly," he says. "She's blond. You're brunette."

I can see where she gets it from.

At seven fifteen, Ben walks into the kitchen.

"Have a good day, my man," Ned says to him. They pound knuckles as Ned leaves.

"Good morning, Sunshine," I say, cutting the crusts off Caroline's sandwich, putting tomato on Ben's, and smearing Joey's with salsa.

"What's today?" Ben asks as he takes a cereal box out of the kitchen cabinet.

"The fourteenth."

"Oh, no." He looks panicky.

"I thought you loved Fridays."

"Today's the day we're doing our Famous Artists presentation. I need to bring my van Gogh costume to school."

"What? Why did you wait till now to tell me?"

"I didn't. I brought home that paper for you to sign last week."

I check the refrigerator door—home to all notices, clippings, and other assorted reminders from my eternal to-do list. Sure enough, the Famous Artists Fact Sheet is there, right underneath a bill from the butcher. I freak a little bit.

"I don't even know what van Gogh looks like! Quick—let's google him."

Ben pulls out his cell phone. Before I can say "how-can-you-find-that-so-quickly-using-just-your-thumbs," he has pulled up a range of van Gogh self-portraits.

"Okay," I say, my eye on the clock. "He wore ascots a lot. Take your blazer to school. And we'll borrow a scarf from Dad."

I go to the hall closet. Ned's antique 1930s white silk scarf is hanging on a padded hanger.

I slide it out from the cellophane wrapper and hand it to Ben. "Make sure you bring it back. It's Dad's favorite."

"How do I tie it?"

"Like this." I drape it around his neck and make a simple loop.

"Now, what about the blood?"

"What blood?"

He rolls his eyes. "The blood from where he cut off his ear, remember?"

I find some gauze in our family first-aid kit. Then I dribble some red food coloring on it and wrap it around Ben's forehead.

"How do I look?" he asks.

"Like you've been in a train wreck," I say.

"Cool," he says with a smile, checking himself out on the selfie side of his cell phone. He puts the blazer, scarf, and gauze headpiece in a shopping bag.

As I finish making their sandwiches, my cell phone beeps. A text message.

I read it.

Thanks again for yesterday. If you need to reach me my number is 914-809-1414. Easy to remember.

CHAPTER 10

I DROP THE KIDS at school. But instead of heading home, I decide to visit my friend Darcy. First I stop at the Human Bean, our local Starbucks wannabe. I order a latte for me, a chai tea for her, a chocolate croissant, and an almond Danish.

On the way to Darcy's, I look in Vince's window. The house is dark. There's no car in front.

Of course. He must be at his wife's bedside.

Darcy is an artist—tall and red-haired, with a smattering of freckles across her face and wide green eyes. Darcy is quite beautiful. But she dresses like come-as-you-are day at Goodwill. So I am not surprised when she opens the door and I see her midsection is covered with hundreds of tiny blue dots.

"Let me guess," I say. "You're making wine from grapes. And you've been stomping them with your breasts."

"Not even close," she says. "I'm spatter-painting a deck chair. But I think I overdid it on the spatter. What's in the bag? Something rich and gooey, I hope."

We sit down at her oak kitchen table. She gets napkins, and I look around. The room is newly painted. It's an odd shade of pink. The color of tongue.

"You like it?" she asks. I lie and say I do.

"You certainly have a knack for this sort of thing," I say. "Maybe you can help our new neighbors get their place in shape."

"The Kelsos?" she asks. "I would...but I still haven't met them. Have you?"

"Just him," I say.

"I saw him once, at a distance," she says. "Saw the kid. Even saw the family cat, sitting on the windowsill—though it could have been a pillow. Never laid eyes on the wife, though."

I tell her about Vince's phone call, and about meeting him yesterday. She looks concerned.

"Hmmm. The whole thing's a little...creepy," she says.

"Creepy? How?"

"The place is a dump," she says. "What kind of family would move in there? Especially with a kid. I've seen the inside. It's like lead paint central."

"Maybe they're short on cash," I say. She frowns.

"So what's the father like?" she asks.

"Nice guy. Not bad to look at."

"How *not bad*?"

"Hmmm. All-American. Blue eyes. Interesting looking."

"Interesting like who?" she asks. "Channing Tatum... or Quasimodo?"

34

"Just sort of . . . preppy," I say.

"Preppy? In a house like *that?*"

I can see where she gets it from.

"Nice voice," I add.

"I bet," she says.

"What does that mean?"

"It means you're blushing."

"What? I am not," I say.

"Now don't go getting all huffy. This is *me* you're talking to. Tell the truth," she says, leaning forward, whispering as if we weren't alone. "Do you have feelings for this guy?"

"Darcy, I just met him yesterday! I've only seen him once."

"But obviously he's seen you," she says, licking chocolate off her fingertips.

"What do you mean?"

"I mean . . . it's just very odd that he asked you to pick up the kid. Why you? And where has his wife been hiding?"

I tell her what Ben heard his teachers discussing. A sudden illness. A middle-of-the-night ambulance.

"When was this?" she wants to know. "Monday? Tuesday? My bedroom faces the front. I would have heard something."

"I don't know. All he said was, they took her away."

"To United?"

United is our local hospital. It's where you go to have a sprained wrist bandaged, or a speck taken out of your eye. But for anything more serious, you go somewhere else. United's one claim to fame is that it's won the Hospital Gift Shop Award three years running.

"I don't know. He didn't say where she was."

"So, for all you know," she says, tossing the Human Bean bag into her recycling bin, "she could be lying in a ditch somewhere."

"Oh, come on..."

"No. *Listen.* You don't think it's strange—a new family in town, keeps to themselves, meets no one. Didn't even move in with any furniture, for God's sake."

"Is that true?"

"No moving van. No U-Haul."

"Well, now that you mention it..."

"One day the house is empty. Then boom, it's got tenants. No one meets the wife. Then suddenly, she's being spirited away in the middle of the night. I'm getting a weird vibe from the whole thing. Hey—can you hand me the Splenda?"

"What a wonderful imagination you have," I say.

"No, really. Think about it," she says, as she taps a few packets against her cup and tears them open. "And then, when they need a favor, do they ask the person who gave them her number and *asked* them to call? No!" she continues, pouring the Splenda into her tea. "This Vince guy goes out of his way to pick someone who didn't even know he was there."

Hell. I am soooo sorry I ever mentioned this to her.

"So, what do you think?" she asks.

"I think...you've been watching too many *X-Files*," I say. Darcy smiles her beautiful Irish smile.

"Maybe so," she says, waving half an almond Danish for emphasis. "But I don't think you've been watching enough of them."

CHAPTER 11

IT'S 6:00 P.M. BEN walks in the door as I'm making the salad dressing.

He has a big smile on his face.

"Hi, honey. How'd the presentation go?" I ask.

"Great. Everybody loved the bandage. They thought the blood looked cool."

"Good for you," I say. "Any mention of Mr. van Gogh's other achievements? His still lifes? His water lilies?"

"Oh. You mean his *paintings*. Yeah, I talked about them, too. But everybody liked the ear story best. Except— Mom, you're gonna kill me."

"Why?"

He rummages through his backpack and pulls out Ned's scarf. In the middle of it is a bright-red food-coloring stain, the size of an orange.

"Oh, no. Your father's going to kill *both* of us. I purposely gave you a plastic bag to put that in."

"I forgot," he says.

"Well, let's not tell Dad, okay?"

Just as I hear Ned's key in the door, the oven timer goes off.

"I'm home," Ned calls out. I grab some potholders and take the chicken out of the oven. A minute later, Ned walks into the kitchen.

"My car is due for an emissions inspection," he says, holding a letter from the state. "You can bring it in Monday, and I'll take yours to work."

"How will I pick up the kids without a car?"

"Wait there while it's being inspected," he says. He wanders over to the liquor cabinet and pours himself a bourbon. "What's new here? What's for dinner?"

"Chicken. Baked potatoes. String beans. And Caroline lost that ring we gave her for her birthday."

"Damnit, Laura," he says. "You let her wear it to school?"

I knew it was going to be my fault. I just didn't know how.

"I didn't 'let' her. She wanted to show it to her friends. Is that so terrible?"

"She lost it. So I'd have to say *yes*."

"And Joey got a sixty-two on his geometry midterm," I continue. I start to set the table.

"Not true," Joey says, suddenly appearing in the kitchen. "It was a sixty-three."

Ned looks at him and shakes his head.

"That's just great," Ned says. "Well, you can kiss any kind of tennis scholarship good-bye."

"It wasn't my fault! It's because the teacher hates me."

"That makes no difference in geometry," Ned says. "Your answers are either right or wrong."

"Should we get him a tutor?" I ask. Both of them stare at me. Wrong thing to say. I'm about to be blamed again.

"I got a better idea," Ned says. "Why limit ourselves to one. Let's hire a *bunch* of people. We'll build a little apartment over the garage. And they can all live here with us."

"He says the teacher picks on him," I say.

"And my boss picks on me. That's life. Get used to it," Ned says to him. "Y'know, if your mother didn't mollycoddle you so much..."

I put down the silverware.

This is starting to be a very unpleasant evening. And just when I think it can't get any worse...it does. Ned goes to pour himself another bourbon. That's when he sees the empty dry-cleaning bag hanging on the kitchen doorknob.

"Did Harry do that tie already?" he asks. Ben and I look at each other. I don't want to lie. But I know what will happen when I tell the truth.

"Not exactly," I say. "We had a little...accident."

That's when it all hits the fan.

"You used my *antique silk scarf*?"

(*Memo to self: Remember what your therapist said. You have control, as long as you stay calm...*)

"Well, it was last-minute, and..."

"Damnit, Laura," he says, slamming the bourbon bottle on the counter. "I ask *so little* of you! Of all of you!"

(*Stay cool*, I tell myself. *He's been under a lot of pressure at work this week. This month. This year...*)

"I bust my ass all day," he continues, yelling. "And when I come home, it's always chaos!"

"Well, I didn't think..."

"No, you didn't!" he says. "What else do you have to do all day, besides be on top of all this crap?"

What else? That's when I lose it.

"You mean, besides making lunches and dinners and dealing with teachers and waiting all day for the cable guy, like I did last week, who—by the way—never showed up?"

"Hah. You want to know what kind of week *I* had?" he says.

"No. I don't," I say. "Because whatever it was—it wasn't as annoying as wasting hours on hold with tech support, or picking out a birthday card for *your* mother—a woman you can't stand!"

"And that took you—what? All of five minutes?"

Okay. Now I'm *really* getting angry.

"Who do you think makes out the checks around here! And calls the insurance company! And does all the garbage that you're just too busy or important to do!"

I punctuate each of these by slamming a plate or a glass down on the table. The table shakes every time.

"Sure, I'll wait for your car on Monday. *You* pick up the kids. See how it feels to spend half your life in a crappy Volvo wagon that, by the way, is due for its eighty-thousand-mile checkup!"

At some point, Ben and Caroline have heard us arguing and wandered into the kitchen to see what's going on.

"See what you've done?" he asks, gesturing to the kids, who cower in a corner. "Are you finished?"

"I'm *never* finished!" I say. "It's called *keeping life to-gether*." I am yelling at this point. "Their life, and your life...and *mine*...*if you can call what I have here a life!*"

I pause. And then I do something I've never done before.

I scrape the chicken off the serving platter and dump it into the garbage.

All five of us stand there, stunned. Me included.

The kids go upstairs quietly. Ned wanders around with a hangdog look. Later, as I walk past him in the den, I see he's sprawled out on the sofa, watching a bunch of talking heads on TV and eating a bowl of Rice Krispies.

I head upstairs and read for a while. As I get ready for bed, I hear a *ping*. I check my cell phone. It's a text from Vince.

Linoleum buckling. Ants taking over the kitchen, he writes. He adds a frowning emoticon. Crappy night here. You?

Same, I write.

Need to run a few errands on Monday, he texts back. I could use some company. Interested? I smile. At least *one person* thinks I'm worth spending time with.

I do a couple of quick calculations in my head. I can drop the kids off, then bring Ned's car in and leave it there. Vince can pick me up at the Emissions Center. Two birds. One stone.

Sure, I write back.

I smile. Things have a way of working out.

CHAPTER 12

BY SATURDAY MORNING, I have cooled down. The kids are busy with friends, sports, TV, computer games, and their iPhones. Even Ned seems a bit contrite when I tell him I am going to take his scarf in. He offers to drive me to Harry's.

I say no. I'm still angry from last night.

I park across from Harry's. As usual, Harry is alone behind the cash register. When he sees me, he does something he's never done before: he comes out from behind the counter and opens the door for me.

"Hi, Harry. Listen. I was wondering if you could..."

"Mrs. Sherman! I have your tie ready. Crisp and clean. Like brand-new."

He reaches under the counter and pulls out Ned's tie, spot-free in a cellophane wrapper.

"You need it in a hurry, *I do it* in a hurry. Harry does his job!" he says. "You tell your friends."

"That's great. But I'm not here about the tie."

I pull the stained scarf out of Ben's shopping bag and hold it up for him.

He screams.

All the color drains out of his face. He puts his hands out in front of him, palms up, and slowly takes a step back.

"Blood?" he whispers.

"What? Oh, no," I reply with a laugh. "Food coloring."

"Don't worry. I'll get it out."

"You think you can? I've heard food coloring is a permanent stain."

"Is tomorrow okay?"

"Well, there's no rush, really. The weather's still warm, so I don't think he'll be needing it for a while. Besides," I add, "tomorrow is Sunday. You're closed Sunday."

"For you, I open."

"No, really. Monday is fine. Thanks. What do I owe you for the tie?"

"Nothing." He shakes his head.

"Nothing?"

"My way of saying sorry. Very sorry." For *what?* I want to ask. Being an asshole?

"Well, that's very nice of you. But really, it's not necessary."

"No, I insist. You leave it to me. I'll get this...this... *red*...out."

"Well, all right. Thank you again."

"And tell your friends," he says. "You make sure you tell them!"

I don't get it. Overnight, he's gone from a dybbuk to Miss Congeniality.

I pull out of my parking space and head home. As I pass Harry's window, I see him standing behind his counter, watching me.

CHAPTER 13

THE GUYS AT THE Emissions Center tell me I can have my car back in a couple of hours. As I get out and hand them the keys, I see Vince's car pull up in front.

He waves. I'm about to open the door and slide in, when he gets out of the car and opens it for me. He is wearing a gray sweater, chukka boots, and jeans. I laugh.

"What are you laughing about?"

"Nothing," I say.

A lie. I am thinking about what a friend of mine once said: If a man opens a car door for his wife, it's either a new car or a new wife.

"Thanks for coming along," he says. "We've got a dreary hour or two ahead of us. Think you can manage it?"

"I'll try," I say. But once we're on our way, the conversation comes easily.

"I thought you drove a Volvo," he says.

"I do. That was Ned's car. And he's..."

"...too busy to bring it in himself? Yeah. We men

are like that. My wife used to complain about the same thing."

I wonder if I should ask about his wife again. Well, of course I should. But I decide not to. Not yet.

"So what sort of errands are we running?" I ask.

"I need to see a few clients."

"What exactly do you do?" I ask. "I mean, for a living?"

"I sell medical supplies," he says.

"What kind?"

"Mostly ostomy products," he says "Colostomy bags, barrier strips, moldable rings. I'm a sales rep for a company that makes 'em."

I shrug. It sounds depressing. Then we talk about movies we've seen...rock groups we like...our kids... the high price of real estate (why they're renting instead of buying)...and where we grew up. (Me: Milburn, New Jersey. Him: Highwood, outside of Chicago.)

Our first stop is a pharmacy a few towns away. Then another one in the next town. I sit in the car and watch through the window. At both places, the scenario is the same: Vince goes in and talks to someone. There's a lot of hand shaking and head shaking. Then he gives them a card and leaves.

"Well, that's it," he says, getting back into the car.

That's it? I think. *Just those two stops?* That took all of twenty minutes.

"So...maybe we could grab a little lunch?" he asks. "That is...if you have the time."

Of course I have the time. He knows it. I know he

knows it. And he knows I know. Whatever little game he's playing . . . I decide I'm going to play, too.

"Well, there's some leftover tuna waiting for me in my refrigerator," I say.

"Do you think we could convince it to wait a little longer?"

I laugh. "Sure."

"I was thinking of La Lavande," he adds. Of course he was. La Lavande is the newest, chicest restaurant within fifty miles. I've been wanting to go there, but it's been totally booked. Some people wait months for a reservation.

I mention this to Vince.

"Yes," he says. "*Some* people."

CHAPTER 14

THE LA LAVANDE PARKING lot is filled with bumper-to-bumper BMWs and Mercedes and, every so often, a lone Porsche or Ferrari.

Inside, every table has a sprig of lavender in a small glass vase.

The maître d' seems to know Vince. They shake hands. He ushers us to a table in the back.

I excuse myself and go to the ladies' room.

I look in the mirror. *Not terrible,* I think. *Not terrible at all.* It took forever to get dressed this morning. I finally settled on my go-to outfit: a black cashmere sweater and black slacks. I like the look. It clings nicely to my backside, which sometimes seems too big, and it perfectly frames my breasts, which sometimes seem too small. But not today.

Did I mention a brand-new black push-up bra? *Victoria's Secret.* Mine, too.

I put on more lip gloss and comb my hair.

I smile at my reflection. Okay. So he really didn't need company for two short errands, and maybe this whole lunch thing was in the back of his mind all along. Is that so terrible? *I'm having a good time,* I think. I can't remember the last time I thought that. It isn't a date. But, damn, it sure feels like one. I'm nervous. I'm excited.

As I head back to my seat, Vince is studying a leather-bound wine list that's almost the size of the table. "I thought we could start with some wine. This is a nice little Médoc," he says, pointing out one of the wines. I take a look. All my eyes register is the name, "St. Julien," and the price, "$85."

"You up for it?" asks Vince.

"Sure," I say. This may be the first eighty-five-dollar bottle of wine I've ever had.

The waiter comes and takes our drink order. Soon he returns with a bottle and two wineglasses. He pours a taste for Vince. Vince takes a sip, swirls it around in his mouth, and nods. The waiter fills both our glasses.

"What shall we drink to?" I ask, lifting my glass. Vince shrugs and smiles sweetly, brushing a boyish lock of hair out of his eyes.

"To friendship. To autumn. And, of course, to you."

I feel my heart clutch. Then again, it could just be my stomach growling.

We clink glasses. I take a sip. Vince speaks.

"Actually, I wanted to talk to you about something."

I nod and nervously slide my wineglass on the table-cloth.

"Vinny had such a good time at soccer. I was wondering—do you think you could drive him there every week?"

Impossible, I think.

"Sure," I say. I can't say no. I don't *want* to say no.

"You're a peach," he says. We clink glasses again and I take another sip. The wine tastes warm and thick and gorgeous. I feel like I'm floating. I look around. The restaurant is fairly empty now; the lunch crowd has left. And the waiter is back with menus.

I order a quiche (*with apple-smoked Canadian bacon*) and a salad (*endive with toasted hazelnuts*).

"Very good, madam," the waiter says, with a small bow in my direction. "And for monsieur?"

"Hmmm," Vince says, studying the menu. "I was thinking about elk."

Say, what?

I look at the menu again. *Seared New England Elk Tenderloin with Parsnip Mousseline.*

"I've never seen anybody order elk before," I say.

"Well, you've probably never been with anybody born in Montana."

"I thought you grew up in Illinois."

A beat. "I did. After we moved from Montana."

For dessert we share *Praline Chicory Coffee Soufflé, Coffee Anglaise, and Warm Beignets.* He pours me another glass of Médoc. Every time I look up, Vince is looking at me and smiling. I tell myself he is just being friendly. Neighborly. Another glass of Médoc and I have almost talked myself into it.

"So why were you so down in the dumps Friday night?" he asks.

"You go first," I say.

"Okay. Vinny doesn't seem very happy at school."

And, of course, he misses his mother, I want to add. But I don't.

"It's a pretty jock-oriented place," I say, remembering what Ben said: *He's a nerd.* "And it takes a while to find your level."

"Yes," he says. "I don't know what I would have done if I hadn't found you..."

If I hadn't found you? The phrase has a hundred layers of meaning.

Vince continues. "I can't even meet other *men*," he says with a smirk. "They all work normal hours. Okay. Now it's your turn."

I think back to Friday night. Caroline's ring. Joey's test. Ned's scarf.

"Well—a bunch of things went wrong. And Ned's been in a pretty crappy mood lately," I begin.

"It's that seasonal affective disorder thing he suffers from."

How does he know that?

"A lot of men do," he adds quickly. "They miss the whole summer macho thing. You know. Golfing. Barbecues..."

"That's what we should do!" I say. "Ned loves to barbecue. And you can meet a couple of the neighbors. What do you think?"

"Well...if it's not a problem..."

"Not at all," I say, wondering if that's really true.

The waiter comes by, bows, and drops off the check.

Vince reaches in his pocket. He pulls out a stack of cash, neatly folded with a sterling silver money clip around it. He peels off two hundred-dollar bills. I must look surprised.

"I don't use credit cards," he says, and shrugs. "Cards are for people who don't have cash."

The waiter takes the money. Vince says, "No change, please." And then what I really hoped might happen, but that I also hoped would *not* happen...happens.

He moves his hand to my hand. He touches my fingertips with his fingertips. Then he turns one of my hands right-side up and studies the lines on it. Slowly, he traces them with his index finger.

"This is your *life* line," he says, running his finger along a line on the fleshy part of my hand. "See how it curves around your thumb? Means you're a rock. People count on you. I can believe that," he says.

He moves his finger up a bit. It tickles. I try not to giggle.

"Now this one here?" he says. "That's the *head* line. Yours splits in half. That says you're sensitive to others. Willing to listen to both sides. Is that the case?"

"I guess," I say.

"Now *this* one...the *heart* line..."

I hold my breath as he traces it slowly, back and forth. "Yours starts high, ends low."

"And that means...?"

He catches my eye and smiles.

"Lot of feelings and emotions under the surface, waiting to break free."

I try to think of something—anything—clever to say. I can't.

"You are a lovely woman," he says. He lets go of my hands.

"But now I guess it's time to let you get back to your life."

CHAPTER 15

MAGGIE'S OFFICE IS IN a gray cement building. I take the elevator up to the fourth floor and enter. The brass nameplate on the door says it all:

MAGGIE TRELEVEN, MSW,
ADOLESCENT AND FAMILY THERAPY

I'm a few minutes early. And it looks as if Ned is going to be late. I sit there and look around at the artwork on Maggie's walls. It is all modern, vague, brightly colored— swoops and swirls that cry out for interpretation. *Kind of like therapy itself,* I think.

Maggie opens her office door and sees that it's just me. "Why don't we give Ned a few more minutes," she says. I am still angry at him for our big blowout last week, but she's probably right: we are here to make peace. I nod.

Six minutes later Ned enters, looking frazzled. "Lot of traffic," he says.

I nod again and we enter Maggie's inner office. Maggie is in her late thirties, slim, pretty, with dark hair pulled back into a professional-looking bun. As usual, she is dressed simply but elegantly: a white silk blouse tucked into a navy pleated skirt.

Ned and I take our usual seats on opposite ends of her aqua sofa.

"So. How are things?" she asks, as if she's a neighbor who just happened to bump into us at the supermarket.

I say nothing. Ned shrugs and says, "Fine." Typical.

"We had a terrible fight last week," I start.

"Tell me about it," she says. And I do.

And then I tell her what happened just last night, when I suggested we invite a few friends over for a barbecue. "He practically bit my head off. He loves barbecuing," I say. "I thought he'd enjoy a chance to do it one more time, while we still have the weather for grilling."

But even as I say it, I'm wondering if it's true. Was I really doing it for Ned's benefit? Or was I just trying to be nice to Vince? The one person who's been nice to me. I keep this thought to myself.

"It struck me as a dumb idea," he says. "A waste of a Sunday. I work hard all week. Can't I have at least *one* day to myself?"

"You can have *every* day to yourself, for all I care," I say, feeling my blood boil.

"Do you really mean that?" Maggie asks.

Yes. No.

"Sometimes," I say.

It goes on like that for quite a while. Neither one of us thinks we get enough respect...enough understanding... enough attention. Maggie just listens.

"The fight, the barbecue idea..." Maggie finally says, her eyes darting between the two of us. "I wonder if those are just symptoms of something else."

Ned and I look at each other. Neither of us says anything.

"What's bothering you the most, Laura?'

I take a deep breath. Where to begin? "Well, I don't know why he..."

"No," Maggie interrupts. "Don't tell *me*. Tell *him*."

I swivel on the couch to face him.

"Okay. I don't know why you even bother coming home anymore, Ned. You're always in a bad mood."

"That's because..."

"I don't care why!"

Maggie stops me. "Let him finish."

"...because my job is making me crazy," he says. "Managing other people's money. Even the smallest mistake can mean millions. And now the place is talking about making cuts."

Maggie nods slowly, sympathetically. "That's a lot of pressure. Laura, do you agree?"

I shrug. Maggie speaks.

"No. Don't just shrug. Tell him."

"Okay. I'm sorry your work is so stressful." I take a deep breath. "But I *hate* how you take it out on me and the kids."

Maggie taps her index finger on her desk, as she always

does when she is about to make an important point. "I think it's important you hear that, Ned. Did you hear it?"

"Yes," he says. And then he does the one thing guaranteed to make me melt: He makes his cute little-boy face— pouty lips, eyes downcast, like he's been caught with his hand in the cookie jar. A face that's hard to hate.

"You're right," he says, quietly. "I have been...a dick. And I'm sorry."

Case closed. Sort of.

"And another thing," I say. "You always..."

"No." She stops me. "No more blaming. We go forward from now on. Both of you need to listen to the other, and then disagree in *positive* terms. We have to stop now," she says, looking at the clock behind us. "But I want you to remember the things we talked about today."

I schedule an appointment for the following week. Ned looks annoyed. Did he think this session was going to cure everything that's wrong with us? But in the car going home, he seems more relaxed.

"I guess I have been a bit of a jerk," he says. A bit? "Want to grab a bite before we head home?"

"Well, I told the kids..."

"Call and tell them to fend for themselves," he says.

"It's better if I text them," I say. "When I call, they don't pick up."

"Ain't that the truth," he says. We both laugh.

So we stop for a burger and beer at Shenanigan's, our favorite local haunt, then sit and talk till ten. It's like the old days—sort of. When we get home, I rummage through my dresser drawer and pull out something Ned gave me years ago—a lacy red negligee—instead of the ripped cotton "Go Huskies" nightshirt I usually sleep in. To my surprise and delight, Ned remembers. "Wow! You still have that?" he asks.

When I come out of the bathroom wearing it, he's waiting in bed with his arms crossed. He smiles. He whistles appreciatively. I crawl in beside him, and we begin to make love—slowly, carefully.

Is this what the women's magazines call makeup sex? If so, I'm all for it. For a while, I can blot out all thoughts of kids, chores, errands—even Vince.

CHAPTER 16

I'M IN THE SHOWER. Washing my hair, shaving my legs. Kiehl's coriander body wash. I'm going to smell nice and natural.

Today is my first official day as Vinny's soccer mom. I haven't seen or spoken to Vince since our lunch.

I step out of the shower. Then the distinctive *ping* of a text message on my cell.

From Vince comes this: I'm bringing snacks 4 team. C U soon.

A few minutes later Vince is at the front door. He's holding three shopping bags. And I'm wearing nothing but a bathrobe, admittedly the most modest bathrobe I could grab—a navy-blue terry cloth that Ned wears, when he bothers to wear one at all. And nothing underneath.

"Is that what you wear to pick up the kids?" Vince says with a very wide smile on his face.

I ignore his comment, and hope I'm not blushing. Then I say, "Those bags are the snacks? Are you feeding the team . . . or the whole school?"

"It's my salesman background," he says. "Get the prospect to smile, and you can sell them anything."

"And what exactly are you selling?" I ask.

"Quite honestly? *My son.* I want the other kids to like Vinny. So if it means bribing the team with fancy snacks and drinks . . . I'm down with that. How's your week been?"

I think about the makeup sex with Ned and look away. Great. It's bad enough that I feel guilty about Vince when I'm with Ned. Now I'm feeling guilty about Ned when I'm with Vince. The bathrobe doesn't help.

"My week was . . . not terrible," I say.

Vince says, "I'm going to put these bags in the trunk of your car."

"And I'm going to go get dressed," I say.

"Don't have to do that for me," Vince says, the same smile lighting his face.

"I'll be down in a minute."

When I return I'm wearing fairly baggy jeans and a fairly baggy T-shirt.

"I liked your other look better," Vince says.

"Gotta go," I say, ignoring his comment. "I don't want to make Vinny late."

Vince holds out his hand to me, as if to shake. But when his hand touches mine, his hold is gentle and there is no shaking.

"Listen . . ." he begins, and then it feels like he's changed his mind about whatever he planned on saying. He lets go of my hand and says, "We're really looking forward to the barbecue on Sunday. Anything I can bring?"

"Nope. Just yourself and Vinny." I pause. "Well—see you Sunday."

Then Vince says, "I've missed you."

I don't remember driving over the speed limit, but I make it to the school in record time. All four kids are waiting for me.

"My dad bought me the shoes and everything else I need," Vinny says, jumping in and tossing a lumpy gym bag onto the seat.

"Great," I say. "And your dad dropped off snacks for the team."

"I know," Vinny says. Then he adds good-naturedly, "He's trying to get the other kids to like me."

I drive my kids to oboe, ballet, and tennis. Then I swing around to the rec center. Coach Mike sees me pull in, waves, and comes running over. Mike is a sweet-heart—craggy-faced, built like a fireplug. And he's a great coach. He's been doing it for twenty-five years. Tough and demanding, but patient.

"Your dad called and said he's packed us up a feast," Mike says to Vinny. Vinny beams as Mike takes the three bags from the trunk and carries them over to the side-lines.

It's a beautiful autumn day and I've got some time to kill. So I park the car and head to the bleachers. Vinny sits on a bench, puts on his shoes, cleats, kneesocks, and shin guards. He is high-fiving two other teammates. I can't wait to tell Vince that his son is fitting in perfectly.

I whip out my cell phone and check my email. Every so

often, I glance up to see how Vinny is doing. He's trying hard to do the warm-up exercises, but he's always a beat or two behind. My heart goes out to him. It's clear he's not a natural-born athlete. But it's also clear that he's having a good time.

A half hour into the exercise routine, I decide to leave. At the same time Coach Mike decides it's time for refreshments. He blows a whistle, and the team runs over and starts rummaging around two bags.

Two bags?

"Where's the third bag?" I ask Mike as I pass him on my way to the car.

"What third bag?"

"There were three. Three bags."

He cocks his head and smirks. He makes a joke. "Maybe it *felt* like three!"

"No. I never lifted them. But I'm sure I saw Vinny's father put three bags in my car."

"Nope," he insists. "It was just two."

Am I going crazy? Maybe I'm wrong. Maybe my mind is playing tricks. Maybe...?

I don't know what another "maybe" could be. Oh, well. I guess I made a mistake. And yet...

I don't get to finish my thought. My phone beeps. It's a text from Joey.

Ur late!!! Where r u??? What's going on???

Yeah. What's going on?

CHAPTER 17

WHEN I WAKE UP Sunday morning, the sun is shining. *The perfect day for a barbecue,* I think.

But then I start to panic.

My mind is suddenly filled with a million what-ifs: What if Vince says something about our outing or about our lunch, which I never told Ned about? What if I slip and do or say something, and Ned realizes how I feel about Vince?

How do I feel about him?

On and on I go. I'm making myself crazy. I feel like a teenager again, self-conscious and awkward around boys. And I hate the feeling.

At two fifteen, everything is cooked, cooling, coming to room temperature, or marinating. I go upstairs to get dressed. Then there's another text from Vince: Positive you don't need anything?

Other than a Xanax, no.

Darcy and her husband, Jake, are the first to arrive.

She shows up carrying a hand-stenciled basket filled with flowers from her garden.

"So where's the guest of honor?" she asks.

"He'll be here," I say.

Darcy smiles and says, "I'm sure he will."

Coach Mike arrives next, carrying a case of Coors. Mike has been divorced for years. Should I have asked him if he wanted to bring a plus-one? Well, too late now.

Mike shakes hands with Jake and Darcy. He hasn't seen them since their son, Alex, graduated a few years ago.

"He likes Stanford?" Mike asks.

"Loves it," says Darcy.

Then I hear the gate open again. I take a deep breath.

Vinny runs onto the deck first. "Where's Ben?" he asks. I direct him down to the basement, where Ben and his video games are.

Then Vince appears. He looks like he just got out of the shower. His hair is wet and slicked back. He's wearing the typical suburban dad uniform: a yellow J. Crew tee, jeans, and Docksides. He's carrying a shopping bag.

"Everybody—this is Vince," I say. "Vince, this is Darcy and Jake, your neighbors on the other side. Mike: meet the man behind all those great snacks. And that's Ned over there—the guy bent over the grill." Ned waves.

"You're the lady who left those delicious brownies," Vince says to Darcy. "So sorry. I meant to send you a thank-you note but..."

"No worries," she says, with a ladylike brush of her

hand. "I'm sure you've had enough to do. How are you liking it here in our neck of the woods?"

They begin a conversation about real estate, shopping, traffic, kids, sports, Vinny, and schools. Ned is busy at the grill, and everybody seems nice and civil to everybody else. I breathe a sigh of relief. I'm about to excuse myself to go into the kitchen when Vince pulls something out of the shopping bag he's holding.

"Almost forgot," he says. He hands me two bottles of Médoc. "I brought you some of that wine you like."

My eyes dart over to Ned, hunched over the grill. Has he heard this? For a moment I imagine him outraged, incensed, seething with jealousy.

But no. Ned is happily fanning the barbecue fire, stirring the charcoal, and not paying attention to any of us.

Okay, I dodged one bullet. I excuse myself and go into the kitchen again to check on the pies. I'm there just a moment when I sense someone behind me. I turn around. It's Vince.

"I need a corkscrew," he says, waving one of the bottles. I turn away, furious at myself for blushing at the word "screw." I point to the drawer where the silverware is kept. "Ned seems like a great guy," he says. Why does he say that? All Ned did was wave.

"Yes, he is," I say. I don't know what else to add. Having him here in my kitchen is making me nervous. Fortunately, he seems to sense this. He heads back out, corkscrew in hand.

As I go outside with a second platter of hors d'oeuvres— sliced salami wrapped around cream cheese and chives, toasted mushroom puffs, a wedge of brie—I see the conversation has gotten around to what people do for a living. Darcy is talking about her artwork, her stenciling, her oil painting. Ned shares the pressures of being responsible for other people's money. Vince nods politely to all of them. Then Jake mentions that he's a cardiologist.

Suddenly, Vince leans forward in his chair, intrigued.

"I've never been to a cardiologist," he says. "And I suppose I should. My dad died of a heart attack when he was barely sixty."

"How long ago was that?" Jake asks.

"Oh—thirty years, give or take."

"Was that his first heart attack?" Jake asks.

"No. He suffered from angina. What I remember most is how he carried those little nitroglycerin tablets around with him and put one under his tongue any time he felt a tingle."

"They don't use them much anymore," Jake says.

"Do you think I should be—what? Checked? Tested?"

"That's always wise, with your family history. Give my office a call, first thing tomorrow. Tell my secretary I said to fit you in."

"Thanks. I'll do that," Vince says. His hair has dried in the sun at this point, and he looks...cute. That curl has fallen into his face as it usually does, and he keeps brushing it back with his fingers.

Like a nervous hummingbird, I dart back into the kitchen. As I'm putting some bowls in the sink, Darcy appears.

"So?" I ask. "What do you think?"

"Delicious," she says. I turn around and see she has taken a fork and dipped it into the potato salad.

"I meant, what do you think of *Vince*."

"I know you did," she says. Suddenly, she turns serious.

"Okay. He's charming. I'll give you that," she says. "But I still don't like it."

"Because...?"

"Because if I was lying in a hospital somewhere, I'd like to know my husband was missing me, or thinking of me, or feeling guilty that he's at a party without me."

Darcy frowns.

"And *not* charming the pants off his new neighbor."

I desperately need to change the subject.

"Jake seems quiet," I say. "Is everything okay with you guys?"

"With us—sure," she says. "But he's preoccupied. He's in the middle of a big malpractice suit."

"Oh, my God," I say.

"Some patient is suing. Claims Jake made a mistake in surgery, and now he can't work. Jake says it's all bull-shit. But until it's resolved, it's hanging over his head and he's a nervous wreck. Anyway, it's all kind of hush-hush. Frankly, I kind of wish he *would* tell someone about it, just to get it off his chest. He said he was gonna ask the guys' advice today."

I look out the kitchen window. Jake is talking. Vince and Mike listen, deep in thought.

"Looks like he's doing that now," I say.

Just then we hear Ned yell, "Dinner is served."

CHAPTER 18

WE'RE READY TO EAT. We all take our seats around the gray wood picnic table.

"To the end of summer," Ned says, holding up his glass. There's a lot of clinking, and I am beginning to relax inside. No cause for alarm after all.

As we finish eating, Joey appears on the deck. He says hi to Darcy, Jake, and Mike. I introduce him to Vince.

"Nice to meet you, son," Vince says, shaking his hand. "You're what now: a junior? How old are you?"

"Seventeen next week," Joey says.

"And he'll be going for his driver's license," Ned adds.

"Ah. The classic rite of passage," Vince says. "I remember when I first got mine. I was fifteen. Of course, the rules in Iowa were very different then."

Iowa?

He sees the surprised look on my face. "My grandparents owned a farm there," he says. "In those days, you could get a junior license at fifteen if you lived more than a mile from school."

"Hard to believe you're getting your license," Darcy says to Joey. "First time I met you, your mom was carrying you around in a Snugli."

"I bet you're pretty good with computers," Vince says. "Unlike us old folks."

"You bet," I say. "We think of him as our live-in IT guy."

"Y'know, Joey, if you've got the time, I could use some help setting up a new piece of software I just got. You familiar with Excel? Spreadsheets?"

"Sure," Joey says, circling around the table and filling his plate.

Why does this please me? Why does it make me nervous?

"That would be great. The company wants me to switch over from my old bookkeeping method, and I don't think I can master it on my own. I'd pay you, of course," he adds. "So you can start saving up for your own car."

"Cool," Joey says. He takes his plate and heads back inside.

"Perfect steaks, Ned," Mike says, sitting back in his chair.

"And great day for a barbecue," Jake adds.

"It *was*," Mike says. "But it looks like it's about to rain." Mike is right. The sky has turned a dark gray.

"Maybe we should head inside for dessert?" I say.

Just then, there's a crack of thunder and a few drops of rain. Then, suddenly, it's pouring. Hard silver drops slash against the deck. Ned runs around grabbing the cush-ions. Darcy, Jake, and Mike gather up the remaining plates and platters and bottles. I hold open the screen door as everyone rushes in and out. I get drenched in the process.

"I've got to close the windows upstairs," I say.

"I'll go with you," Vince says. Before I can protest, he's following me up the stairs, to the second floor.

By the time we get there, rain has already soaked a small part of the carpet. Vince moves quickly, slamming the windows shut in the hall bathroom, the boys' rooms, and Caroline's room.

Last stop: my bedroom.

We walk inside. He stands there for a moment, taking it all in: the lace curtains, the cream-colored duvet on the bed, the antique French mirror over the dressing table.

"Nice," he says. Nice? Does he mean the room? The af-ternoon? Being there with me? All of the above?

He looks around and sees my red lace nightgown hang-ing on the closet door. Then he looks at me and laughs.

"Well now," he says. "I guess I'll have to adjust my fan-tasies."

A small shiver passes through me.

Slowly, quietly, as if he has all the time in the world, he walks across the carpet and closes the window on my side of the bed. Then the one on Ned's side.

"A California king-size bed," he says. "You and Ned like that?"

"Yeah, most of the time," I say. "Sometimes it feels...I dunno...too big. A little..."

"Lonely?"

I say nothing. But Vince speaks.

"You don't know what lonely means until...you know...with my wife gone..."

There is a crackle of thunder behind him. Then a bolt of lightning that lights up the room. For a split second, he is backlit, a lone figure standing in the rain on the York-shire moors. He is Heathcliff.

And I am his Catherine.

He takes a step toward me. With a finger, he lifts my chin.

"Don't be afraid," he says, his eyes locked on mine. "You never have to be afraid of *me*."

He runs his hand through my hair. Then down my ear. And across my neck. He is tender. Oh, so very tender.

I freeze. Time stops. The moment seems to go on forever.

But then, with the back of his hand, he leans in and gently wipes a few raindrops off my cheek. I am relieved. Or heartbroken. Maybe a little of both.

Then we both head downstairs, as if nothing has happened.

CHAPTER 19

THE SHOP WAS CALLED Gussied Up. That was the first thing that annoyed Marlene.

Gussied Up sounded cute and fun. But the gowns they sold there were elegant and expensive—ridiculously expensive. Way more than what Marlene and her husband paid in rent.

The women who came in and tried them on and admired themselves in the store mirror rarely looked at the price tags. That annoyed Marlene, too. But she was in no position to say anything.

She needed a job. They needed the money.

When a man came into the store, Marlene and the other salesgirls were instructed to fawn over him. Offer a glass of champagne. Direct him to a chair where he could sit and watch his wife—girlfriend? mistress?—try on gowns and twirl for his amusement. Women with men always spent more, she was told.

And men alone spent the most.

So when Marlene sees the man walk in, she rushes to his side, picturing a big, juicy commission. He is nice-looking. Early forties, she guesses. Nice smile. He eyes a rack of fancy cocktail dresses.

"May I help you find something?" she asks.

"I'm looking for a gift for a lovely lady," he says. "I want her to know just how lovely . . . by getting her something special."

He is such a gentleman. Marlene sparks to him immediately.

"Were you thinking of a gown?" she asks.

"Probably not the best idea. I don't know her size."

"We have some lovely handbags and scarves," Marlene says, gesturing to a display against the wall. "Does she have a favorite designer?"

But the man is shaking his head. "I don't know. I don't know her that well."

He thinks for a moment.

"I have an idea," he says. "Why don't you show me the thing you like most in the store."

Marlene smiles. She knows exactly what she should show him.

She uses her key to open a glass counter, and pulls out a gold metal belt, studded with green and blue emerald-cut rhinestones, and decorated with sterling and gold filigree. "It's a one-of-a-kind Art Deco piece," she says.

She stretches it out on the counter. "It was custom-made for a very wealthy woman," she says, holding it up so he can get a closer look at the French pavé settings.

"Is it gold?" he asks.

"Pinchbeck," she says. "A kind of gold alloy invented in the eighteenth century. But the buckle part is eighteen karat. Magnificent, isn't it."

"Yes," the man says. He looks at the price tag. Marlene assumes he will flinch or decline graciously. He does neither.

"This is perfect," he says.

"Very good, sir."

"Please," he says. "Call me Vince."

"All right then... Vince," Marlene says. She clips the price tag off, then gently rolls the belt into a circle and wraps it in silver tissue paper.

To her shock, he reaches into his pocket and pays with cash. She has never seen that much cash before.

"Have you been working here long?" he asks, as she puts the belt in a large gold box.

She cuts off a long piece of gold and silver ribbon and begins to make a bow.

"No. Just a few months."

"I get it. Looking for something to do with your downtime."

She laughs. "Not quite. I needed..." She stops midsentence. She doesn't know how much to tell this man, but he seems so kind. "My husband has been ill for a while."

"Nothing serious, I hope." He frowns.

"Well—he's on disability. But..." She stops herself again. If the shop owner knew she was talking to a customer about herself, she wouldn't like it.

"Does he intend to go back to work?"

"Yes. Eventually," she says.

"But not until the lawsuit is settled."

Marlene snaps her head around. Suddenly, she feels very afraid.

"What...?!"

"I mean—that's what it's all about, isn't it, Marlene?" Vince continues.

How does he know her name?

"Your husband is a deadbeat. Always was. Even before the surgery. Missing days. Calling in sick a lot. One of those guys who's always looking for a free ride. Am I right?"

A chill goes through her. Who is this man? What does he want from her?

"You know," the man continues, "insurance companies are onto people like you. Filing false claims. Making false accusations. It really isn't right, how you can ruin a good doctor's life with just one little lie."

"No!" Marlene says, her voice starting to crack. "It's not like that! That surgeon made a mistake! My lawyer says..."

"Marlene. Please!" Vince holds up his hand. "Do not insult my intelligence by referring to that ambulance-chasing brother-in-law of yours as an attorney, when both of us know the truth."

She has finished wrapping the belt. She hands it to him. She is close to tears.

"What do you want?" she asks. She can barely get the words out.

"I want you to tell your husband to withdraw his case," he says.

"I don't think I..."

He leans in and grabs her wrist. She winces.

"Go home. Tell him a man came into the store and gave you a deal. A simple trade. He drops the case, and he gets to keep...the thing he loves most."

He is still holding on to her wrist. "That seems fair, doesn't it? I think you understand what I'm saying."

Marlene can hardly speak. She is shaking so much. She nods. He lets go of her wrist and turns to go.

"By the way," he says, turning back. "You can keep this, too." He hands her the wrapped package. "Consider it your very generous settlement."

He laughs. Then he walks out the door.

CHAPTER 20

IT'S BEEN OVER A week since the barbecue. Vince has written me several texts and emails.

Laura, I miss u.

Where r u?

Come on, girl. We have to talk.

Do we?

Not until I figure out what I want to say.

Yet I can't help checking my messages twenty times a day, to see how desperate he's getting. How much he misses me. How much he wants to see me again. I'm like a lovesick schoolgirl with her first crush. And it feels...well, exciting. Before Vince, most of my messages said things like "Teacher needs to see you."

Or "Working late 2nite. Asshole client."

Suddenly, I hear honking outside my door. It starts out slowly, then gets more insistent. Someone is leaning on a horn, full blast. What the hell...?

I go to the door, determined to yell at whoever is creating such a racket. I should have known. I see Vince's car. The honking stops.

Vince rolls down the window and waves. Shit.

I walk to his car, unsure of how to play this.

"Hey," I say. "What's up?"

He is not smiling. "You know," he says quietly, "I don't like to be ignored."

Something doesn't feel right. But then he laughs, and he's the old Vince again. The angry voice is just a tease.

"You're a tough lady to reach," he says, turning on the charm. "Didn't you get my messages?"

"Yes, but..."

"Look. I was a little out of line on Sunday, scurrying up the stairs like that. So if I said or did anything to upset you..."

"No, really. It's fine. I've just been so busy," I say.

Both of us know this is a lie. Busy with what? Broiling lamb chops and folding boxer shorts?

"I want to make it up to you," he says. "Get in."

"What? *Now*?" I am leaning on his car. I take a step back.

"I said get in." That tough-guy voice again.

"Really, you don't have to..."

"I've got a big surprise planned," he says.

"I can't now," I say. "I've got to pick up..." But he cuts me off.

"Taken care of," he says. "I called Darcy. She's gonna bring the kids home. So come on. No more excuses."

I just stand there.

"Scout's honor," he says holding up three fingers. "You're gonna love it. Trust me. Get in."

So I get in. Is this a good idea? I don't know. A second later I'm buckling my seat belt.

Vince turns and we drive through town.

"We need to talk," he says.

"About...?"

"About my wife," he says. He looks over at me as we pass a row of fancy Victorian gingerbread houses opposite a small park. My favorite part of town.

"Okay," I say. He parks the car and I follow him out. We sit on a park bench. He is staring off into space for quite a while. Then he turns toward me.

"The truth is, my wife left me. Walked out on Vinny and me, over a year ago. Decided she just didn't want to...be with us anymore."

He turns away and I see him wipe his eyes with the back of his hand.

I am stunned. I don't know what to say.

"She's living—I don't know. Somewhere in Florida, I think. We haven't heard from her since. It's been terrible for me and Vinny. I still have a hard time even talking about it."

"So she's not...?"

"Sick? In a rest home, somewhere? No," he says sadly. "That's what I tell people. But I wanted *you* to know the truth."

My heart is breaking for him. He's lonelier than I could ever imagine. A minute ago I thought I was being kidnapped. Now I just want to throw my arms around him and tell him it's all gonna be okay.

So I do.

We sit like that for a while, hugging each other, cheek to cheek. I smell his aftershave—something spicy. Patchouli, maybe. Or musk. He runs his hand across my back. Then up along the back of my neck. He whispers my name over and over again. "Oh, Laura . . ."

I want this moment to last forever. Is that all I want? I'm ashamed of what I am thinking. But he seems so very unhappy.

Then he pulls away.

"Well now," he says, taking a deep breath. "Now that that's out of the way—do you want to know where we're going?"

"You mean there's more to this car ride?"

"You think I spirited you away just to tell you that? We're going into the city," he says. We go back to the car and he makes a left turn onto the highway.

"New York City?" I ask.

"Unless you'd rather go to Cleveland." We both laugh.

"What's in New York?" I ask.

"Look in the glove compartment."

I pop it open. Next to the registration and manual is an envelope. I open it.

It's two center orchestra seats to *Hamilton*. Today's matinee. Starting at two.

"I know how you love acting, music, all that stuff," he says. "So I thought maybe this was something you might want to see."

Might? The show of the century? Is he kidding? Last month I asked Ned about getting tickets. His response? "At five hundred dollars a pop? I'd rather watch Netflix."

The show is thrilling and gorgeous and full of wonderful moments. And Vince seems to really enjoy it. He applauds loudly.

And at one point, during a touching moment, he reaches over and takes my hand. We look at each other and smile. Has any moment in my life ever felt this joyful, this peaceful?

I don't think so.

We chat about the show all the way home. He pulls into my driveway. I can see the kids through the living room window, sitting on the couch. Caroline is reading a book. Joey and Ben are watching *Game of Thrones*. Nobody seems to be missing me.

"This was a lovely afternoon," I say. "Thanks. And Vince..."

"Yes?"

"Thanks for leveling with me about your wife."

"Thanks for listening," he says. He leans over to my side and gives me a quick and gentle kiss on the cheek.

One of the mysteries of Vince: how can a kiss this chaste and friendly feel so...well...so incredibly hot?

I stand there for a moment as he drives off. Now it's back to the lamb chops and the boxer shorts.

I miss him already.

CHAPTER 21

NED AND I ARE supposed to meet at Maggie's. But at the last minute, he texts:

Meeting running late. Can't get away. Go w/o me.

Ordinarily, I would be pissed. But today I am glad for a private session.

I need to talk to her about Vince.

Maggie knows something's up. She sees it in my face, as I sit down. I want to tell her everything. But I don't know where to begin.

"See, there's this guy..." I say.

Damn. Bad enough I feel like a teenager. Now I'm starting to *sound* like one, too.

"This *man*. He's new in the neighborhood. I drive his son places. He's charming and funny and nice to me. And his wife walked out on him, a year ago..."

"Go on," she says.

"Do I have to spell it out? Ned has been a dick and I spend time with a nice man who seems genuinely fond of me. He says I'm his only friend."

Her eyebrows go up a bit on that line. But then they settle down again.

"And I think I'm falling in love with him."

"Tell me about it," she says.

Then the floodgates open. Every fear and feeling and fantasy of the last few weeks comes tumbling out.

As I ramble on, I know what Maggie's thinking: how could I possibly hope marriage counseling would work, when all along my heart was elsewhere?

But if Ned hadn't been acting so awful these past few months...

"So this is Ned's fault?" she asks.

"Well—sort of," I say. "What I like about Vince is it's all so *easy*. He really cares about me. We don't get bogged down in the awful stuff."

"Awful stuff, like...?"

"Oh, you know. Dentist appointments. Mortgage payments. Blaming each other for things the kids did."

"The stuff of life," she says.

"Well, yes..." I say. "But it's more than that. I mean— what do I do here, Maggie? Nothing's happened between us—yet. But would it be so terrible? I mean, yes, for the kids, if they ever found out. They would be devastated. And Ned—it would be awful for him. Maybe. I don't know anymore."

She doesn't say anything.

"Oh God, Maggie. Don't just sit there nodding. Tell me what to do here! I'm a wreck!"

"You want me to give you permission to have an affair," she says.

I say nothing.

"You know I can't do that," she says quietly, smoothing down the pleats of her skirt. "Only you can decide. But if we keep talking about it . . ."

"No!" I say. It comes out louder than I thought it would. "I am *so damn tired* of talking, and thinking about this, and slinking around behind Ned's back, and feeling guilty about what I want to happen, and being angry at Ned for . . . for . . ."

"For not being more like Vince?"

"For not *being* Vince. A nice simple guy who loves me and has a good time with me."

"Once a week."

Oh. Low blow.

"Okay," I say. "Once or twice a week. What are you saying? That Vince would turn into Ned if we were married? That that's how all marriages get, over time?"

"Laura, I didn't say that. I just asked . . ."

"Help me, Maggie. *Please!* I feel like my whole life has turned upside down, ever since I answered that phone call."

And then, all of a sudden, my cell phone rings.

I look at it, prepared to let it go. But it's not Ned or Vince or any of my friends.

It's Ben and Caroline's school.

"I have to take this," I say to Maggie. Damn. What has Ben done now? I bet he mouthed off to one of his teachers. Or maybe he failed something.

I press Talk.

"Mrs. Sherman?" I hear a voice say.

"Yes," I say. I'm prepared to hear the worst about my son.

"This is Principal Wallace's office. We need you to come to school. There seems to be a serious problem...with Caroline."

CHAPTER 22

WE ARE SITTING IN Principal Wallace's office. Evelyn Wallace is a heavyset woman with short curly hair. She wears navy suits a lot. Even on a good day, she could pass for a prison warden.

Principal Wallace is usually cheerful—just what you want in a person who spends her life around small children.

But today she is not smiling.

And neither are we.

"This is outrageous," I say. Ned nods.

"There's no way our daughter could be involved in something like this," he says.

Mrs. Wallace is holding a small plastic bag. In it are a bunch of pills.

"I understand your concern," she says. "But these were found in her backpack."

How dare Wallace suggest such a thing!

"That's impossible," I say. If I sound huffy or pissed, it's because I am.

She shakes the bag. The pills dance around.

"I don't know how they got there!" Caroline says. She is crying. She'd been sitting on the bench outside Wallace's office crying even before we arrived. Her face is bright red.

I lean in closer and study the bag in Wallace's hand.

"Hah! That's not even the kind of *bag* we use," I say. "I never buy the ones with zippers." Case closed. Or so I think.

"We have two witnesses," Principal Wallace says. "Your daughter accidentally dropped her backpack when she was getting up from her desk, and this bag fell out."

"It isn't mine!" Caroline says, still sobbing.

"A boy sitting next to her picked it up and handed it to the teacher," Mrs. Wallace says. "The teacher brought it to me."

Ned has been seething. Suddenly, he explodes.

"I want the name of that boy!" Ned yells. "And I want to talk to that teacher!"

Good. I want him to make a scene. I want him to yell and scream and show this woman how wrong she is. My little girl? My baby? The whole thing is preposterous.

"What kind of pills are they?" I ask.

"Ritalin," the principal says. "Twenty milligrams. I showed them to the school nurse."

"Then I'll speak to her as well!" Ned yells.

"Mr. Sherman," the principal says, in the kindly voice we're more used to. "I know children these days are under a lot of pressure to do well. And your Caroline has always been...a perfectionist. So it's easy to understand..."

"Let's get one thing straight," Ned says. "My daughter does not take drugs."

It's clear our protests are falling on deaf ears. Or, even worse, the ears of a person who has already made up her mind.

"There are many children in the school who require medication," she says. "But the protocol is for a parent to give the prescription bottle to the *nurse,* who then doles it out."

"I don't think you heard me, Mrs. Wallace," Ned says. His face is almost as red as Caroline's. "I said my daughter *does not take drugs!*"

There is a pause.

"Not that you're aware of," she says quietly.

That's when Ned loses it.

"What are you saying?" he says, jumping up suddenly. "That my daughter is a drug addict? That's she's selling these? Giving them away?"

I'm torn between wanting him to reach across the desk and slug her . . . and afraid he just might.

"Please, Mr. Sherman. I'm just saying . . ."

But there's no stopping him.

"If I get my lawyer on the phone, I can have you removed just like that!" He pounds his fist on her desk. "How *dare* you suggest that my daughter, a *goddamn eleven-year-old* . . ."

"Mr. Sherman! There are children around!" Mrs. Wallace says. She stands up. Now they are eye to eye. "I'm not suggesting anything! I'm only saying . . . we have a drug-free school! If Caroline needs Ritalin to focus . . ."

"They're not mine!" Caroline wails. "I don't know how they got there."

"Let's get out of here," I say. Ned takes Caroline's arm and leads her to the door. He turns toward Principal Wallace one last time.

"You will be hearing from my lawyer about this. I can promise you that!"

I follow him out the door. Caroline is still crying.

"Dad, I swear..."

"I know you didn't," he says. "This is all a terrible mistake. And if she dares put this on your permanent record..."

He walks us to my car without finishing his sentence. "I'll meet you at home," he says. "I've got to...take care of a couple things."

"You're not heading back to the office, are you?" I ask. "It's after four."

"Yes," he says. But then a moment later: "No." He turns and heads to his car.

I get in my car and Caroline gets in next to me. "Mom, those aren't mine. Honest." She's still sniffling.

"I know. Honey, I believe you." And I do believe her. Really.

But then whose are they?

CHAPTER 23

NO DOUBT ABOUT IT. Tonight will be a "Freezer Night."

After our meeting with the principal, I'm too wiped out to cook. So I open the freezer and throw together a meal made up of anything I can microwave.

It's a haphazard menu, even for us. Frozen pizza. Frozen Brown 'N Serve sausages. (Can you put breakfast sausages on a pizza? Well, I'll find out soon enough.) Fish sticks. Two dozen pigs in a blanket. And chunks of frozen cookie dough for dessert.

The kids don't care. And Ned doesn't, either. Neither one of us has the energy to make conversation at dinner. As the boys chat away, Caroline is quiet. Her face is still puffy from crying. I look over at Ned. He looks like I feel: totally spent. Worse than spent. *Squandered*.

Later on, when I go upstairs, Ned is already in bed reading. It's the first time we've been alone together since our meeting at the school. I can't stop thinking of how the principal looked at us. The expression on her face as she shook that bag.

"What are we gonna do?" I ask him.

"I don't know," he says. "I don't want to talk about it now."

I feel the fury rise up in me.

"Oh. And you think *I do*?"

He shrugs and goes back to his book.

"Damnit, Ned. This is important! What do you think is going on?"

He doesn't answer.

"I mean, do you think...there's any chance that she...?"

"No!" He says. He slams the book shut and turns to face me. "Jesus, Laura! She's practically a baby! *No way* she would have those pills in her backpack. Hell, the kid can barely swallow a Tylenol. No way she's taking drugs behind our back!"

"Well, then how come...?"

"Forget about it," he says. He goes back to his reading. Book open. Case closed.

Forget about it? Does he really think I can do that?

"Okay, then. What *do* you want to talk about?" I ask. "The weather? The situation in Iraq? *Game of Thrones*?"

If my life were a movie, a little animated red-devil character would jump onto my shoulder at this point and whisper in my ear: "Go ahead! Tell him about *Hamilton*! Tell him about *Vince*! Tell him...*everything*!"

But of course, I don't.

"I do have one piece of good news," he says. "That guy Vince came by my office this week."

Wait. Did I say my life was a movie? Wrong. Minute by minute, it's turning into an episode of *The Twilight Zone*.

"What did he want?" I ask. I can barely get the words out.

What I really want to ask is: Did he mention me? Did he tell you how we hugged? Did he tell you we held hands in the theater, or how he kissed me good-bye?

"He asked if I'd be willing to take him on as a client. You know. Handle some of his money."

"And you said . . . ?"

"Sure. Why not. A commission's a commission. So we're going to get together again next week and talk strategy. I need to find out his level of risk tolerance."

"When was this?" I ask.

"Wednesday."

"This *past* Wednesday?" The day Vince poured his heart out to me? The day the two of us went into the city?

"Yes," he says.

Fear, anxiety, and adrenaline are racing through my body. There's just one thing I can do to distract myself: start my Lamaze breathing.

Of course, it doesn't help me any more now than it did during childbirth.

Ned may be lying about this, I think. Or is he? Did Vince stop by before he picked me up? I can't ask Ned too many questions. He'll wonder why I'm asking.

Maybe Ned is wrong about the day. But if he isn't, why

didn't Vince tell me what he had done? He sends me ten, twelve texts a day. Why didn't he mention this in any of them?

One of them is lying to me. Maybe both of them are.

(*Memo to self: It's too bad you didn't pursue your acting career. Look how you're able to maintain a straight face when, inside, your entire life is falling apart.*)

Ned goes back to his book and reads a few more pages. He yawns. Soon he turns out his light. He's asleep in a matter of minutes.

Me? I know I'm going to be tossing and turning for hours.

CHAPTER 24

WHY ON EARTH DID I agree to this?

I know why. I thought it might clear my head to get away for a day.

Besides, it sounded lovely on paper. A bus ride into the city. An afternoon on the water. A picnic lunch at the Statue of Liberty.

Of course, I forgot about the downside: I would be chaperoning ten noisy, rambunctious second-graders on a class trip, a group that doesn't even include my own kids. A bunch of kids who delight in being annoying and ob-noxious, from the time we board the bus at school all the way down to Battery Park.

I brought a *Vogue* and a *Vanity Fair* to read on the bus. That's a laugh. I spend the entire ride breaking up fights. Making sure Dylan doesn't pick his nose — or, if he does, not to wipe it on Sophie. Getting vomit bags ready for Lacey, who gets carsick.

If I think a ride on the ferry will quiet them down, I am wrong. The water is rough. On the ride over, both Lacey *and* Tyler need vomit bags. Like an overtaxed mother hen, I get dizzy trying to keep an eye on my ten charges. They scatter between the benches and the rails. It's my job to make sure no one falls overboard.

And then I see the guy in the black suit.

He is sitting a few rows in front of me. A young man, mid-thirties, dressed like an undertaker. Black shoes, white shirt, black tie. He is wearing dark sunglasses and reading a newspaper.

The only person on the entire ferry who's completely alone.

Every so often, out of the corner of my eye, I see him move the paper to the side and look at me. The one time our eyes meet, he quickly turns away.

Call me crazy, but I could swear the guy is watching us. Watching *me*.

An admirer? A stalker? A pervert? This is New York. He could be all three. He is good-looking, if a bit bland. Certainly ten years younger than I am. So it's flattering. But odd.

Once the ferry docks at Liberty Island, he disappears in the crowd.

I help my group of kids off the boat and stand guard as they make bathroom visits. Mrs. Bolton, the teacher, announces that tickets to the top of the torch have been sold out for months. So we're only climbing as high as the pedestal.

This meets with a lot of groans, but I'm delighted. I'm carrying all their lunches. Two shopping bags filled with sandwiches, juice boxes, chips, and fruit, to lug up all the stairs.

When the photo taking is finished—a few New York harbor shots, and several hundred selfies—we head back down for lunch. Mrs. Bolton and I sit at a picnic table to eat. The kids prefer eating on the grass.

Then they line up for the final leg of our historical journey: a visit to the gift shop.

But as the kids make a beeline to all the Statue of Liberty green foam crowns, the rubber souvenir bracelets, and the *I* ♥ *Lady Liberty* T-shirts, I see him again: my Man in Black. Just standing there.

It's as if he's been waiting for me to show up.

Who is he? What does he want? Nothing to be afraid of, I tell myself. There are hundreds of people milling around. This is a public place.

Unless he's a sniper. Or a hit man. Or a terrorist.

Come on, Laura. Get a grip.

We board the ferry back. I look around and breathe a sigh of relief. My stalker is nowhere in sight. It's rush hour, so the bus ride back takes forever. Some of the kids start to doze off. The rest are tired, hot, and cranky. By the time we pull into the school parking lot, I'm feeling that way, too.

And then I see him again. In the school parking lot.

Same man. Same suit. Same sunglasses. Only this time, he's sitting in a parked Subaru in front of the school.

Okay. Now I'm really scared. Who is he? What's he doing in front of an elementary school at 6:00 p.m.?

And what do I do if he follows me home?

I don't give him a chance. Once the last kid is off the bus, I run into the school. I'm looking for someone who'll come with me, so I don't have to walk out alone.

I'm in luck. Mr. O'Brien, the gym teacher, is still there. He's over six feet tall, and a weight lifter. If anyone can protect me, he's the one.

But when we get outside, the man is gone.

Mr. O'Brien smiles and walks back inside. I jump in my car and lock the doors. Have I ever made it home in less time? I don't think so. Just to be sure I haven't been followed, I drive around the block a few times before pulling into my garage.

Who was he? I have no idea.

But something tells me he knows who I am.

CHAPTER 25

SAFETY VALVE. SAFETY NET. Safety first.

Every time Archie Monahan hears the word safety, he has to smile. A "safety" was what they called a condom back in the 1940s, when his father first opened Monahan Drugs.

Archie remembers all the young men who came in, asking to speak to his father. How they looked around nervously as his dad opened a drawer in the back. Then paid and left quickly, hoping they wouldn't bump into anyone they knew. How shocked his dad would be, Archie thinks, if he could see how things have changed. An entire shelf of condoms with names like Skyn, Rough Rider, and Pleasure Plus. Textured, ribbed, and studded. Some even glow in the dark.

And right next to them: Lubricants. Ovulation kits. Home sperm tests. Contraceptives. Vibrators.

Archie hears the front bell ring. That means a customer. He's prepared to give his usual welcome . . . when he sees who it is. He frowns.

"Hello again, Archie," says the man.

"Hello, Vince," Archie says.

The man extends his hand to shake. Archie ignores it.

"I was wondering if you've had a chance to think about the offer I made the last time we talked," Vince says. Archie makes a face.

"I thought about it. The answer is still no."

"Hmmm. Perhaps I didn't explain it well," says Vince. "What I'm promising is . . ."

"I know what you're promising," Archie says. "And I don't want any part of it."

Vince shrugs and wanders around the store. Archie stands and watches him. Vince picks up a tube of toothpaste and a bottle of avocado-scented shampoo. Then he circles back to the pharmacy counter to pay.

"You see, the thing is . . . I would understand your reluctance, under ordinary circumstances," Vince says to him. "Except, as of last month, your circumstances are anything but ordinary. Am I right?"

Stunned, Archie looks at him for a moment. Then he turns away.

"Sorry to hear about your boy," Vince says solemnly. "Damn shame, after all those commendation medals. A real hero he was, too. Where'd it happen? Afghanistan?"

"Iraq," Archie says. He practically spits out the word.

"Your son, God rest his soul, isn't around anymore to take over the store. And those two lovely grandchildren of yours— Luke and Justy? They're gonna need you, Archie. Now more than ever."

Archie says nothing. He just stands and stares. His eyes and his mind are somewhere far away.

"Stella can't handle them alone. Certainly not financially. And let's face it—business isn't what it used to be. Those big chain stores are killin' guys like you."

Archie has heard all this before. Slowly, he walks over to the phone.

"Forgive me, but you're not a young man anymore, Archie," Vince adds. "What's going to happen to all of them when you're gone?"

"I want you out of here," Archie says quietly. "I'm gonna count to three. If you're not out, I'm calling the police."

"And tell them what?" Vince laughs. "That a man came in and offered you a deal that'll put you on Easy Street? So you and Millie can travel, buy things for the grandkids, save for their college? Go ahead, Archie. Call them. And put the phone on speaker, so I can hear them laugh!"

Vince takes a step toward him. *Is he going to hit me?* Archie wonders. *No, he thinks.* People like Vince don't do that. They kill you with words, not fists.

Vince leans in closer, so they're almost eye to eye. "Let me ask you something," Vince says. "What would your dad have done, with an offer like this?"

"Don't you dare bring my father into this!" Archie is yelling now. "I'll have you know, my father was the most de-cent...honorable..."

"Easy, old man." Vince backs off a little. "All I meant was: Did he ever take a vacation? Buy a car that wasn't second-hand?"

"You know what my dad would do? He would toss you out on your ass!"

Vince shakes his head in disbelief.

"You're throwing away a golden opportunity," he says. He takes a few dollars out of his wallet and pays for the toothpaste and the shampoo. "Nobody has to know about it. It'll be our little secret. You'd be the silent partner here. I'm the one taking all the risks."

"Get out!" Archie says. He points to the door. His voice cracks.

Vince shakes his head in disbelief. He shrugs.

"I thought we could do this the easy way," Vince says. He heads to the door. "But if you're determined to make it hard for me..."

He leaves before he finishes the sentence.

CHAPTER 26

BY TUESDAY NIGHT, WE'RE already arguing about it.

"Nobody your age needs his own car," I say. "They won't even let you have one at school till you're a senior. So what's the big rush?"

"What will I drive when I go out with my friends?" he asks. "Not your crappy Volvo."

I resist the urge to tell him that he and his siblings are the ones who made it crappy. Sticky car seats. Potato chip crumbs. Muddy shoes.

"And Dad won't let me drive his new BMW," he says.

I am in the middle of sweeping. I stop. I put the broom down. I lean against a wall.

His new *what*?

"Uh, what makes you think Dad is getting a new BMW?" I ask.

"He told me," Joey says. "I asked if I could drive his car, and he said no, he's trading it in."

This can't be right. Ned is getting a new car? We just paid for an emissions checkup on the old one.

"So if I can't drive *your* cars," Joey says, smearing peanut butter on three slices of bread for his pre-dinner snack, "I guess I'll just have to use Vince's."

He sees the shock on my face. He misreads it as confusion.

"You know. *Vince.* The guy next door? He said when I got a license, I could use his car anytime I want."

"Uh, I don't think that's a good idea," I say. He stares at me, waiting for a reason. I say the first thing that comes into my mind. "I doubt his insurance would cover a second driver."

But Joey is already shaking his head.

"Chill, Mom. It does. I've been driving his car for a couple of weeks now," he says. "Helping him make deliveries."

(Note to self: that fluttering sound you hear is your whole life, spinning out of control…)

"I thought…you were helping him…with his computer," I say. It's getting hard to put together a cohesive sentence.

"Yeah. That took, like, an hour. But then he hired me to help with his business."

I'm still leaning against the kitchen wall, trying to process all this. Ned told me nothing about his new car. Vince told me nothing about Joey. And Joey—who usually tells me nothing, *ever*—spilled the beans about both of them.

I look at the clock. It's almost seven. Where the hell is Ned, when I desperately need to talk to him? How many asshole client meetings can one mid-level executive have?

When he walks in, he's in an unusually chipper mood.

"Hi," he says, all smiles. "Smells good. How was your day?"

I know I should wait. I know he likes to check the mail and pour himself a drink before he listens to my daily Family News Wrap-Up. But the anger is bubbling up inside me. I can't control myself. If I don't say something now, I'm going to explode.

"When do you get to pick up your new car?"

He freezes mid-pour. "How do you know about that?"

"Joey told me."

"I was going to surprise you," he says. He takes a sip of the bourbon. Then another.

"You were going to surprise *me*...with a new car for *you*?"

The irony of this seems to escape him.

"Wait'll you see it!" he says. He's like a kid in a candy store. "It's the five-twenty-eight-i sedan. Black sapphire. Mocha leather seats..."

I haven't seen him this happy in a long time. He goes on and on about enhanced Bluetooth, key memory, even a moon roof. And all I can think of is the years I've wasted clipping coupons.

"It's a beauty," he says. He is all smiles.

"And what does this little beauty cost?" I ask.

"Zero percent down," he says. Even *he* knows that this is not an answer.

"Ned—is this something we can afford?"

"I told you—I've got a new client. His portfolio is huge."

"Are you talking about...Vince?"

That's when it turns ugly.

"What do you care where the money comes from?" he yells. "Goddamnit, Laura. I make it all! I should be allowed to spend it the way I want!"

Bourbon in hand, he goes upstairs and slams the bedroom door.

Years ago, as a joke (sort of), I started making a list of all the things we fight about. Careless things (being out of stamps). Annoying things (his habit of leaving used dental floss on the bathroom sink). His mother. My brother. His drinking. My eating. On and on and on.

I thought we'd pretty much covered the gamut of things to argue about. But tonight, eighteen years into our marriage, there's a new one: a fifty-thousand-dollar car that I knew nothing about.

I am trying to sort this all out when the phone rings. It's Darcy. "Boy, I'm glad you called," I say. "I need to talk to you."

"Me first," she says. And then she shares a startling piece of news.

Coach Mike, our friend, our mainstay, our hero...has just been arrested for dealing drugs.

CHAPTER 27

THE NEXT MORNING, I text Vince.

Very upset. Must talk. Call when you can.

Seven minutes later, he rings my bell. He's holding flowers.

"You haven't been answering my texts again," he says. There is the beginning of a frown. "But see how quickly I answered yours?" Back to a smile. "May I come in?"

I take a quick look up and down the street to see if any of my neighbors are watching. There's no one around. Just me and the man I'm crazy about, standing on my doorstep.

And I'm crazy enough to let him in.

He hands me the bouquet. "Where did you get these?" I ask.

"Darcy's garden. I didn't think she'd mind."

He sits down on the couch. Do I sit there, too? He sees me hesitate. He pats the spot next to him and smiles.

I decide to sit on a chair. He shrugs. "Suit yourself," he says. "What's going on?"

I cut to the chase. "Exactly *when* did you go to see Ned?"

This startles him. "Why do you ask?"

"Was it this past Wednesday?"

He looks confused.

"Wednesday I was with *you*." He gives me his sweetest heart-melting smile. "Don't tell me you've forgotten *already*..."

But I'm in no mood for charm.

"Why didn't you tell me you were going to see him? And what's with you and Joey? Why are you driving my kid around, sneaking behind my back?"

"Whoa," he says, holding his hands up in front of him. "One thing at a time. About Joey: he wants to buy his own car. And I know you're not crazy about that idea. So yeah, he's working for me. But we decided not to mention anything about it for a while."

That makes sense. But I still don't like it.

"The Ned thing? Look: I know it hasn't been great between you two lately."

"You heard us arguing last night?"

"Honey—the truth? I hear you arguing a lot," he says. "I thought I could maybe do something to help. And I didn't tell you because... I wanted to surprise you."

Why the hell does everyone want to surprise me?

"Besides," he says, "I thought it was Ned's place to say something, not mine."

Good answer. Smooth answer. The guy should run for office. He's totally unflappable.

"I just thought, if I threw a little money his way, things might get easier for the two of you."

Okay. Now I'm angry. I get up quickly, holding the flowers.

"Laura—wait..."

"I need to put these in water," I say. I hurry to the kitchen to get a vase. Is that what this is all about? I'm some sort of...charity case?

"Get back here!" he calls out to me. And when I don't, he comes into the kitchen. I reach up to a shelf for a vase. He grabs my shoulders and turns me around to face him.

"Listen," he says.

"No. *You* listen!" I say. "You hijacked my family! I don't understand what's going on. Joey is even more distant. Ned has begun lying to me, for the first time ever. I can't deal with any of this." I start to pull away. "I want..." I hesitate.

"What?" he asks. "Tell me. Anything."

"I want my life to go back to the way it was! Before I met you!"

Suddenly I see fear in his eyes.

"You don't mean that," he says. "Please, don't say that. Don't do this to me."

And then he does something he's never done before. He pulls me toward him and kisses me on the lips. Slowly.

I whimper quietly. Or is that him? I'm not sure. I open my eyes. His eyes are still closed.

"Laura," he says, gently. "I've waited forever to do that." Great. Now, on the list of Vince's Positive Attributes, I can add one more: *Mind Reader*.

He takes my hand and leads me back to the living room. My heart is beating so fast, I'm having trouble breathing. I'm scared, because I don't know if I can trust him.

No. That's just part of it.

I'm scared because I've never been kissed like that by anybody, ever.

Not. In. My. Whole. Life.

A million thoughts are colliding in my brain, each more thrilling and terrifying than the next. And all of them are variations on the same theme: *Now what? Alone in My House, with Nowhere to Be Till Two Thirty*, I think. It sounds like the title of a country song.

And as he pulls me down to the couch, I think of another one: *I Want Him Out of My Life, But I Can't Stop Kissing Him.*

His fingers cup my face, stroke my neck. Then he gets more adventurous. His hand wanders down and fondles my breasts, and I let him. I think I am going to die of desire. We sit there for a while, making out (do they still use that expression?) like teenagers.

"Please don't go away," he whispers. He's practically pleading. "You're the best thing that ever happened to me."

"You should get out more," I say, trying to make him laugh. It doesn't work.

"Since I met you, I've felt more alive than I have in years," he says. "But if I'm hurting your marriage or causing you pain..."

"No," I say. Who am I kidding? He's the kindest, gentlest, loneliest man I ever met. I could never give him up. Not now.

His hand moves to my thigh, but I swat it away. Yes, I'm firing on all cylinders. And if my heart and my hormones had their way, I would give myself to him in an instant. Except—I can't. Not yet. Not until—

Until what? I don't know. Something is stopping me.

There are so many things I want to ask him—Why did his wife leave? Why, with all his money, is he renting such an old run-down place?—but I don't. I tell myself it's because I don't want to ruin the moment.

But maybe it's just that I don't want to know the truth.

CHAPTER 28

ANOTHER MONDAY. ALMOST HALLOWEEN, and today's to-do list reads like a scavenger hunt. A black cape, a blindfold, and a pair of nunchucks for Ben, who wants to go as a ninja. White face paint for Joey, who'll dress up as a ghoul. A silver headpiece, blue cape, and red tube dress and wristbands for Caroline. (She wanted to go as a cheerleader. I argued for Madame Curie. We finally compromised on Wonder Woman.)

As I'm pulling out of my garage, Darcy comes running over, waving her hands.

"Wait up!" she yells. "Great news!" I roll down my window. She's all smiles.

"They dropped the case!" she says. "I just spoke to Jake. That malpractice suit? Done, done, and done!"

"That's wonderful," I say. "What happened?"

She shrugs. "Nobody seems to know. Jake's lawyer got a call from the other lawyer. The guy just changed his mind."

"Just like *that*? I wonder why?"

"Who cares! Where you headed?" she asks.

"To the party store to buy Halloween costumes. Want to come?"

"Thanks, but no. I've got a celebratory dinner to plan."

"Well, congratulations," I say. This really is good news for them. The trial had been hanging over both their heads.

The party store is jammed, of course. A veritable wonderland of glitter, polyester, and hideous rubber masks. I am debating between two pairs of nunchucks (would Ben want plastic or polystyrene foam?) when my cell phone rings. A man identifies himself as Karl Wallace, an assistant pharmacist at Walgreens.

"I'm calling to let you know we've taken over all the prescriptions from Monahan's Drugs, now that it closed."

Monahan's is closed?

Monahan's has been a fixture in the community since...well, since forever. It still has the same dark wood paneling, the same old-fashioned wooden ladder that slides across the floor on little wheels. Even the same soda fountain and green leather stools since it first opened. When the kids were little, we used to take them to Monahan's every Sunday for ice cream cones. And now it's closed. The end of an era.

"Is Mr. Monahan retiring?" I ask.

"I don't know what his plans are," the new druggist says. "But we have all your family's prescriptions on file here, when you need them."

"Thanks for calling," I say.

Monahan's is located right on the main street in town. It's what's realtors would call Prime Retail Property. Once I finish at Party House, I decide to drive by and see if there's any indication of what the store is going to become. I hope it's not another bank. We could use a good restaurant in this town. A hip shoe store. Maybe even a Trader Joe's.

As I drive past Monahan's in search of a parking space, I see a sign on the door.

TO ALL MY VALUED CUSTOMERS it says, in big black letters. I am surprised to see that Archie has decorated the shop for Halloween. There's a huge spider web in the window, the entire height of the store. How odd that he would bother doing that if he was planning to close.

But as I get out of the car and get closer, I see it's not a decoration at all. The entire front window is completely cracked—shattered in the shape of a spider web, radiating out from the middle.

My eyes wander down. A chill goes through me.

Right in the very center is what looks like a bullet hole.

CHAPTER 29

REINHART, WILSON, AND SLADE *has its offices in one of those angular steel and glass buildings that looks like it might topple over at any moment.*

But inside, the financial services firm is as sturdy as a rock.

The company has two thousand employees worldwide and manages twenty-seven billion dollars in private money. Its offices are sleek, elegant... and very, very quiet. The thick beige wall-to-wall carpeting makes every noise as silent as a handshake.

Alice, the seventh-floor receptionist, makes it a point to remember every name and every face she comes in contact with.

But today, there's a new one.

"Welcome to RWS. How may I help you?" she asks.

"My name is Parker Paulsen," the man says. "I'm here to see Ned Sherman."

"Do you have an appointment?" Alice asks.

"No," he says. "But I don't want to impose on your good graces. If you could just point me in the direction of his office..."

"I'm afraid I can't do that, sir," she says. "We have strict rules about unescorted visitors."

"See, the thing is, I'm an old fraternity buddy. Ned and I haven't seen each other in, gosh, must be twenty years. I'm just in town for the day and wanted to surprise him."

Alice frowns. Cold-calling is against company policy. But this man looks—well, like a potential client. Nicely dressed. Oxford button-down shirt. Brooks Brothers tie and jacket. She's waffling.

"Take a look at this," he says. He pulls out an old photo of himself in his college days. The photo is dog-eared and worn. "That's me on the left—and there's Neddy," he says. He points to another young man in the picture.

Is that Ned, with hair down to his shoulders? He's wearing a baseball cap that says "Chicago Cubs." And she knows Ned went to Northwestern.

"Well . . . all right. Whom shall I tell him is calling?"

"Just say it's an old fraternity brother from Phi Ep."

She rings Ned, who picks up on the second ring.

"Mr. Sherman—one of your old fraternity buddies is here. He says he wants to surprise you."

Ned is intrigued. He knows a lot of his frat brothers have done very well over the years—better than he's done. Could it be Corky Ballentine? Nico Ross? Or that Parker guy—what was his last name again? All Ned remembers about him is that he was independently wealthy.

"I'll be right out," he says. You just never know where a new client might come from these days.

As Ned gets to reception, he sees the man has his back to the door.

As he gets closer, the man turns and comes rushing at him. He swallows Ned up in a bear hug.

"Ned Sherman!" he says. "You old son of a gun. Why, you haven't aged a day!"

Ned freezes. He turns pale. The man sees the shock registering on Ned's face. He looks at Alice.

"You see? I told you he'd be surprised! Well, c'mon man," he says to Ned. "Let's not just stand here. Take me to your office. We've got a lot of catching up to do!"

Ned looks around. The security guard is nowhere in sight. But even if he was...

They walk down the hall to Ned's office. Ned is sweating. What is Vince doing here? What does he want? Up till now he's been able to keep his dealings with Vince separate from his professional life. But now...

Ned walks into his office. Vince follows and shuts the door behind them.

"Listen," Ned says in a loud whisper. "You can't just waltz in here like this."

"Oh, no?" Vince asks. "I already did!"

He lunges at Ned and grabs him by the throat, spinning him around till he has him in a powerful choke hold. Ned begins gasping for air. He can't breathe. And he can't scream—but even if he could, should he? That would bring people in, asking questions. And that's the last thing he needs.

"I got your message," Vince tells him, tightening his grip on Ned's neck. "But I gotta tell you: It's too late. Nobody walks away from me. You got that?"

Ned tries to answer him. He can't. His head is wedged tight between Vince's arm and his body.

"You're in too deep, my friend. And there's no going back. Understand?"

Ned starts to nod yes . . . but Vince is closing off his windpipe. Ned feels himself start to faint.

Then just as quickly, Vince lets go. Ned begins to sputter. Is he going to throw up? God, he hopes not. He knows his face is red.

Vince takes out a pocket comb and begins combing Ned's hair back in place.

"So don't go getting any fancy ideas. Y'hear? I need to know I can count on you. You're like my right ball. And Ned . . ."

"What?"

"Whatever crap you're using on your hair," Vince says, looking at his comb in disgust, "get rid of it. It's way too greasy."

CHAPTER 30

I AM TRYING TO make sense of all the changes in my little suburban world. But the more I try to sort it out, the harder it gets.

A beloved coach, arrested. A bullet hole in Monahan's window. Ned's secret slush fund. A bunch of random things, happening all at once, totally unconnected.

Or are they?

So I start doing what I usually do when I need to keep my body as busy as my mind: I clean. With a vengeance.

Armed with a spray can of Pledge, Windex, a few dust rags, and a half gallon of Mr. Clean, I slowly make my way around the house. As all the how-to-clean manuals advise, I start at the top (mirrors, picture frames) and work my way down (tabletops, kitchen counter) till I get to the bottom (rugs, floors).

Next, the kids' rooms upstairs. Now I really have my work cut out for me. All three of them are slobs. I tackle Joey's room first. It's a jungle of clothes, electronic gear, sports equipment, and leftover food, surrounded by posters of various rock groups—all of whom look like serial killers. I strip the bed and use lemon-scented polish on his dresser. At least part of the room will smell good.

On a whim, I start to organize his closet. Starting at the top, I pull down a shelf's worth of T-shirts and fold them, then straighten out the clothes on hangers. The bottom of his closet is filled with sneakers, tossed in a heap. Like a good mother, I pull them out to sort them into pairs. That's when I see the bag tucked way in the back.

Like a not-so-good mother, I open it and look inside.

The bag is filled with pills. There must be thirty bottles in all. All of them have labels hand-written in pencil. Some names I recognize: Percocet. Oxycodone. Some are just initials: R2. G. C. Big O.

My first thought: *These are all candy pills.* The kind that used to come in Fisher-Price medical kits, when the kids were young.

My second thought: *Who am I kidding?* These pills are real, all right.

But what are they doing in Joey's closet?

There's got to be a logical explanation. Joey's a good kid. Maybe he doesn't even know they're there. It's possible, right?

Oh, please, God, tell me it's possible...

I collapse on his desk chair, pushing aside all the clothes on it...and all thoughts of what this could mean.

Suddenly, Joey walks in the room. He sees me holding the bag.

"Where did you get these?" I ask.

"What are you doing in my room?"

"These are dangerous drugs, Joey. Who gave them to you?"

"Who gave you permission to go through my things?"

"Did Coach Mike give you these?"

He snickers. He throws his backpack on the bed, turns to me, throws his head back, and starts to laugh.

"Don't be ridiculous," he says. "*I* gave them to *him*."

I am suddenly terrified of the tall, lanky teenager standing in front of me. My firstborn. My baby. When he was an infant I tied a red ribbon to his stroller—an old superstition to ward off evil spirits. I guess it worked for seventeen years.

But now . . .

There's so much I want to say. So much I need to ask. But all I can manage to blurt out is the dumb threat I used when they were little. "Just wait till your father gets home!"

And then I hear it again. That mean, awful, evil laugh.

"Yeah. *Ask Dad,*" Joey says. "He'll tell you aaall about it."

Does Ned know about this? Is he somehow involved? Oh God. The money for the new car! Suddenly, it all begins to make sense.

I've got to call Ned. Now. No. I can't. I have to wait till he gets home so we can deal with this in person.

But I've got to talk to someone . . .

Of course. *Vince.* He'll know what to do. How to make sense of all of this.

I text him. He doesn't answer. I text him again a few minutes later. Still no response. So I dial his number. He doesn't pick up.

I'm about to leave a message when I get a better idea: Go to him. Sit on his doorstep until he gets home.

This time, I don't care how many neighbors might be watching.

CHAPTER 31

I RUN TO VINCE'S house and ring the bell. Nobody answers. Maybe he's in the back, I think. Or in his garden. Not gardening, of course. Pulling up weeds? Well, it's possible.

I go to the back. He's not there, either. And I can't tell if his car is in his garage.

I peer in his windows to see if I can spot him. No luck. I even yell his name. Nothing.

I'm desperate. I've got to talk to someone. So I cut across Vince's backyard to Darcy's.

Just as I am about to ring her bell, I see a caravan of police cars heading my way.

Oh God — they're coming to arrest Joey!

But as I run back home, I see the cars have stopped in front of Darcy's house. *Good,* I think. *They got the address wrong.* This will buy Joey and me a little time to figure out what to do next.

And what *should* we do?

Do I help him escape? Does he turn himself in?

Inside the house, I call Joey's name. No answer. Did he see the caravan? Is he gone already? I go to my living room window and look out. A dozen policemen are standing on Darcy's front lawn, as well as two men in business suits. One of them holds a bullhorn and talks into it. I can't hear what he's saying, but I see Darcy's door open. Several cops rush in. A few minutes later, they come out again. But they're not alone.

They've got Darcy's husband, Jake, in handcuffs!

As they push him into one of the squad cars, Darcy runs out of her house, yelling. She jumps into her car to follow them. Then one by one, all the cars drive away.

All except one.

The door to that car opens, and a man gets out. I feel myself break out in a cold sweat. I know that walk, that suit. It's my Man in Black. The Statue of Liberty stalker.

Who is he? What is he doing here? He's not a cop. Is he a plainclothesman? A reporter?

As I hide behind the curtain, I watch him. He pulls a small piece of paper out of his pocket and checks something on it. He looks around slowly.

Then he walks to my front door and rings the bell.

CHAPTER 32

I DON'T ANSWER. I won't answer. I can't answer.

Not until I figure out what he wants. And what I need to say.

So I stand behind my curtain and watch the Man in Black ring my bell. He rings several times and waits. Did he see me duck into my house? I'm not sure. Whoever he is, he's the soul of patience. He stands there for quite a while. Finally, he turns and gets back into his car and drives off.

It's almost six o'clock. Still no Vince. No Ned. No Joey. I go into the kitchen. On an ordinary day I would be getting dinner ready right about now.

But today has been anything but ordinary.

As I pass the refrigerator door, I see something scrawled on the calendar. I get closer. It says *PTA Meeting 6:30*. I have to smile. Months ago, when life was normal, I signed up to chair the annual Kiddie Carnival at the kids' school. And tonight is the kickoff meeting. Great. A couple of hours to argue the merits of face painting versus dunk tanks.

And try not to think about your whole family in jail.

I pull into the school parking lot. But just as I am about to walk up the steps to school, I hear a voice say, "Mrs. Sherman?"

I turn. It's the Man in Black.

CHAPTER 33

THIS TIME THERE'S NO escaping him.

"Yes?" I say. I'm too frightened to be afraid.

"I'm Special Agent John Witten. With the FBI," he says. He pauses a minute to let that sink in.

"We're trying to nail a drug dealer who's been working the area. His name is..."

I hold my breath. Oh, please, God, don't let him say Joey Sherman. Or Ned Sherman.

"...Nick Milligan."

I laugh. Did he see how terrified I was? Did he read anything in my eyes?

"Sorry," I say. "Can't help you. I don't know anybody by that name."

I knew this whole thing was a mistake. My husband, my son, involved in something sinister? *What was I thinking?* The feds are going after somebody named Nick Milligan. A total stranger.

"He goes by other names as well," Witten is saying now.

He takes a small pad out of his pocket and begins to read. "Burt Polley. Dennis Barton. Lou Corley."

I shake my head to all of them.

"Here's a picture of him," he says. He pulls out a mug shot of a nice-looking man in his forties. Front view. Profile. No. Can't be. This is clearly a picture of . . .

"Vincent Selko," he says.

And the earth opens up. I am sucked to the bottom. I know I am standing in the school parking lot, except I have fallen down into the very reaches of hell.

"Charming guy, from everything we hear," he says. "Able to con a lot of people into doing his dirty work. Down at headquarters, we call him the Suburban Manson."

He puts the picture away carefully in his wallet.

He keeps talking. I know, because I see his lips moving. But I'm only catching bits and pieces of what he says.

"Your family . . . tailor-made . . . husband in finance . . . teenage son who drives . . . and *you* . . ."

He doesn't have to say it: a lost, lonely housewife looking for love in all the wrong places.

Vince using Ned, using Jake, using Joey—maybe I can believe that.

But using *me*, after all the things he's said and done?

No. There's *no way* he could have made all that up.

"Why are you telling me all this?" I ask.

"Because . . . we need your help."

"No!" I say. I shake my head violently.

Witten pauses a moment. "Mrs. Sherman," he says,

very quietly, "we have your son on tape. Making deliveries, with Vince in the car." I can tell by the way he stares at me that he's telling the truth.

"And your husband has been laundering money for him. Several million dollars in overseas investments."

"What do you . . . want me to do?" I ask.

"We want you to wear a wire."

"I can't do that!" I say. He thinks it's because I'm frightened, or in denial. But that's only part of it.

If I'm wearing a wire, Vince will feel it when he hugs me.

"Well, here's the thing," Witten says carefully. "If you work with us—that'll go a long way toward helping your son and your husband. They're looking at jail time. *Serious* jail time. But if you agree to help us reel this guy in . . ."

"What you're asking me to . . . this is just too . . . I can't . . . I need to talk to . . . think about . . . " I say. It's more of a sputter than a sentence.

"Of course," Witten says.

This is all too much for me. I want to sit down but there is no place to sit. Instead, I lean against a car and put my head in my hands.

I start to sob.

"I know this is hard to hear," Witten says. His tone is so gentle, I expect him to put his arm around me. But he doesn't. "You need to know: The guy is dangerous. He's destroyed a lot of people who got in his way."

Destroyed? Does he mean blackmailed? Killed? Or just broke their hearts.

"And . . . he may know we're on to him."

"What do I do?" I ask.

"You'll hear from us. Meanwhile? Just stay away from him," he says as he heads back to his car.

Then he adds, as if he knew the truth: "*If you can.*"

CHAPTER 34

THE KIDDIE CARNIVAL MEETING. The other mothers look up as I enter. They stare. I must look even worse than I feel. I stumble through some lame excuses. A sudden emergency...a sick kid at home...my mother is ill. I'm babbling. Do they believe me? Who cares.

Then I run out. I dial Ned's office. I get his answering machine and leave a message: *Come home! Urgent!* I leave the same message on his cell as an email and as a text. Where the hell is he?

I call his secretary's cell, since it's after hours. She gives me a number where Ned can be reached. It seems familiar. But my brain is racing too fast to stop and sort it out. I dial it. And I hear a voice message: "You've reached the office of Dr. Maggie Treleven..."

Say, *what*?

Ned is in a session with Maggie? Ned, who hates therapy and was only going because I insisted?

Or—wait. Maybe it's a whole other scenario. Is he seeing her behind my back? Are they having an affair?

No. Impossible! But even if it's true—no time to deal with it now.

Somehow, I am able to drive back home. I send Ned more texts, more emails, more messages. Still no response.

All I can do now is wait. And wait. The clock is ticking.

Then suddenly, I hear a car in the driveway. Thank God! Ned is home!

But as I run to the window, I see it's not Ned at all.

It's Vince.

CHAPTER 35

TODAY, I'M FRIGHTENED. Does he know what's happened?

Just to be on the safe side, I grab my cell phone and press Video to start recording. I put the phone in the living room, on the table next to the lamp.

Vince rings the bell.

"Hi," he says. He smiles. "Okay if I come in?"

"Sure," I say. I try not to seem jittery. If he senses I am, he'll know something's up.

"Are you alone?" he asks. I nod yes. Then he leans in and hugs me. We stand that way for quite a while.

"I've missed you," he says. "Is everything okay?"

No.

I want to say: The FBI thinks you're a drug dealer. I think Joey is peddling drugs for you—unless he's not. My husband is somehow involved or having an affair with our therapist. Maybe both. Maybe neither. And the cops want me to wear a wire so they can reel you in.

But I say nothing.

"Something wrong?" he asks.

I try not to look at him. I don't want to get lost in those blue eyes.

"Tell me the truth," I say. "Did you do it?"

He looks—what? Confused? Frightened? In my state of mind, I can't quite tell.

"Do what?"

"All those things...they said you did."

Now he looks concerned. "Who have you been talking to?" he asks.

"The FBI."

"Whoa." He takes a step backward. "The FBI was here?"

"They arrested Jake," I say.

Now things are really beginning to spin out of control.

"Do you know anything about...any of this?" I ask. "The pills? The ones Joey has in his room? Are you involved...Is Ned...?"

I can't even get the words out. I'm sweating like crazy. How could I ever wear a wire? I'd electrocute myself.

But he seems relaxed. "C'mere," he says. He pulls me toward him and onto the couch. There's a part of me that really wants us to just dissolve into kisses.

But all the other parts are afraid.

As I pull away, I accidentally knock into the side table. My phone drops to the floor. Like the gentleman he's always been, Vince picks it up. He looks at it. He sees it's been recording. He frowns. Now what?

He slams the phone down on the coffee table, shattering the screen.

Then he slaps me across the face.

I cry out with shock and pain.

"You bitch," he says. "Were you trying to trick me?"

"Vince! No!"

He jumps up and grabs my arm. He's holding it too tight.

"That hurts!" I say. But he's dragging me to the front door. "Wait! Where are we going?"

He doesn't answer.

I try to pull away. But he's way stronger than I am. I scream.

"Shut up," he says.

He slaps me again.

On the way out the door, I stumble. I trip on the pavement, scraping my knees. They start to bleed.

But Vince is in a hurry. He picks me up by my hair and drags me toward his car. I'm trying to kick him and pull away, but he grabs my other arm and twists it behind me. He opens his car door and starts to push me inside.

Suddenly there's a loud horn.

It startles him. He lets go of me and I run in the direction of the horn. It's Ned! He's seen what is happening and drives up over our lawn. Frazzled, out of breath, I open the door and jump in.

"Drive!" I say to Ned.

Because there's no time to say anything else.

CHAPTER 36

NED PULLS OUT AS fast as he can...but Vince is faster. He gets in his car and zooms toward us. I feel a jolt and hear a sickening crunch. Vince has slammed his car into our rear bumper!

Even worse, he's backing up slowly. He's going to do it again!

"Drive, drive!" I scream, as if our lives depended on it.

Because right now, they do.

Vince isn't just trying to slow us down or even stop us.

Somehow, he's turned into a madman. And he's trying to *kill us*.

There's so much to ask Ned. So much to tell him. But for now we just need to get as far away from Vince as possible.

Ned floors the pedal. Our car screeches down our quiet suburban street.

My heart is racing. I look back. Vince's front bumper is smashed in. Smoke is seeping from under his hood.

But Vince quickly straightens out and accelerates directly toward us.

"Go faster, Ned!" I say. "He's still coming!"

"Laura, this is crazy. We have to call 911!"

He's right. But I realize with horror that my iPhone is still on my coffee table, where Vince smashed it. "I don't have my cell!"

"Take mine," Ned says, reaching for his front right pocket.

"No, *I'll* get it. You focus on the road. Just get us out of here!"

I grip the car door to steady myself as we make a squealing left turn at the end of the block. We're soon flying down another tree-lined street, passing station wagons parked in driveways, bikes strewn across lawns, children playing in front yards.

Vince is still on our tail—and getting closer.

I manage to pull Ned's phone from his jacket pocket and fumble to call the police . . . but I can't. There are no bars. No service.

"Look out!" I scream as a silver minivan starts backing out of a driveway right in front of us. I reach over and smack the horn as Ned swerves. We just miss it.

But so does Vince. Who's still coming for us.

"Let's head to a busy street," I say. "With lots of cars, people. *Somebody* will see us. *They'll* call the cops."

"I'll turn on Ridge Road," Ned says.

"No!" I say. "Take a left here! It'll be faster!"

"Here? That's a sidewalk—and a park, with a fence! And—"

"*Trust me!* Do it now!"

Ned cuts the wheel sharply and our car leaps up onto the curb. We both bang our heads on the roof as it lands.

"Go, go!" I scream.

Ned listens. We pick up speed...

And then we crash directly through a rickety chain-link fence!

Thankfully, the lawn is empty because the sprinklers are on. Our tires slip and slide like crazy when they hit the wet grass. The sprinklers pelt us with water like the inside of a car wash. I reach over and turn on the windshield wipers.

"Park Street is just on the other side," I say. "Once we get there—"

Suddenly two loud pops ring out behind us. They sound like fireworks, like on the Fourth of July. I'm confused, but only for a few seconds.

Because I hear a third pop—and our rear windshield shatters.

"Oh, my God!" I scream. "He's shooting at us!"

CHAPTER 37

I DUCK LOW IN my seat...*Bang!* Another shot. This one ricochets off our trunk.

I look in my side view mirror: OBJECTS IN MIRROR ARE CLOSER THAN THEY APPEAR. Vince's arm is sticking out the window, aiming a gun right at us.

Oh God. How close *is* he?

Ned zigzags back and forth, trying to dodge the bullets. We're like human targets in one of Ben's video games. I scream as Vince shoots twice more. Both shots miss us. Then we reach the end of the park.

There's another chain-link fence ahead of us. "Hang on!" Ned yells.

We crash through it and take a sharp right onto busy Park Street. Cars honk and veer out of our way.

Bang! Another shot hits us—this one on the side somewhere. Ned swerves across both lanes to avoid the next one—and into oncoming traffic!

This is crazy. I've been stopped on this street for a dangling license plate. *Where are the traffic cops now, when we need them?*

We smash into someone's mailbox. It goes flying, sending letters fluttering through the air like snow.

"Just keep going!" I plead. "We have to lose him, we have to—"

And then suddenly, I hear it.

"Aaagghhhh...!"

An animal cry. A sound filled with pain and fear. Half wail, half scream.

An inhuman sound.

Except...it's coming from Ned!

There's a giant red spot on his right shoulder, getting bigger and bigger. It looks like a large red corsage. But it's far worse.

He's been hit!

"Ned—are you okay?! Ned! Answer me!

CHAPTER 38

I CAN TELL HE'S in incredible pain. He's moaning in agony, maybe going into shock. Every instinct tells me to stop the car and help my husband before he bleeds to death.

But I know if I do, we'll *both* die.

"It'll be okay, Ned! It's going to be okay!"

I lean over and grip the wheel so we don't crash.

Vince's car pulls up next to us on the driver's side.

He rolls down his right window. And aims his gun at us.

Drenched in my husband's blood, my heart racing, I get one final crazy idea. I pray to God it works. I let Vince's car get a little closer . . .

Then I jerk the steering wheel to the left as hard as I can.

We crash into each other and we both go spinning like tops.

I hear metal crunching. Tires squealing. Glass shattering.

Ned and I are tossed around until finally our car comes

to a stop. I feel dizzy and dazed. My whole body aches, head to toe. But I'm alive.

Is Ned?

I reach over and take my husband's bloody hand. I give it a squeeze.

A few seconds go by. The longest in my life.

Then, weakly, Ned squeezes back.

Thank God!

I hear police sirens in the distance. I look out through my shattered window. Vince's car has rolled onto its side.

And Vince himself is slumped in the driver's seat. Not moving.

Am I in shock? I must be. Because I am about to do something crazy.

I push open my mashed car door and stagger out. Slowly, I start walking toward Vince.

Because there is something I need to ask him.

CHAPTER 39

A HALF HOUR LATER.

Ned is on a gurney. He is connected to tubes, with a mask over his face. Heavy bandages are wrapped around his shoulder. He is still bleeding, slipping in and out of consciousness...but alive.

I am on a gurney as well, lying quietly, a little woozy. They have given me a shot of something to stop the pain in my arm. My injuries are not life-threatening, they say.

So for the moment, all the available EMTs are surrounding Vince's Honda. It barely resembles a car at this point. They have been using a crowbar and a blowtorch to crack it open and get him out. I hear voices, noises, the whir of machines.

Vince is hanging upside down in his seat, still unconscious. The way he was when I first wandered over. He hasn't moved since his car rolled over onto its side.

Finally, the last piece of his car door crashes to the ground. They lift him out and put him on a third gurney.

There is blood in his hair, on his face. Blood is seeping from his ear. But then I see his lips move.

That means he's alive. Am I glad? Am I sorry?

No need to think about that now. I will have a long time—the rest of my life—to decide.

As I lie there, bits and pieces of the past few months with Vince float by me. The fancy French restaurant. Our first kiss. *I can see where she gets it from.* Darcy's early warning.

I think about that old parable of the man eating the apple. It is delicious—the best apple he's ever had. But just as he reaches the center, he finds a worm. Does this mean the apple wasn't wonderful? Does it negate every delicious bite that brought him joy up till then?

My family life is shattered. The two men I cared most about in the world lie broken and bleeding.

My life, with Vince in it, tasted wonderful.

But there is something I still need to ask him. Something I need to know, before I can ever move on.

CHAPTER 40

AGENT WITTEN WAS RIGHT. The surveillance tapes clearly showed Joey delivering drugs. So he agreed to testify against Vince. As a minor with a clean record and no "priors," Joey was given six months' probation, and was required to do community service for a year. The good news: he seems to enjoy it. I wouldn't be surprised if he winds up being a social worker someday. Well, maybe.

Jake never wrote fake prescriptions. He gave Vince blank pads, so his sentence was reduced to a misdemeanor. He lost his license for three years, and there's no guarantee the hospital will take him back. Darcy hasn't talked to me for quite a while. She still blames me for everything that happened with Vince. We're trying to ease our way back into some semblance of a friendship. But it will take time.

Vinny was sent to live with his mother. It turns out Vince had abducted the boy on one of his alternate custody weekends. The heartbroken mother had been searching for him all that time.

Ned was tried and convicted of laundering the proceeds from controlled substances—a Class B felony. He got two years in prison, plus a huge fine that wiped out most of our Roth IRA.

Vince's old house—the house next door—was sold to a young venture-capital couple who tore it down and are building a McMansion. I would be pleased by this, and what it does to real estate values, except I don't live there anymore. Once Ned was indicted, he lost his job at Reinhart. We sold the house soon after. No regrets there.

Well, maybe one: I would have wanted to move back into the city. But I promised the kids we'd stay in the suburbs till they all finished high school. I figure I owe them that.

Will I ever get over the guilt I feel, bringing Vince into our lives? I'm not sure. And I'm not sure what will happen once Ned gets out. It's clear to me now that our marriage had problems long before Vince entered the scene. Ned says he's willing to work on it. But I don't know if there's anything left anymore.

It's like that line from "The Gambler": "You gotta know when to hold 'em, know when to fold 'em."

So that kind of brings you up to speed on everybody involved.

Oh. Except for Vince.

EPILOGUE

FROM THE OUTSIDE, THE MacDougall-Walker Correctional Institution could pass for a Holiday Inn. But once you push your way through the heavy glass doors and walk through a metal detector, you know it isn't.

I put my pocketbook through an X-ray machine and submit to a serious body frisk. Then I fill out a bunch of papers, sign the visitor's log, and am sent to a waiting room. Along with many other visitors—family members, friends, clergymen, and attorneys—I wait.

Then I see him.

He is dressed in the classic orange jumpsuit, escorted by a prison guard who looks as if he doesn't know how to smile. I am seated at a wooden table. Vince sits down on the other side. He doesn't seem surprised to see me.

"They told me I had a visitor," he says. "I knew it would be you."

"How's it going?" I ask. I remember what I had read

in the local papers. In *Law & Order* terms: they threw the book at him. Forgery. Blackmail. Intimidation. Trafficking. Possession of controlled substances with intent to sell. Child abduction. Attempted manslaughter.

I think of the lovely afternoon he and I had on that park bench, a million years ago. He won't be seeing one of those anytime soon.

Vince looks older, tired, but as appealing as ever. That boyish lock of hair that kept falling into his eyes is gone—shaved away in a prison buzz cut. But he still has the same smile.

Here I am, seated across from the man who almost destroyed me and my family. Yet hard as I try, I can't hate him. We make small talk—the food there, his cell, what Joey is up to. And then I ask him the one question that's been burning in my brain.

"Did you ever care for me at all, or was I just part of the plan?"

He throws his head back and laughs.

"My God," he says. "All you women are the same!"

All you women . . . ?

"A guy says a couple of nice things to a broad, and she's ready to follow him anywhere. You gotta learn to toughen up, Laura. Or else, the next guy who comes along . . ."

But I don't let him finish.

"Guard!" I call out. The guard comes over as I get up to leave.

"Laura, wait!" Vince calls out. But I'm already out the door.

The visit lasted six minutes. Just long enough to learn what a fool I've been these last several months.

And now?

These days, with Ned not there, I have a lot more time for myself. Time to figure out what makes me happy.

Maggie will be a help with that. And no, she and Ned weren't having an affair. He needed to come clean to someone; she was the perfect choice.

I joined a support group. That should help, too. Maybe I'll go back to acting, like I always wanted. Or maybe I'll write a play about everything that happened.

I think it would make a hell of a story.

THE KILLER'S WIFE

JAMES PATTERSON

with **MAX DiLALLO**

PROLOGUE

DETECTIVE ANDREW MCGRATH STANDS in front of his open liquor cabinet, shaking. Inside are just a few old bottles, most of them covered with a fine layer of dust. McGrath may have his share of vices, but booze has never been one of them.

Tonight, however, he's desperate to have a drink.

Partly it's to settle his nerves. But also because it's tradition. When McGrath first traded his patrolman's badge for a detective's shield nearly eleven years ago, his colleagues at the San Luis Obispo Police Department all pitched in to buy him a nice bottle of Scotch. A *very* nice bottle of Scotch. A Macallan 25-Year-Old Sherry Oak, which retails for about a thousand bucks.

The catch?

He was only ever allowed to drink it after he'd solved a murder.

Since then, McGrath has popped it open roughly once or twice a year. San Luis Obispo, a scenic town of about forty-five thousand tucked along California's hilly central coast, rarely sees serious crimes.

But tonight, the book has just been shut on the toughest, most taxing homicide case of McGrath's career. He's a veteran detective, but this pushed him to his limits— then *past* his limits. He is exhausted. Utterly drained. Shaken to his very core.

So once he unscrews the cap from the heavy glass bottle—after all these years, still about three-quarters full—McGrath doesn't pour a nip into a tumbler.

Instead, he takes a long, hearty gulp right from the source. Thick, amber rivulets trickle down his chin. The taste is rich and floral, sharp and smoky.

But the feeling is bittersweet.

Wiping his mouth on his sleeve, McGrath carries the bottle into his sparsely decorated living room. Nestled next to each other on the sofa, beneath a threadbare old quilt, are his elderly parents, Leonard and Evelyn McGrath. A late-night talk show is flickering softly on the TV, but both his parents' eyes are closed.

They look so calm, McGrath thinks. *So at peace.*

So different from how *he's* feeling.

With his free hand, McGrath gently lifts and retucks the blanket around their shoulders, careful not to disturb them. He turns off the television.

And, in the silence, hears something outside that makes him stop in his tracks.

The distant whine of a police siren.

Strange, given the late hour. To avoid bothering the

town's residents, police officers are instructed to use only their flashing lights between the hours of 10:00 p.m. and 6:00 a.m., except in extreme emergencies. So McGrath's curiosity is piqued.

But as he hears the siren getting louder, getting closer, he understands.

It's a professional courtesy. A friendly warning.

The cops are on their way for *him*—but he's been expecting them all night.

McGrath steps into his front hallway now. Without putting down the bottle of Scotch, he unholsters his sidearm, a jet-black Glock 22. He ejects the bullet cartridge, and places it and his gun side by side on the entry table.

Then he steels himself, and opens the door.

An unmarked white Chevy Impala and two squad cars are pulling into his driveway. Four uniformed male officers and a female plainclothes one—Detective Gina Petrillo, smart, feisty, ballsy, the only woman investigator on the entire force and therefore one of its toughest—exit their vehicles and approach.

"Evening, gang," McGrath calls to them. "Lovely night, isn't it?"

Gina takes a moment to try to control the storm of emotions raging inside her. Shock. Confusion. Fury. Betrayal.

Then she readies a pair of handcuffs.

"Detective Andrew J. McGrath," she says stiffly, "you have the right to remain silent. Anything you say can and will be used against you in—"

"Oh, Jesus, Gina, stop it." McGrath holds up the palm of his empty hand like a crossing guard. "Just tell me straight. What am I being arrested for?"

Gina responds with a vicious scowl. This was a colleague she once believed in. A man she once trusted. Once loved like a brother.

"Murder, Andy. But you already knew that, didn't you?"

With a resigned shrug, McGrath takes a final swig of the exorbitantly priced Scotch.

"Actually," he replies, "it's *worse* than that."

Without warning, he hurls the glass bottle to the ground, letting it shatter on his concrete front steps. Gina and the officers leap back, startled. But McGrath stays still as a statue.

"*Much* worse. Come on inside."

CHAPTER 1

Six weeks earlier

"KNOW THE THING I love most about this job?" asks Gina.

She's in the passenger seat to my right, rummaging through the plastic bag at her feet, which earlier held our grease-soaked KFC drive-thru dinner.

We've been sitting in this stuffy parked car together for the past five mind-numbing hours, so I answer sarcastically. "The nonstop thrills?"

Gina removes a crumpled paper napkin stained with barbecue sauce from the bag. She folds it inside out, then blots her glistening brow.

"You're close. The glamour."

It's true. Real police work *isn't* glamorous. Or very exciting. Definitely not how it's portrayed in the movies. Most of the time, our chosen profession is about as hip as digging ditches, as riveting as collecting trash—except that a hole in the ground won't ever lead you on a dangerous high-speed chase, and even the smelliest, foulest dumpster in the world won't ever pull a gun on you.

But real police work is what's required to catch a very real bad guy.

Like the one who's been terrorizing our quiet community on and off for nearly two years.

"Red Bull?" Gina asks as she reaches into a small plastic cooler behind her seat.

She already knows my response—*No, thanks. How can you even drink that crap?*—so I don't have to say it. Taking just one skinny, sugar-free can for herself, Gina holds it against her face for a few seconds, then cracks it open and gulps it down.

I admit I could use a little pick-me-up, too. After tailing and staking out our current person of interest for nineteen days straight—no breaks, no days off—I'm definitely feeling worse for the wear.

I can only imagine how Gina's holding up—my loyal partner of almost seven years, and my best friend for decades. We went to San Luis Obispo High together, if you can believe it, less than a mile down the road. Gina's a trooper: she and her girlfriend are raising two stinking-cute twin toddlers at home, and I don't know how she does it. Sure, I've got my aging folks I help take care of, but at least they can change their *own* diapers.

"Looks like another wild and crazy night in the Pierson household," she says.

Gina is peering through a pair of binoculars. I raise my own to look for myself.

Through the second-floor window of a modest Spanish-style bungalow down the block, we watch as

Michael Pierson and his wife, Ellen, get ready for bed. They change into almost-matching pajamas. They brush their teeth side by side at the bathroom sink in chilly silence. They exchange a chaste peck on the cheek. Then they slip under the covers and shut off the lights.

"That right there is why me and Zoe are *never* getting married," Gina says. "And they don't even have kids! I get depressed just watching."

"Well, your relationship's a little different," I say. "Neither of you is a serial killer. At least as far as I know."

"You really think he's our guy, huh?" Gina lowers her voice, adding somberly: "And you really think those poor girls are dead?"

I do. On both counts.

There's been only circumstantial evidence so far linking Pierson to the ongoing string of abductions. But after I interviewed him twice at the station, he just felt ... *off* to me. I can't say why, but something deep in my gut tells me he's behind them.

For one, he's vice principal of San Luis Obispo High School, where all the young female victims were students, and he knew them fairly well. Two witnesses also put Pierson near Santa Rosa Park—where the most recent missing girl was last seen, out for a jog—on the night she disappeared, twenty-two days ago.

Like the three young women before her, she vanished without a trace.

But goddamnit, I'm going to prove Pierson is guilty!

That son of a bitch is going to pay, no matter what it takes.

And if by some miracle those girls *are* alive... I'll find them, too.

It's getting late, and I'm starting to feel a little foggy. I shut my eyes and rub my face, trying to fight it. Maybe I'll take a quick power nap. Maybe I'll have a Red Bull after all. Maybe I'll—

"Shit, Andy!" Gina exclaims, punching me hard in the shoulder. "Look!"

CHAPTER 2

GINA AND I WATCH with surprise as Michael Pierson exits his front door.

That might not seem like anything special. But over the past nineteen days we've spent surveilling this guy, his behavior has been so predictable, you could set your watch by it—as long as you didn't fall asleep first. Pretty much all Gina and I have seen him do is drive to and from school, drive to and from the supermarket, pick up some dry cleaning, do some yard work, and go to bed early. (As far as I can tell, he also hasn't made love to his wife once this whole time—which is criminal in *my* book, but not according to the California Penal Code.)

Tonight, Pierson has finally changed up his routine. In a very big way.

He was wearing pajamas less than an hour ago. Now he's got on jeans, a gray sweater, and a blue Golden State Warriors baseball cap, the brim pulled low. He's also carrying a small black duffel bag and speaking nervously on a cell phone, although we're much too far away to hear him.

"*That's* new," I say.

"Yup. I always thought he'd be an Angels fan."

I roll my eyes. My partner has two modes: sarcastic and *very* sarcastic.

"I mean his cell. Pierson has an iPhone. That's an old *flip* phone."

"Damn, you're right. Gotta be a burner. But who's he talking to?"

No idea. But the real question is, where's he going?

We watch as Pierson finishes his conversation, hangs up, then gets into his silver Honda Civic parked in his driveway. As he begins pulling out, I glance at my watch. It's 11:26 p.m. This is by far the latest we've ever seen him awake, let alone outside his house—let alone *going* somewhere. Something is most definitely up.

After his Honda passes us, I count to five, then start my engine. Keeping my headlights switched off, I pull a gentle U-turn. And follow.

San Luis Obispo—or SLO, as a lot of us locals call it— is a lovely place to live. But it isn't exactly a thriving metropolis. This late on a weeknight, the streets are empty, and I have to keep a good distance between my car and Pierson's. The last thing I want to do is spook him.

"He's making a left on Conejo Avenue," Gina says.

I don't tell her she's stating the obvious. If he continues straight, it's a dead end.

I simply nod and make a left up that hilly street myself, then keep an eye on the Honda as it continues to snake through this sleepy patch of residential homes.

Pierson soon makes a left onto Andrews Street, the road that leads into town...but then he hooks another left, looping back around.

"What's he doing?" Gina asks.

I have no idea. But soon, we find ourselves back on Pierson's block.

"Damnit!" I exclaim, pounding my fist against the steering wheel. "He's going home. He must've seen us. Shit."

"Or maybe he just wanted to take a little drive," Gina says. "Go in circles for a while. Clear his head."

"Or maybe...this is his ritual," I say. "He's psyching himself up before he strikes again."

Gina and I let that lie there as Pierson's car nears his driveway and starts to slow. It looks like he was taking a spin around the neighborhood after all. False alarm.

Except—he doesn't stop. He continues past it, then makes another left on Conejo, then heads down Andrews again.

And this time, he keeps going.

Gina rubs her hands together in excited anticipation. "Okay, we're back in business."

I'm a little antsy myself. This is uncharted territory— for Pierson and us, too.

The Honda heads east along Monterey Street, one of SLO's main thoroughfares. We pass a few shopping centers. A video rental store, shuttered long ago. A greasy taco joint right across from a hip new green-juice bar. (That's California for you.)

Pierson approaches an empty intersection with a stale

yellow light. Instead of slowing, he accelerates. It turns red—but he speeds right through.

"Let's pull this asshole over," Gina suggests. "Maybe see what's in that duffel."

I slow down but don't stop as I reach the same quiet intersection, to make sure the coast is clear. Then I speed through the red light myself.

"No, not yet. This is our chance. I don't want to blow it."

After a few blocks, Pierson turns off the main road and stops in front of a modest two-story apartment complex, the color of burnt coffee. I stealthily pull over about a block farther down, a discreet distance away but with a decent line of sight on him.

Maybe thirty seconds later, a woman exits one of the second-floor apartments and scurries down the stairs. She's wearing a baggy sweatshirt with the hood up.

"Here comes company," Gina says. "But I can't get a look at her. Can you?"

I can't, either. Not from this angle. *Damn.* Her face is totally obscured.

Until she opens Pierson's passenger-side door.

"Jesus..." I mutter.

As the woman turns to get in, the dome light casts an eerie glow across her face.

I see now that she's just a girl. A *teenager.* Bright-eyed and apple-cheeked.

I also get a glimpse of the writing on her sweatshirt.

SAN LUIS OBISPO HIGH SCHOOL

CHAPTER 3

"NOW WE *GOTTA* PULL this asshole over," Gina pleads. "She could be his next—"

"You don't think I know that?" I snap, surprised and a little embarrassed by the edge in my voice. "But if we collar him now..."

I trail off, because Gina knows exactly the classic police dilemma we're in.

A high-school vice principal picking up an underage girl around midnight looks sketchy as hell. But there might be a perfectly reasonable—and legal—explanation. They *could* be having an affair. Or Pierson could be helping her flee an abusive family and move into a shelter. Either way, it's not proof Pierson abducted or harmed any of those *other* poor girls. It won't bring them back. And it won't put him away.

"Run this address," I tell my partner. "Find out who she is. I won't let her out of our sight. I promise."

Gina gives me a troubled look, but agrees. She opens

the dashboard-mounted laptop between us and gets to work.

Meanwhile, I keep my eyes glued to the silver Honda, still just sitting there in front of the apartment complex. I'd give anything to know what's happening inside.

"Come on, *come on*," I whisper. "Get out of the damn car. Just walk away."

No such luck. The Honda shifts into drive and pulls back onto Monterey.

A few seconds later, Gina and I are trailing it again. Now I leave only about one block's distance between us. I'm not taking any chances.

"Okay, I think I got her," Gina says, her acrylic nails clattering across the laptop keyboard. "Brittany Herbert, age seventeen. Goes by Britt. She's a junior at SLO High. Lives in apartment 2C with her mom and stepdad. I found her Facebook page. Is this her?"

Gina flips the screen around to show me the profile picture of a teenager posing with some girlfriends, all puckering their lips for the camera, happy and carefree.

I'm positive that's the same young woman I saw get into Pierson's car.

This potential next victim has been identified. It just got *personal*.

"She lists her cell phone on her profile, too," Gina says. "Maybe we text it."

"And say what?" I ask. "'Hi, Britt, we're two undercover cops following the car you're in. Don't freak out, but your vice principal might be about to murder you'?"

"Fine," Gina says, exasperated. "We'll do this your way. But damnit, Andy, you're taking a major risk here. I'm warning you..."

I nod, stiffly. The pressure's on.

Pierson's Honda cuts through SLO's unimposing downtown, then heads toward the 101 freeway, which basically cuts San Luis Obispo in half. I start to worry that Pierson might merge onto it and try to spirit the girl out of town. I'd follow this bastard all the way to Canada if I had to, but the farther out they get from our jurisdiction, the tougher it will be to keep tabs on him and Brittany—and possibly call for backup.

Thankfully, the Honda cruises below the underpass and stays within the city limits. For now. But it keeps going, heading northwest, toward the town's hilly outskirts.

Soon, I can start to make out some tree-lined ridges off in the distance.

Which makes my stomach drop.

I know *exactly* where they're going.

CHAPTER 4

BISHOP'S PEAK. AT OVER fifteen hundred feet, it's the highest point in the region by far. With its stunning views of the city, it's a popular draw for hikers, picnickers, and bird-watchers alike.

It's also a *nightmare* for law enforcement.

The surrounding hillsides are rugged and treacherous. They stretch on for miles, a maze of winding trails and steep switchbacks. The tree cover is dense, the vegetation thick, the wildlife dangerous. And especially after sundown, the place gets darker than the North Pole during a lunar eclipse.

In other words, it's the perfect location to kill a teenage girl and dump her body.

"Relax, man," Gina says, touching my arm. After so many years of working together, she can practically read my mind. "This isn't his spot. We combed the peak for miles in every direction. Not just three weeks ago, but *every* time. Remember?"

I couldn't possibly forget. These hills are such an obvious choice to stash a kidnapping victim—dead or alive—that each time a girl has gone missing, the SLOPD pulled out all the stops. Most recently, we deployed multiple search parties, two circling rescue helicopters, even some K-9 units borrowed from the county sheriff. Officers worked around the clock for three days. We didn't find a thing.

Still, that's ice-cold comfort right now as the Honda reaches the end of the winding paved street...and rumbles onto a dirt service road.

If Pierson and Brittany just wanted to be alone for an hour or two, there are plenty of motels they could have gone to instead. What are they doing *here*?

I tighten my grip on the steering wheel and keep their car in my sights.

Up the hillside we go, higher and higher. Since my headlights are still off, it's getting almost impossible to see where the road ends and the steep ridge below begins. I have no choice but to drive even slower. If Gina and I crash, Brittany's all on her own.

We round a particularly steep bend. When I think I've steered through, there's suddenly a sick jolt—my front left tire is slipping off the road! Gina lets out a little gasp as I jerk the wheel to the right, barely keeping us from tumbling to our deaths. Cursing under my breath, I drive on.

"Hold up," Gina says, pointing her index finger to the sky. "I think they stopped."

Did they? I can't tell. The Honda is just around the next ridge, momentarily out of sight. But I do notice the glow of its headlights is gone.

Why here? Why now?

No clue. But if there was ever a time to make our move, this is it.

I shut off the engine. "Let's roll," I say to my partner, who is already quietly opening her door—and drawing her sidearm. I do the same.

Crouching low, we creep slowly along the side of the wooded hill separating us from Pierson and Brittany. Trying to move through the underbrush is like traipsing through quicksand. I feel the prickly brambles and cacti scratch my skin through my clothes, but I ignore them and keep moving.

Finally we reach the crest. I look down at the Honda below—*with horror*.

Pierson is standing by the open passenger-side door, heaving Brittany's limp body into his arms.

"Police! Don't move!" I shout as Gina and I charge down the hill.

Pierson looks genuinely shocked to see us, a real deer in the headlights. He immediately releases the girl's lifeless frame, letting her slump back into her seat.

Then he takes off running.

I nearly trip over myself rapidly changing direction downhill, trying to cut him off.

I'm no Usain Bolt, but thankfully neither is Pierson. I lunge for the son of a bitch and tackle him to the ground.

Shoving his head into the dirt, I quickly holster my service weapon and snap handcuffs on him in seconds.

I look back at the Honda, fearing the absolute worst.

"How is she?" I call to Gina, who is kneeling beside Brittany, frantically searching for her pulse, lifting her eyelids to inspect her pupils. "Britt, can you hear me?" Gina says. "You're safe now. Don't be scared, Britt. It's all over."

I look back down at Pierson, his face dirty and bloody, his expression stony.

"You piece of shit!" I shout. "Did you kill her? Like you killed all the others?"

Pierson spits out a piece of gravel. Then his lips curl into a chilling grin.

"Actually, it's *worse* than that. *Much* worse."

CHAPTER 5

"COFFEE, BLACK. ON THE HOUSE."

Gina thrusts a steaming Styrofoam cup of joe into my hands. I almost spill it all over myself, since my attention is elsewhere: I'm standing at the edge of a roped-off section of hillside, roughly fifteen feet by twenty, watching a team of crime-scene investigators wearing white full-body evidence suits carefully comb through it.

They're looking for a mass grave they suspect might be underneath.

What a goddamn world.

"Thanks," I reply, turning to face my partner. I have to squint a little, since she's backlit by the rising sun. We've been at this all night. "Except I take three creams and four sugars, Gina. You've only known that for years."

My partner shrugs. "I know your doctor wouldn't mind the change."

"Yeah, yeah," I mutter, and take a careful sip of the bracingly hot, bitter beverage. Like Gina's beloved sugar-free

Red Bull—another little can of which she's guzzling at the moment—I don't know how people can drink *this,* either.

"Speaking of white coats," I say cautiously, "any update on Brittany yet?"

"I just got off with the hospital. She's stabilized, resting comfortably."

Relief floods every cell of my body.

"Thank God. Okay. We need to get down there, talk to her as soon as she's awake."

"Doctors say it could be a while. Midday at least."

"That's fine. Have her labs come back?"

Gina tilts back her Red Bull can and drains the last few drops.

"Not yet. But based on her condition, they think Pierson slipped her some kind of sedative. Could be Rohypnol, maybe a ketamine derivative. My guess is, he hid it in that fifth of Smirnoff that was under the passenger seat, covered in her prints."

"Sick bastard," I mumble, simmering with rage. I bite down on my bottom lip, so hard it draws a few drops of blood.

"Detectives, a moment?"

The voice belongs to the bespectacled Dr. John Hyong, the SLOPD's chief forensic pathologist. He's walking toward us, peeling off his latex gloves. The way the rising sun reflects off his white jumpsuit and hood, he looks almost…*ghostly*. Which is grimly appropriate, actually. He's been leading the team of techs searching for bodies for the past six hours.

"Find anything?" I ask, almost afraid to hear his response.

Hyong shakes his head.

"No trace. Our subterranean sonar imaging has also been inconclusive. We're expanding the perimeter another ten feet all around. However, if we still don't find—"

"I appreciate the update, John," I say, deliberately cutting him off.

Because I know what this "expert" is going to say.

Hyong doesn't think we'll find *shit* buried in these hills. I practically had to beg him even to start a search. Hyong agreed only as a favor to me. He didn't think the rocky hillside would make a good burial spot in the first place—and the police had already combed this ground multiple times.

I can't say I blame him. There's no evidence that Pierson took any of the other four victims up here.

In fact, there's still no evidence linking Pierson to the other girls' abductions at all.

But damn it, I was right about that creep this time!

Would he really drive Brittany Herbert all the way to Bishop's Peak on a whim?

I don't think so. There's a method to his madness, and I'm going to figure it out.

And I'm going to find those girls. They've gotta be here somewhere.

Gotta be.

CHAPTER 6

I KNOW I SHOULD wait for my partner to do this, but I can't.

I should probably stop home first, too. Take a hot shower, grab a change of clothes, give my grimy teeth a quick brush. But I can't do that, either.

There's too much at stake. And no time to lose.

So while Gina swings by her place for a bit to help her girlfriend get their twins fed, dressed, and off to day care, I drive back to the Piersons' house.

I want to have a little chat with Ellen.

The woman I'm convinced is the killer's wife.

From our weeks of surveillance, I know Ellen usually gets up around six thirty. She goes for a quick jog around the neighborhood, has a light breakfast with her husband, then around eight heads to school—not San Luis High, where Pierson works, but Hawthorne Elementary, where she's the school nurse.

Sure enough, when I pull into the driveway a few minutes before seven, the kitchen light is on. I spot Ellen inside wearing workout clothes. She's holding a cordless phone to her ear and pacing anxiously.

Probably because she has no idea where her husband is.

On my way over, I spoke to the desk sergeant back at the station, who told me Pierson turned down the chance to make his one call. He hasn't spoken to his wife, to the high school, to a lawyer—anybody. He's just been sitting in his cell all night.

Does that sound like an innocent man to you, or a guilty one?

"Fine," I said to the sergeant. "His choice. Let him rot."

It feels a little strange to walk right up to the Piersons' front door and ring the bell. I'm so used to sitting in my car with Gina down the block, watching it from the shadows. Seeing the place up close like this, I notice a few details I didn't before. Like the mismatched screws holding the metal mailbox to the wall. The novelty welcome mat, old and fraying, with a yellow floral design around the word ALOHA.

The door opens, and Ellen stands there for a few seconds in stunned silence.

Up this close, I notice some new details about *her,* too. Like the dusting of freckles across the bridge of her nose. And her subtly mismatched eye color: the left one is a faint emerald, the right one aquamarine.

"Mrs. Pierson? I'm Detective McGrath, SLOPD. I, uh...do you mind if..."

I'm suddenly a little tongue-tied myself. Something

about this woman has caught me off guard. I always thought Ellen was nice-looking, if a little plain. But now I see there's a magnetism about her.

"Is this about my husband?" she asks. "He was gone when I woke up. His car, too. I called his cell, but it was charging on the kitchen counter. Is he all right?"

"He's fine. But he's . . . been arrested."

"Arrested?" Ellen covers her mouth with her hands as if she's just seen a ghost. "No. No, that's ridiculous. He didn't do it!"

I feel my right eyebrow arch of its own volition.

"I didn't tell you what he was arrested *for*, Mrs. Pierson."

Ellen looks rattled. Scared. Caught?

"Why don't we go inside and talk?" I say.

Ellen leads me into their quaint living room and right away begins nervously tidying the place up. Not that it needs it. In fact, the room is meticulously clean and orderly. Even the old magazines on the coffee table are in perfectly neat stacks.

"I—I'm sorry the place is such a mess. I had no idea anyone would be—"

"Please," I say, gently touching Ellen's forearm. Her skin feels clammy but supple and warm. "Let's have a seat. I'd like to ask you a few questions."

We settle next to each other on a sagging beige couch.

"Does the name Brittany Herbert mean anything to you?"

Ellen squints, thinking, then shakes her head.

"What about Claire Coates, Samantha Gonzalez, Maria Jeffries, or Patty Blum?"

Now Ellen shuts her eyes tight.

"Those names mean something to *everyone* in this town," she says. "They're the four girls who . . . who . . ."

Ellen can't finish the sentence. So I do it for her.

"Who all disappeared over the past twenty-two months. Presumed dead. Patty went missing just three weeks ago."

"I know. My God, it's so awful. Those poor girls. But what does this have to do with me and Michael?"

"We need your help finding the bodies, Mrs. Pierson."

"*My* help? What are you talking about?"

Ellen isn't making this easy. I have a feeling she knows a lot more than she's letting on. But I have to play this carefully.

"You and your husband have been married for six years. But tell me: How well do you *really* know him? Do you think he'd ever be capable of—"

"Absolutely not!" Ellen exclaims, springing to her feet. "You think *he* . . . ? This is crazy! Whatever you think Michael did . . . he's a good man. He's innocent!"

Ellen glares at me with her bicolored eyes, now wet with tears.

Her emotion is so real, so raw, I almost want to believe her. Almost.

CHAPTER 7

I QUICKLY BACKPEDAL AND try to calm Ellen down. I assure her our investigation is ongoing and that no charges have been filed yet against her husband in connection with the four girls' disappearances.

But then I tell her about his arrest last night.

About the underage student he picked up around midnight. How he drove her to a deserted patch of woods and drugged her to near cardiac arrest. Whether Michael Pierson is involved in those other four abductions or not, he sure ain't a Boy Scout.

Ellen, her shoulders trembling, her voice cracking, sits back down on the couch and agrees to answer my questions.

We start with what she remembers about last night—which isn't anything out of the ordinary. She's just about done telling me what little she recalls about the nights the four *other* teens went missing, when I hear two vehicles pull up in front of the house.

I turn and look out the living room's spotless bay windows. Three uniformed officers are exiting a pair of squad cars. Gina is with them, clutching a trifolded sheet of paper.

"My partner's here," I explain to Ellen. "With your permission, we'd like to search your house and yard. You can wait right here until we're finished."

Ellen stammers a bit, then nods.

"If you think it might help, go ahead. Please."

"Thank you, ma'am," I tell her. "We appreciate that."

What I *don't* tell her is that I was asking simply as a courtesy, trying to curry a little extra favor with her. That document in Gina's hand is a search warrant, signed by a county magistrate.

I greet my partner and the officers at the front door and bring them up to speed on my dealings with Ellen. Then we divvy up the house and yard, snap on some latex gloves, and get to work.

But when I reenter the living room, I see that one of the bay windows is wide open.

And Ellen is gone.

"Shit, we got a runner!" I say, reaching for my service weapon. "Gina, cover the front. You two, the sides. I'll take the rear, see if she—"

"Are you looking for *me*?" comes Ellen's shaky voice from the kitchen.

I hurry in and there she is, innocently setting out a row of mugs along the counter. She looks both confused and embarrassed to have caused such alarm.

"It was getting stuffy in there, so I opened a window. And I thought I—I'd make some fresh coffee for you all if anyone wants some."

Ellen, the school nurse. Behind her, I see Gina step into the opposite doorway and roll her eyes.

"That's not necessary, Mrs. Pierson," I say, trying to control my irritation. "Why don't you wait in the living room. Like I *asked* you to."

Over the next ninety minutes, our search goes down without incident. Me, Gina, and the officers turn every square inch of the house inside out, looking for any clues that might link Pierson to Claire's, Samantha's, Maria's, or Patty's disappearance—or even better, that might lead to finding them alive.

We carefully bag and tag every possible piece of evidence, including Pierson's iPhone and laptop. An old paper datebook that may help reveal his whereabouts at the time of the crimes. Some unmarked bottles of pills in the bathroom. A stack of old SLO High School yearbooks filled with signatures—including one signed by Maria Jeffries, the third victim—that might shed light on the vice principal's relationships with the girls. One of the officers even finds a purple scarf that resembles the one Samantha Gonzalez, the second victim, was allegedly wearing the night she went missing.

All are tantalizing clues. But none is conclusive.

Then we do an additional search, a "structural sweep," pulling up rugs and carpets, moving furniture, checking every crack and crevice to make sure we didn't miss any hiding spots built into the house itself. Like a trick wall in the back of a closet. A secret nook under a staircase. A trapdoor that leads to a hidden soundproof room where four teenage girls have been locked away for two years.

Nothing.

I regroup with Gina in the attic, where it's stiflingly hot and muggy. My partner has just finished inspecting the roof and rafters and has come up empty-handed.

"I don't know whether to be relieved or pissed off," Gina says. "What a waste of time. We didn't find a damn thing."

"We still have to search the backyard," I say. "Could get lucky."

But Gina frowns. She pulls off her latex gloves with a snap and rolls them into little white pellets.

"You're really still convinced Pierson's our guy?"

I am. I can't say why exactly. Call it a hunch. Call it an instinct. Call it years of hunting down bad guys.

But I absolutely am.

"What's all that?" I ask, pointing to a little drafting table in the corner of the attic. On it are some wooden frames, glass panels, and a few small tools and tiny boxes.

"Apparently," Gina answers, "Mrs. Pierson is something of a lepidopterist."

"Huh?"

"A butterfly expert. A collector. Have a look yourself."

I head over to the workstation and see that pinned inside many of the framed glass panels are various preserved, drying butterflies. There must be dozens at least, each a different shape and size, every color of the rainbow, beautiful and delicate.

So Ellen Pierson collects butterflies.

And her husband collects teenage girls.

CHAPTER 8

ELLEN FELT LIKE SHE was living inside a terrible dream.

Her husband was missing. A detective was at her front door, sturdy and good-looking, but polite at first.

Yet his confidence grew as he explained the shocking reason he was there.

Michael had been arrested—for drugging a female student and attempting to dump her lifeless body in the woods near Bishop's Peak.

As if *that* wasn't hard enough to believe, the police also suspected he was behind the disappearance of those four *other* poor teenage girls who'd gone missing over the past two years, a crime spree that had set the entire town on edge.

Michael, a dedicated educator, her loving husband. Could it really be?

"He's a good man," Ellen insisted to the detective. "He's innocent!"

"We need your help finding the bodies, Mrs. Pierson," the detective said.

Ellen sent a hurried text to the principal of her elementary school saying she'd likely be coming in late, if at all, citing "personal reasons." Now she's gone numb from head to toe, watching the police tear her home apart, top to bottom.

This can't be happening…

Part of her wishes she could transform into one of her beloved butterflies, then float right out the open window, unseen.

Another part of her wants to scream and shout, flip over the sofa, hurl the coffee table clean across the room.

Instead, Ellen just sits there on her overstuffed couch, a human statue, forbidden by the police from even making a pot of coffee, praying that this all really *is* just a nightmare and she'll wake up any minute. That Michael will be snoring softly by her side, not sitting in a jail cell. That Brittany Herbert will be home, too, not lying in a hospital bed. That her husband's laptop, his anxiety medications, the purple scarf he bought her for Christmas four years ago, will all be in their proper places, not in plastic evidence bags on their way to a forensic lab.

The search finally ends, and the detectives and officers leave.

At least, Ellen *thought* they were leaving.

Instead, she sees they've simply relocated to outside, where they continue their invasive search in her backyard. Sifting through her rosebushes. Rooting through her vegetable garden. Poking holes in her lawn.

With the police outside, Ellen begins to clean up—

which will be a herculean task. Every room she walks through is an absolute mess. Every drawer and closet has been rifled through. Every single item she owns has been examined and moved out of place.

As her numbness begins to wear off, she starts to feel angry. Confused. Violated.

She knows what will calm her down: her butterflies.

So Ellen heads up to the attic, to the old desk in the corner where she stores and works on her collection. Of course the police rifled through her tools and framed glass shadow boxes. But they seem to have been gentle enough. Ellen notices a few of her colorful winged specimens have come unpinned, but thankfully none looks damaged.

Taking a deep breath, she selects a pair of tweezers and begins carefully restoring the butterflies to their proper places. She figures if she can reinstate some semblance of order to this tiny slice of her life, maybe the rest will follow.

She's wrong.

Barely five minutes have passed when she hears some kind of commotion out in her front yard. She peers through a tiny window overlooking her lawn and sees the two detectives and other officers buzzing around like bees on honey.

One of them is also yelling, barking orders. The words are faint and muffled, but Ellen can just barely make them out.

And they fill her with dread.

"We found something!"

CHAPTER 9

BONES.

Loosely packed topsoil.

The putrid smell of rotting flesh.

I know right away we've just stumbled on a shallow grave—right in the middle of the killer's backyard.

As Gina and the other uniformed officers start cordoning off the Piersons' backyard with yellow crime-scene tape, I'm already on my cell dialing Dr. Hyong.

"Hello, Detective, we're just wrapping up at Bishop's Peak," he says as soon as he picks up. "I'm afraid we didn't find anything. So I'm officially ending the search. I was going to call you this afternoon to tell you, after I grabbed a few hours of sleep."

"Sorry, Doc," I reply, "but no rest for the weary. I'm gonna need your team to pull a double shift. Because here at the Pierson place, we definitely just found *something*."

Within the hour, Hyong and a half dozen fellow white-suited crime-scene techs arrive and set to work. They carefully mark off the grave site, then begin to excavate, photograph, and catalog the brittle, buried remains.

Standing on the periphery of the property with Gina, I'm simmering with a mix of emotions. I'm glad my instincts were right. We finally have the proof we need to connect the other girls' disappearances to Michael Pierson. We can nail the bastard!

But seeing Hyong and his colleagues sift through the soil, I feel a well of deep empathy for the victims all over again. And fury that those poor young girls had their precious lives cut short.

"We're gonna have some new questions for Pierson after this," Gina says.

She offers me a pack of chewing gum, which I decline. She shrugs and folds a stick into her mouth, and the faint smell of hot cinnamon is soon tickling my nostrils.

Anything to replace the smell of death.

As we continue watching the forensic team, I get an odd sensation—like someone is watching *me*.

I turn and look back at the house. And what do you know? Ellen is staring down at us from an attic window. Her expression is cold, blank, like a mannequin's.

"I'm going to have a few more questions for *Mrs.* Pierson, too," I say.

"Detectives?" Hyong suddenly calls to us. He's heading our way, removing his face mask, and shaking his head.

With concern, Gina and I hurry over to meet him.

"John, what's wrong?" I demand.

"Those bones don't belong to any of our victims."

"What? But how do you—so you're saying—"

"No," he interjects. "They're just the remains of a dog."

CHAPTER 10

I'M BACK ON THE old beige couch again, sitting next to Ellen, who's twirling a fresh Kleenex in her hands. A tiny mountain of them has accumulated beside her.

"He told me...he told me Ruby ran away," she whimpers.

"And how long ago was that?" I ask.

"Four months, two weeks, and five days. I remember it perfectly. I'd just spent the weekend in Fresno. It was my nephew's third birthday. Michael had to stay here, catch up on some work. When I came home, he sat me down, right on this very couch, and broke the awful news."

I nod; her story checks out. Dr. Hyong isn't a forensic veterinarian, but he estimated, given the state of the dog's decayed corpse, that it was buried between four and six months ago.

With a gentle sniffle, Ellen adds, "She...she was such a good girl."

I want to give this woman a moment to compose herself. Her pain and shock seem genuine to me. But Gina, perched on a love seat nearby, interjects. Harshly.

"Wish you remembered the nights those *real* girls went missing half as well."

I know where my partner is going with this, so I shoot her a quick glance—*Hey, back off.* But she's on a roll.

"Chances are looking better and better that your husband killed them, too."

Ellen's bicolored eyes grow wide with horror.

"What do you mean, my husband killed them...*too*?"

Great. This was the other piece of info Hyong gave us about the dog's remains. I was planning on sharing it with Ellen later, when the time was right, or maybe not even telling her at all. But Gina just spilled the beans.

"Our forensic expert, Mrs. Pierson," I say delicately, "observed a prominent indentation on the left side of Ruby's head. He believes it was caused by blunt-force trauma."

"Hard enough to crush Ruby's little skull," Gina says, not helping.

"Her death was quick and painless," I add, possibly fudging the truth a bit. "But intentional. And cruelty to animals is often associated with cruelty to people. I know this is all hard to hear. But now do you see why it's so important you tell us everything you can about your husband?"

Ellen blinks a few times, processing this latest chilling revelation, but stays quiet.

Through the bay window facing the street, I see Hyong

and his team stripping off their white jumpsuits, packing up their response vehicle, and getting ready to leave.

It's a harsh reminder that after all this, we're *still* no closer to finding any evidence that links Pierson to the disappearance of Claire, Samantha, Maria, or Patty. And we're no closer to finding those girls, dead or alive. *Damn it!*

"Mrs. *Pierson,*" I snap, starting to succumb to my frustration, "we need your help. You're married to that man. Think. Hard. Talk to us. *Please.*"

Ellen stares right at me. Her lips part slightly, as if she's going to speak, as if she's finally going to give us something we can work with. I lean forward in anticipation.

Then Ellen leans forward, too. And bursts into heaving, ugly sobs.

CHAPTER 11

PRECISELY TWENTY-THREE MINUTES ago, Ellen pulled her Camry into the Hawthorne Elementary School faculty parking lot. She's been sitting in it ever since, willing herself to simply open the car door, get out, and head into the school that she loves so much, just as if it were any other day.

Of course, it's *not* any other day. Not even close. It's her first day back since that handsome detective knocked on her door last week and turned her whole life upside down.

Since then, Michael has been formally arraigned. But he is still refusing to speak to the police, to his court-appointed lawyer, or even to his own wife.

Detective McGrath is the opposite; he can't seem to talk to Ellen *enough*. He's been calling her every other day to check in, hoping she might remember some new detail that could help his investigation. But so far, she hasn't.

Reporters, too, won't leave Ellen alone. They've been

knocking on her door at all hours, trailing her everywhere she goes, begging her to break her silence and give an interview, which she has steadfastly refused to do.

But the damn press won't give up! Just this morning, to get to school unseen, Ellen slipped out the back door before dawn, hopped the fence on the far side of the yard, then sped off in her car, which she had deliberately parked a few blocks away from her home. And yet, Ellen could have sworn she saw one of them following her today. *No, I'm just being paranoid,* she told herself. *Or maybe all this stress is starting to play tricks on my mind.*

Ellen had wanted to come back to work to feel some semblance of normalcy in her life again. Just sitting around at home, helpless, was driving her nuts. But now she just feels foolish. And overwhelmed. She rubs her tired, bloodshot eyes. *Maybe this was a mistake,* she thinks. *Maybe I came back too soon. Maybe—*

"Good morning, Nurse Pierson!" comes a chorus of children's voices.

Ellen sees a gaggle of kids walking past. They're giggling and waving, tickled to see the school nurse outside the building and not wearing her trademark white coat.

Their laughter and innocence tug on Ellen's heart. Hard. It's an adorable reminder of why she became a school nurse in the first place: to keep these precious kids healthy. *They need you,* Ellen tells herself. *So quit wallowing and get moving!*

At last, Ellen does. She exits her car, approaches the building, and enters.

Walking through the halls to her office, however, is an unsettling experience.

Most of the students she passes greet her happily, like the ones outside. But the glares she gets from her fellow faculty members are fierce and unrelenting. Certainly they have all read the local papers and have been gossiping in the teachers' lounge for days. They all know Ellen's husband has been accused of some truly heinous crimes. But far from showing sympathy for their colleague, their expressions range from shock to judgment to horror.

Ellen shifts her eyes to the ground until she finally reaches the nurse's office. She hurriedly unlocks the door, then slams it shut.

The school day begins, and gradually Ellen falls back into the familiar routines of the job she loves, tending to student ailments large and small. She gently cleans and bandages the scraped elbow of a whimpering first-grader named Mackenzie, who fell while playing basketball. She "treats" a third-grader named AJ—who Ellen knows has a history of pretending—for his sore throat by giving him a couple of pieces of candy she's stashed in a cabinet. And she reassures a nervous fifth-grader named Carlos that the pimple on his nose might be a little embarrassing, but it's a perfectly normal part of starting puberty.

Ellen is a few hours into her morning, reorganizing the first-aid closet, when her cell phone buzzes. She's gotten a text. Pls see me asap.

Ellen's heart skips a beat. It's an unusual request, especially at this time of day. She starts to text back but decides it's better to simply do as she was asked.

After another long, even more unpleasant walk through the halls, Ellen reaches her destination. James Warrick, a distinguished and still nice-looking man despite his thinning hair and middle-aged paunch, is sitting in his office behind a messy desk.

"Ellen, hi," he says when he sees her in the doorway. "That was fast. Come on in. And why don't you shut the door, please?"

Ellen does both and tries to smile.

"I haven't been called to the principal's office since I was a little girl."

She waits for James to reply, but he doesn't. Normally they have a friendly, even flirty rapport. But Ellen quickly realizes this is going to be a very different kind of conversation.

"Look, this isn't easy for me to say," James begins. "I feel awful. And I can't imagine how *you* must be feeling. But given what's happened...on behalf of the school board...I'm asking you to take some additional time off. Indefinitely."

Ellen is too stunned for a few seconds to speak. Then she stammers: "You're *asking* me? Or...you're *telling* me?"

"Parents have been calling me all week. Teachers are worried, too."

"Worried about *what*?" Ellen demands, struggling to tamp down her rising anger.

"Ellen. Be serious. How would *you* feel if the nurse at

your child's school was married to a kidnapper and attempted murderer? How can I possibly—"

"My husband is innocent until proven guilty!" Ellen
snaps. "And so am I, Jim! Isn't that how our system works?"

James sighs. "Please don't make this harder than it has
to be. Listen..."

He reaches for one of her hands, which have involun-
tarily curled into fists—but Ellen angrily yanks it away.

"I can't believe you're doing this. After everything we've
been through!"

James's face softens. He wants to do the right thing by
her. But he has hundreds of students, parents, and teachers to think of, too.

"I'm sorry, Ellen. You know I am. But until this whole
thing blows over, there's nothing else I can do. Except
wish you good luck."

CHAPTER 12

SUSPENDED, FOR NOTHING!

Stumbling out of the principal's office in a daze, Ellen truly can't believe it. Another pillar of her life has just come tumbling down.

She shudders to think what might be coming next.

After the longest, most humiliating walk through the halls yet, Ellen returns to the nurse's office and begins to gather up her belongings. Pausing briefly to eye the rows of neatly organized translucent cabinets full of medications and first-aid supplies, she gets the sudden urge to smash them all to bits in a fit of rage.

But of course she controls herself. Ellen hopes to get her job back when all this drama blows over, and going postal is a surefire way to prevent that.

So instead, she swallows her shock and shame, scoops up her purse and uneaten lunch, and scrams. James told her the substitute nurse who covered for her over the past week would be arriving within the hour. Part of Ellen feels a pang of guilt about leaving the nurse's office unattended, even for such a brief time. Yet the thought of having to face her replacement is simply too much to bear.

Ellen scurries down the hall one final time, then pushes open the school's rear exit and steps outside. The bright midday California sun makes her squint, but its rays feel warm and soothing. Small comfort, but she'll take it

Ellen starts heading to her car in the faculty lot— when she sees something that stops her in her tracks. A man with curly black hair, wearing a wrinkled blue button-down, is leaning against her Camry, scanning his smartphone and smoking a cigarette.

He looks about forty. He looks familiar, too, although Ellen can't quite put her finger on how she knows him.

Then it hits her. He's a goddamn *reporter,* one of the many who have been knocking on her door for days. So she *was* followed this morning after all!

Ellen turns back, praying he won't notice her, but it's too late.

"Mrs. Pierson, wait!" the man exclaims, tossing down his cigarette and hurrying her way. "I'm Mike Curr, with the *SLO Tribune.* I'd just like to ask you a few—"

"I said *no!*" Ellen shouts, swatting the man out of her face. "Leave me alone!"

She nearly knocks him over as she plows past him, then slides behind the wheel, starts the engine, and screeches out of the parking lot, narrowly missing a gatepost.

Racing down San Luis's quiet streets toward home,

Ellen feels a growing knot in her stomach, knowing she'll have to face a phalanx of additional reporters waiting for her. It won't take long for them to realize she was suspended, either, and plaster that across every front page in town. She just can't handle that right now.

So instead Ellen pulls a U-turn. She takes South Street to Madonna Road, then hooks a right into Laguna Lake Park. It's a lush open space, one of her favorite spots in the city. The perfect place to unwind. To decompress. To think.

Ellen turns off her cell phone, then dons a floppy beach hat and a pair of oversized sunglasses—a crude disguise, but better than nothing—and spends a few hours ambling along the scenic lakefront and the park's gently sloping trails. She passes bikers, joggers, stroller-pushing parents, even a class of first-graders on a field trip—thankfully from a different elementary school, so she doesn't know any of them or their teachers. It's relaxing, but strange and painful, too, seeing all these other people carrying on with their lives while hers lies in tatters.

Finally, with the sun edging toward the horizon, Ellen decides she's ready to go home. All she wants to do is work on her butterfly collection for a bit, then curl up in bed—and not wake up for a very, very long time.

As she nears her home, in addition to the cluster of reporters still camped out in front, she sees an official-looking white Chevy Impala parked in her driveway.

And as soon as she pulls beside it, Detectives McGrath and Petrillo step out.

McGrath has been calling her fairly regularly since last

week, but he hasn't paid a house visit since the police searched her home and dug up her backyard. So Ellen immediately knows something is afoot. She watches them order the press to back off, which she appreciates. Then she steels herself as they approach her.

"Good evening, Mrs. Pierson," McGrath says with a rakish but polite smile.

Ellen struggles to keep her composure. "Hello again. Is something wrong?" Realizing the absurdity of her words, she backtracks. "I mean, something *new*."

"No, ma'am," McGrath answers. "We just have a few more questions for you. I was going to ask you to come down to the station. But I figured you'd be more comfortable in your own home."

Comfortable. That's not something Ellen has felt all week. And she probably never will again.

"Let me ask *you* something, Detectives," she says. "Do I *have* to answer these new questions? What would happen if I refused?"

McGrath sighs and runs his callused hand through his thick mane of hair.

"And here I thought we were becoming friends."

"Friends?" Ellen scoffs. She can't hold back anymore; she lets him have it. "You think my husband is a killer. And you think I'm involved. You're trying to cozy up to me so I let down my defenses. So I slip up and give you some clue or piece of evidence you can use against us. Well, if that's what you consider friendship, you might be stranger than I thought!"

McGrath looks irritated, but Petrillo cracks up.

"You're wrong about that, Mrs. Pierson," she says. "He's a *helluva* lot stranger."

But Ellen is in no joking mood. She promptly spins on her heel and marches into her house, slamming the door shut behind her.

CHAPTER 13

ELLEN DOES NOT OPEN that door for the next five days.

She has become a shut-in. A hermit. Too overwhelmed to venture outside her house. Too scared to confront the growing horde of reporters out front. Too despondent to even change out of her pajamas.

She's been spending her days in the attic, hunched over her colorful assortment of butterflies. Sorting and cataloging, cleaning and preserving, building and polishing their glass display cases.

She's been spending her nights in a haze of red wine and tears.

For food, Ellen has been subsisting on what was already in her cupboards, mostly staples like beans and pasta and cans of tuna fish.

For company, she's been rereading her favorite romance novels and streaming old sitcom reruns. Her friends have, by and large, abandoned her, so she's stopped reaching out and unplugged her home phone. Her jailed husband still refuses to speak with her, and she's begun to give up hope on that front as well.

Tonight Ellen is curled up on the sofa, wineglass in hand, watching an ancient episode of *Married...with Children,* thinking about how dumb and insignificant Al and Peggy's marital problems seem compared to her own— when her doorbell rings.

The sound startles Ellen out of her stupor. She pauses the show and checks the clock: it's after 10:00 p.m. She certainly isn't expecting any visitors at this hour. A few reporters still bother her from time to time during the day, but never this late at night.

It must be a prank, Ellen thinks. *Or someone trying to mess with me.*

So Ellen ignores it. She's about to restart the show when the doorbell rings again. It's followed by knocking, gentle yet firm. Then a familiar man's voice.

"Ellen? It's me. I know you're in there. Can we talk? I just—I want to know how you're doing. Please open the door."

Every muscle in Ellen's body tenses. She *definitely* wasn't expecting...*him.*

Ellen considers ignoring her visitor until he gives up and goes home. But it's been days since she's had any contact with another human being. And she's moved that he thought to stop by and check on her, even if it's mostly out of guilt. She decides seeing a semi-friendly face can't hurt. Right?

"Hi, Jim," Ellen says, opening the door for the same person who, just a few days earlier, had summoned her to his office via text message and suspended her for something her *husband* had done. Tonight James's tie is loosened. His shoulders are slumped forward. And his eyes betray a concern for her that was absent earlier in the week.

"This is quite the surprise," Ellen continues. Then, suddenly embarrassed by her makeup-free face and unwashed hair, she adds: "Clearly I wasn't expecting anyone."

James offers a tender smile. "Could've fooled me. I think you look lovely."

He's a terrible liar, but Ellen appreciates the sentiment.

"I just stopped by to see how you were doing. How you were handling it all. I tried calling, but there was never any answer. Your cell, too."

Ellen remembers that her phone died a few days ago and she never bothered recharging it. She shrugs.

"I'm fine, Jim. Considering."

"Listen. I feel awful about your job. I want you to know—"

"If you really felt that bad, you wouldn't have suspended me," Ellen says, deliberately putting him on the spot.

"That's not fair," James answers. "Parents, teachers, the board—you have no idea the kind of pressure I was getting. I tried to stand up for you as much as I could."

Ellen wants to believe him. She wants desperately to have a friend right now, an ally, when the rest of the world has turned its back on her.

"Why are you *really* here, Jim?"

"I told you. I wanted to apologize. Again. And make sure you were all right."

Ellen tucks a few strands of hair behind her ear. "Thank you. I appreciate that. More than you can know." Then she adds: "Does your *wife* know where you are?"

James looks down at the doorstep. He nervously shuffles his feet.

"Now, that's *really* not fair, Ellen."

With a coy smile, she reaches out and takes James's hand.

"You know I don't always play by the rules."

CHAPTER 14

ELLEN WAKES UP IN bed—alone. She feels a bit groggy. Her head is gently throbbing. She must have had more wine last night than she realized.

After taking a moment to steady herself, she hobbles into the bathroom and does something she hasn't done all week.

Ellen takes a good, long look at her reflection in broad daylight.

It practically makes her wince.

Her glassy eyes have plum-colored bags under them. Her skin is splotchy. Her hair is greasy, tangled. She knew she'd let herself go these past few days, but not *this* far.

Okay, she thinks. *Enough. No more wallowing. Time to pull it together.*

Ellen starts by taking a scalding-hot shower for almost thirty heavenly minutes. She briefly feels guilty for wasting so much water, knowing California has been suffering a major drought. But she hasn't bathed once in nearly a full week, so it's a reasonable indulgence.

Next comes vigorous brushing—both her sticky teeth and her knotty hair.

After that, it's makeup. Normally not a vain person at all, Ellen goes to town this morning. She dusts her cheeks with pink blush. Slathers her lips a shade of ruby red. Coats her eyelids a deep forest green, adding a Cleopatra-style flourish at the edges.

Lastly come clothes. By habit, Ellen begins to put on a variation of her typical school-nurse attire: sensible khakis, a simple blouse, a comfy pair of Keds. But no. Today that just won't do. After rummaging through her closet—and forcing herself to ignore her husband's clothes at the other end—she finds an old sundress, yellow with a red floral print. She hasn't worn it in years, and frankly, it's a little short and a bit too low-cut for a woman her age.

But what the hell? Ellen thinks. *I'm doing this for nobody but me.*

And it works. Striking a pose in front of her bathroom mirror again, Ellen can't believe the transformation. She looks a thousand times better. But more importantly, she *feels* better. She feels—almost—normal again.

Ellen pads down the stairs into the kitchen and puts on a pot of coffee. Through a side window, she glimpses a few reporters still camped outside along the sidewalk. She starts to grumble under her breath...until she sees them all move aside to let a car pull into her driveway.

It's a white Chevy Impala, which she recognizes right away.

Out steps Detective McGrath. By himself. And somehow, he's gotten even better-looking since the last time she saw him—the healthy amount of salt-and-pepper scruff he's sporting gives him an extra rugged, manly air.

Ellen wasn't expecting him today, but she's not upset to see him, either. She opens the front door for McGrath before his finger can even ring the bell.

"Mrs. Pierson, I—oh, wow," he says, clearly caught off guard by her appearance, and fighting the urge to glance her up and down. "You going somewhere? You're . . ."

"Like a human being again?"

McGrath smiles.

"Do you mind if I come in?"

"I could use the company. But I'm guessing this isn't a social visit."

McGrath shakes his head. Of course it's not. Ellen knows *exactly* why he's here. To ask her more questions. To gather more evidence against her husband.

Ellen is soon pouring two cups of piping-hot coffee. Once again they're seated beside each other on her couch. But this time, she feels . . . different. She's less shellshocked. More comfortable.

But more tingly, too.

"It's good to see you again, Detective," she says, "but I'm afraid you're wasting your time. As I've been telling you for weeks, I don't remember anything more about—"

"No, I get that, Mrs. Pierson. And the details you *have*

been able to remember about the nights of the disappearances—they've been very helpful. But today..."

McGrath takes a careful sip of his coffee, then gently sets it back down.

"...with my partner working another case, I'd like you to tell me more about your husband *generally*. The kind of man he is. How you met. The state of your marriage. That kind of thing."

"How we met? Our marriage? I don't quite see how that—"

"I don't mean to pry. I'm just trying to get a fuller picture of our suspect. Because to be frank with you, ma'am..."

McGrath leans in a bit and gives Ellen a smoldering gaze.

"...I can't for the life of me figure out why any man would ever go after a couple girls when he's got a *woman* at home like you."

Ellen shifts on the sofa. She tugs at the hem of her sundress. She doesn't know if McGrath is using his sex appeal as a new tactic, or if he's hitting on her, or both. Part of her is offended by this approach. But part of her—fine, *much* of her—is flattered.

"Well, to be honest," she says, "Michael is...a lot like *you*, Detective. Not on the outside. But he's very loyal. Focused. And determined. We met about seven years ago at a California state teachers' conference. In Sacramento. We couldn't believe we had both been living in San Luis Obispo—and working in education—for so long and hadn't met. He asked me out that night, but I said no. I had just gotten out of a rocky relationship and wasn't interested in dating yet. But Michael persisted. He kept calling me and calling me. Sound familiar? Anyway. Finally, I said yes. And I'm glad I did."

McGrath now looks at Ellen a little icily.

"You're 'glad' you went out with, then married, a serial killer?"

Ellen blushes. "You know what I mean."

"And how has your marriage been recently? Specifically, the past two years. Since the abductions began."

Ellen's eyes fall to her mug. She stares at the milk and coffee swirling together, like mini storm clouds brewing on the horizon. She begins to choke back tears.

"Every relationship has its ups and downs. But my husband always seemed like such a sweet, caring, wonderful man. I loved Michael. Even now, a tiny piece of me . . . still does. And maybe always will."

McGrath rubs a callused hand over his scruffy beard, thinking.

"Has he still not talked to you since he was arrested?"

Ellen nods, almost embarrassed.

"In that case, I have some news about him you might want to hear."

CHAPTER 15

I WONDER SOMETIMES WHAT'S really going on in their heads.

What they're really thinking about when they look up at me with those puppy-dog eyes but are so clearly talking nonsense that I can see through it a mile away.

"The turkey is burning!" my mother, Evelyn, is exclaiming.

She's rocking her ninety-five-pound, eighty-six-year-old frame back and forth in her easy chair, flailing her arms and struggling to get up.

"Ma, shhhh, relax," I coo as gently and sweetly as I can.

"And the stuffing, too! And the sweet potatoes and, and— oh, Andy, Thanksgiving is ruined, and it's all my fault!"

I place my hands on her shoulders and guide her back into her chair. I do so as delicately as if she were an antique porcelain doll.

"It's all gonna be fine, Mom. I'll take care of it, I promise. Don't worry."

This seems to settle her. It usually does.

As she and my dad have both gotten worse over the last couple years, I've found that responding to them with facts or logic or reason doesn't work. The actual words I say basically don't matter at *all* when either one of them gets like this. As long as my tone is tender and my energy is calm, I could recite the Gettysburg Address to my parents and it would chill them out and bring them back to reality.

I've just about gotten my mom soothed when I hear the toilet flush in the bathroom down the hall. Then comes my father's booming voice.

"Snap out of it, Evie!" he barks, shuffling into the living room still rebuttoning his pants. "Thanksgiving? It's March. Do you hear me? It's springtime!"

"Oh, of course it is, Leonard!" my mother snaps, waving her hands in the air like she's at a revivalist church service. "I know that. I'm talking about *next* year!"

I let out a long sigh, my patience wearing thin.

"Let's all stop with the yelling, huh?"

I love my parents. I really do. But dealing with them isn't always easy.

They refuse to move to an assisted-living home, so I'm the one who has to do the assisting in *their* home. I try to swing by as much as I can, but working overtime these last few weeks on the Pierson case has mostly kept me away. But now, here I am.

"Andy, tell your father and me more about that nice girl you met. She worked in real estate, didn't she?"

Ugh. This time I have to grit my teeth as I speak patiently and pleasantly.

"Mom, you're thinking of Kelly. We broke up two years ago. Remember?"

My mother's expression gets spacey for a few seconds as she processes this.

"You know I just want you to be happy is all."

"You deserve to have a special woman in your life, son," my dad chimes in. "Just like I do."

My mother warms and puts her bony hand on his.

"Her name is Gloria," he says. "She's a real doll. I'll introduce you sometime."

With a laugh, my mother playfully swats him. Despite myself, I chuckle, too.

But the thing is, lately, I *have* been thinking about a special new woman in my life—a helluva lot more than I thought I would be.

Her name is Ellen Anne Pierson. She sure is an intriguing creature. Married to a psychopathic, pedophilic serial killer for years and never had a clue.

Or so she says.

Except more and more, I'm really starting to believe her.

And if she *is* telling the truth, just think about what she's going through! The shock. The denial. The loneliness. The pain.

For a sweet, attractive, bighearted woman like that—a school nurse, for God's sake—it's gotta be overwhelming.

I guess I've been starting to feel sorry for her.

And maybe—Jesus, I can't believe I'm even saying this—maybe I've been starting to feel something *else* for her, too.

CHAPTER 16

"SIR, I WILL ASK you one more time. Do you fully understand the severity of the crimes of which you have been accused?"

When facing the formidable, no-bullshit superior court judge Linda Knier, plenty of suspects tremble in their shackles. But not Michael Pierson. That smug son of a bitch is just standing there in his orange jumpsuit, saying and doing nothing.

Hang on. Scratch that. I'm wrong. Even though I'm sitting in the very back row of the courthouse, I can make out that he's literally twiddling his thumbs.

"He does, Your Honor," answers John Kirkpatrick, Pierson's rumpled, perpetually disheveled lawyer. "And my client strongly denies any and all allegations. Furthermore, given that so much of the evidence the State has outlined against him is circumstantial at best and mere conjecture at worst, we urge the court to toss out each and every count with prejudice."

I shake my head. *Defense attorneys.*

I've encountered Kirkpatrick a few other times. He even cross-examined me once on an assault-and-battery case. By all accounts, he's a good and decent man. And I know it's wrong to condemn attorneys—especially public defenders, who don't have much say in it—for the clients they represent. But the fact that the guy can stand up there with a straight face and say Michael Pierson should walk free makes me sick to my stomach.

And apparently, most of the spectators feel the same way. His comments trigger a chorus of groans and boos from the packed gallery. These onlookers include Brittany Herbert's mother and stepfather, of course, as well as the parents of Claire, Samantha, Maria, and Patty. Black, white, Hispanic, rich, poor—the families of Pierson's victims represent a cross section of San Luis's diverse community, united in their shared grief and desire for justice.

Judge Knier holds up her hand, and the commotion simmers down.

"Thank you, Counselor," the judge responds. "But the court disagrees. I will take under advisement your motion to dismiss the ancillary counts against your client. But the primary charges against him very much still stand. A jury of Mr. Pierson's peers will decide his guilt. Your motion for bail is also denied. Defendant is to be remanded into custody until the start of trial. We are adjourned."

Crack-crack-crack goes her gavel. And just like that, the hearing is over.

Kirkpatrick tries to hastily confer with his client as a

burly bailiff cuffs Pierson and starts to cart him off, but the bastard couldn't seem to care less.

Instead, he looks back at the gallery and makes eye contact with Ellen. She's been sitting in the third row on the far left side, as still and silent as a statue. He gives her a solemn nod, and I see her quickly mouth something back to him.

Wait—that was the first time they've made contact since his arrest.

What did she say?

It looked like "Good-bye."

But it also kind of looked like "You'll die."

Or maybe: "Should I?"

Shit. This could be important. I gotta find out. Fast.

CHAPTER 17

"MRS. PIERSON, HOLD UP!"

I'm racing through the courthouse hallway after Ellen, my boots slapping against the white marble with every step. I'm already feeling out of breath, but I'm very happy I found her.

Just after Pierson was led away, Samantha Gonzalez's mother, Maria, buttonholed me and asked if there was any new evidence in her daughter's case. In the approximately 3.2 seconds it took me to politely say, in my badly broken Spanish, *"No, señora, now excusa-me,"* Ellen is gone.

Now, scurrying down the hallway, Ellen glances back at me, but she doesn't slow down. In fact, she slips on a pair of sunglasses, ties a white scarf around her head, and quickens her pace.

Is she *running* from me?

"Mrs. Pierson," I call out again, "I just wanna talk to you!"

But still she pretends to ignore me and keeps moving. Damn it!

She's pretty fast, too—until she gets caught up in a gathering crowd of reporters all hollering questions at her. In no time, they've practically got her surrounded. Poor Ellen tries to snake her way through, but she can't.

Which gives me the opportunity to snap into action.

"Police! Everybody step back!"

Hurrying over, I wave my silver badge in the air with one hand while moving the reporters aside with the other until I reach Ellen, who's now cowering, practically frozen.

"Mrs. Pierson will not be answering any questions!" I bellow. Then I drape my arm around Ellen's slender shoulders and start pushing our way through the horde like a human snowplow.

"And if any one of you keeps giving her a hard time, now *or* at her house? I will *personally* arrest you for aggravated harassment and disturbing the peace, and you will *never* get another quote or tip from the SLOPD until I retire. Anybody wanna test me? Go right ahead!"

That does the trick, all right. Even though most of these reporters are smart enough to guess I'm probably bluffing, they back off anyway and let us pass.

Once we're out of the thick of it, I steer Ellen away from the main entrance and down a side hallway.

"Wait . . . wh—where are we going?" she stammers, still overwhelmed by it all.

"I know a side exit," I tell her. "It'll spit us out right

next to the employee and law-enforcement parking lot. I'll drive you home, Mrs. Pierson, okay?"

"What about . . . my car?"

"I'll have it towed." With a smirk, I add: "To *your* place. It's no sweat. I'm a cop, remember?"

Ellen gives me a grateful look, along with a smile.

It's only then that I realize, even though we're far from those crazy reporters now, I've still got my arm wrapped around her.

CHAPTER 18

NOT TWENTY MINUTES LATER, I'm turning onto Ellen's street. Her house comes into view. And she gasps.

It's an unbelievable sight.

There isn't a single reporter or news van out front anymore.

"I...I don't know how to thank you, Detective," she says as we pull into her driveway. "They were *monsters*."

"They just want to find the facts. Know the truth. Can't say I blame them."

Ellen seems to get my message. When I shut off the engine, she finally takes off the sunglasses and scarf she's been wearing since the courthouse and turns to me.

"Is this the part where I invite you inside, and since your partner is still working that other case, you ask me some even *more* probing, personal questions?"

"Maybe. But let's start with one you *do* know the answer to."

"I'll try," she says moments later as I follow her into the kitchen. "That's what I mouthed to him as he was led off. *I'll try.*"

Ellen heads straight for the sink and pours herself a tall glass of water. She drinks it down in a few big gulps. She starts to fill the glass up again, then stops and opens the freezer. From the back she pulls out a half-empty bottle of Grey Goose vodka. Fancy stuff. She pours a healthy amount of *that* into her water glass and guzzles it just as fast. It seems to settle her nerves almost instantly.

"You'll try *what*?" I finally ask as she wipes her mouth with her forearm.

"To survive. To get through this nightmare. To stay strong. To move on. I think that's what Michael was trying to tell me with his look. I wanted him to know I would."

As I watch Ellen put away the vodka and rinse out her glass, I can't help but be fascinated by this strong, beautiful woman.

"Detective," she says softly, "do I ever get to ask *you* any questions?"

"You can ask me anything," I answer. "If there's something you want to know about the investigation, or police procedure, or—"

"That's not what I'm talking about. I mean, questions like... 'With so much crime and hate and ugliness in the world, how do you get up every morning and still do your job?' Or, 'Is there any line you *wouldn't* cross if it meant solving a crime?' "

Ever so slightly, Ellen pouts her lips.

"Or . . . 'Is there a special someone in your life?'"

This woman! If she's trying to throw me off, I will not let her succeed.

Breaking the tension, I say: "Your butterfly collection, I presume?"

I've just spotted a couple items sitting on the table on the back porch. They look like frames of some sort, beside a few bottles of paint and brushes. Without letting Ellen answer, I head out to get a better look.

"After I've cataloged and filled a new shadow box with specimens," she explains as she follows me, "I like to stain the frame. I use different colors for different woods. It's too stuffy to paint up in the attic. All the fumes. So I do it out here."

I glance out at the backyard now and see all the uneven mounds of dirt where Dr. Hyong and his team dug up the dog grave we stumbled on. It was just a few weeks ago— but it feels like ages.

Then I look back at all the colorful butterflies in their freshly stained frames.

"It really is a wonderful collection, Mrs. Pierson."

I turn to face her and look directly into her sad, tired, but still entrancing bicolored eyes.

What kind of woman, I wonder, takes pleasure in collecting dead things?

CHAPTER 19

SOMETIMES I WISH I was one of those cops who drink.

Watching Ellen chug that vodka the other night—and seeing her flooded with such instant relief—actually made me a little jealous. Sure, I'll have a beer or two or four with some pals once in a while, but the hard stuff just isn't my style. Which is why my liquor cabinet looks so pathetic. Rifling through the couple of dusty bottles in it from God-knows-when, none of them really appeals to me.

Except that Macallan 25-Year-Old Sherry Oak. It's the gift all the guys in the department got me years ago, right after I got my detective's shield. It's the extra-extra-good shit I'm only "allowed" to pour after I've solved a murder case.

That's the drink I'm dying to have right now.

After almost five weeks since Pierson's arrest, I'm more convinced of his guilt than ever...but I'm still no closer to finding those other girls.

I know I should be focusing more on the case. Me and Gina should be out there hunting down more leads. Scouring the town and woodlands for more clues.

But instead, all I can think about is Ellen.

The goddamn killer's *wife*.

She's such an enigma. The more time I spend with her, the less I get her.

Most of the time, she seems like an open book. But every once in a while, I feel like she's hiding something, even though I can't put my finger on it. I can't tell if she's as steely as she seems, or as delicate as one of her butterflies.

But either way, there's something about her that's simply . . . intoxicating.

Jesus, McGrath, stop it. You're talking crazy!

I finally cave and grab a grimy old bottle of Jack Daniel's that's probably been sitting in my cabinet since the first George Bush administration. I slosh a bit into a tumbler and shoot it back—and nearly gag.

Can hard alcohol go bad?

Can an *innocent woman* go bad?

CHAPTER 20

AFTER HER SCUFFLE WITH that horde of reporters outside the courtroom—which ended only thanks to her white knight, Detective McGrath—Ellen thought her war against the press was over.

She had no idea it was about to get worse.

By the following morning, even *more* members of the media appeared in front of her home. The courthouse episode seemed to energize them, not discourage them. They took to knocking on Ellen's door at all hours of the day and night, preventing her from getting any decent sleep. (Maybe this was a deliberate tactic to wear her down.) Even just opening the blinds to peek outside for a few seconds subjected her to a hail of screams and taunts.

If Ellen was afraid to leave her house before, now she was terrified.

On more than one occasion, she thought about calling McGrath. She assumed he hadn't been serious about his threat, but she figured he would at least keep an eye on her place. Come to think of it, she hadn't heard from him since that day. Had he gotten too busy? Had he lost interest in her as a source of information? Or had the unexpected intimacy of their last conversation spooked him and pushed him away?

It doesn't matter. With or without him, Ellen knows she can't keep living this way, a prisoner in her own home. And as the start date of her husband's trial draws closer, this hell will only get worse—unless she puts an end to it now. Herself.

Standing in her kitchen, so bone-tired that she's brewing a rare pot of midday coffee, Ellen knows what she has to do. A simple act of defiance to show the press who's boss. She flips off the gas, opens her freezer, and downs the remaining few gulps of Grey Goose straight from the bottle—a little liquid courage that she very much needs.

Then she unlocks her front door and steps outside.

"Mrs. Pierson! Any comment on your husband's charges?"

"Will you ever apologize to the families of his victims?"

"Do you plan to stand by that monster's side at trial or divorce the bastard?"

The questions come fast and hard, hurled like rocks and glass bottles by an angry mob. Ellen's instinct is to duck and hurry back inside, but she resists it with every ounce of her strength.

"Will your husband be mounting an insanity defense, Mrs. Pierson?"

"Can you confirm reports he's been put on suicide watch?"

"How could you live with him for so long and have no idea who he really was?"

Ellen still refuses to take the bait. *I can do this,* she thinks.

Keeping her head held high, she walks calmly down her driveway, past her car, then steps onto the sidewalk. Now that she's on public property, the reporters swarm around her like vultures, surrounding her on all sides.

Still, she forges on, moving slowly and steadily down the block. But then the questions begin to get even worse. The reporters are growing frustrated by her silence and are desperate to get a rise out of her.

"How do you respond to claims that you knew about your husband's crimes and kept quiet?"

"If you're really innocent, why won't the police leave you alone?"

"Is it true you helped him pick his victims out of the yearbook and were there when he killed them?"

Ellen feels her lip start to quiver now. Her hands ball into fists. The notion that she had *anything* to do with what happened to those young women is sickening. Humiliating. And infuriating.

She feels the urge to start screaming at those vicious reporters to be quiet, to leave her alone, to show a little human decency. But making a scene when a dozen cameras are rolling is the *last* thing she needs.

Ellen walks faster now, keeping her eyes straight ahead. *Let me just make it once around the block,* she thinks. *Just give me that tiny victory. Please.*

But the reporters smell blood in the water.

"Did you and your husband get off on hearing those poor girls scream?"

"Where the hell are the bodies, Mrs. Pierson? Where did you bury them?"

And that's it. All Ellen can take. The final straw.

But instead of having a meltdown in the middle of the street, she turns and starts to run. Shoving the reporters out of her way, she races back home.

Once back inside, she slams her front door, locking and bolting it. Then she collapses in a heap of tears right there in her entryway.

McGrath. He's the only one who might even begin to understand what she's going through. He's the only one who'd listen if she called him. Ellen crawls toward her kitchen, toward her cell phone, resting on the counter. All she has to do is pick it up and dial to hear a friendly voice, to see a friendly face, to—

No. She can't. She won't.

At least not yet.

CHAPTER 21

NIGHTFALL IN THE HILLS of San Luis Obispo is a quiet, peaceful time. It's one of the things Ellen has always loved most about living here.

But tonight, she finds the silence outside her home deafening.

She's been tossing and turning for hours. The two tall tumblers of Scotch she had made her fuzzy but not sleepy. The old sitcom reruns she tried watching were agitating, not distracting. And now, a few minutes before 3:00 a.m., Ellen feels the walls of her little home closing in on her. She can't breathe. She needs to get out. Get some oxygen. This instant.

Those damn reporters camped outside can go to hell.

Ellen bolts out of bed. She throws on a pair of jeans and a black sweater. She ties her wild mane of hair in a sloppy bun. Then she grabs her car keys and, before she has time to change her mind, bursts out her front door toward her Camry.

This unexpected development clearly catches the sleepy press off guard. Which was exactly Ellen's intent. "Hey, she's going somewhere!" one of them shouts as Ellen starts her engine and peels out, the squeal of her tires piercing the quiet night.

Free at last!

Ellen tears down her street, blowing past the homes of all her dozing neighbors, who have long since shunned her. She rolls down all her car's windows and lets the cool air hit her face from every side. It's exactly the kind of refreshment she needs.

Ellen applies the brakes as she approaches a yellow light at the intersection of Andrews Street and Monterey. She flips on her turn signal to make a left, even though she doesn't know exactly where she's going. For now, she just wants to drive and enjoy the freedom of the open road.

After a few seconds stopped at the red light, however, that freedom disappears.

In her rearview mirror, Ellen spots a small caravan of cars and news vans speeding toward her. Those goddamn reporters are following her!

Ellen furiously pounds her steering wheel. *Come on!*

But no. This time, she is *not* going to give in to them. Not a chance.

Making sure the intersection is clear, Ellen blows right through the stoplight, crossing Monterey Street and heading onto Grand Avenue. Most of the press is still stopped at the red, but damn it—a few run the light, too, and keep following!

Gotta get away, Ellen thinks as she barrels along this four-lane thoroughfare. *Gotta shake them!* But how?

Up ahead, Ellen sees signs for on-ramps to the 101. Which gives her an idea.

She knows it's crazy...but she also knows that at 3:00 a.m. on a weeknight, the freeway should be practically empty. And if she happens to get pulled over, well, she's been growing chummy lately with a certain SLOPD detective who could probably help her get off with just a warning.

Ellen takes another look behind her and sees two local news vans and three other cars on Grand Avenue, coming up fast. So she decides it's worth a shot.

Making a wildly sharp left to head southbound—via the *off-ramp*—Ellen is soon racing down the freeway...in the wrong direction!

Honk-honk-hoooooonk!

Horns blare and tires screech as the few cars that *are* on the freeway at this hour brake and swerve like crazy to avoid plowing into her.

Ellen quickly gets over to the shoulder. She flashes her brights and honks her own horn as a warning to other oncoming vehicles, but she doesn't slow down one bit.

Soon she's pushing forty-five miles per hour, which is about as fast as she feels safe driving in this insane condition. But she knows it will be only a matter of minutes before one of the stunned drivers she passes calls 911. So she'll have to get off the freeway as soon as possible.

The hard part, though, is over. She checks her rearview

mirror. Not a single news van or reporter's car is following her! None of them had the balls, which fills Ellen with a burst of pride.

She keeps driving, the wind roaring through her Camry, the cacophony of horn-honking never stopping.

Up ahead, finally, Ellen sees an exit. The sign is facing the other direction, of course, but she knows it's for California Boulevard. The off-ramp gets closer...closer...

But Ellen steers clear of it. It would spit her out too close to the Grand Avenue off-ramp she used. And the press might be expecting her to do that. They might very well be there waiting for her. Definitely not worth the risk.

So Ellen continues speeding along. Her sweaty hands stay glued to the wheel. Her steely gaze stays fixed straight ahead. Her icy resolve stays as strong as ever.

She passes another exit, Santa Rosa Street. Then a third, Osos Street. Ellen considers driving even farther this way, possibly out of town—

But then she hears a distant police siren.

Shit!

Okay. No more time to mess around. The next exit is for Broad Street, and Ellen decides she has no choice but to take it.

Pumping the brakes as she nears it, she pulls a wide, insanely dangerous U-turn across the two right lanes. Scraping the side of her Camry against the guardrail, she accelerates down the off-ramp and onto this sleepy residential street.

Ellen heads a few blocks down, then finally pulls over,

stopping under the cover of a giant oak tree. She shuts off her engine. She leans her head back.

And she lets out a long, guttural scream.

Adrenaline is surging through her body. Tears are leaking from her eyes.

How the hell did this happen to her life?

But for right now . . . what the hell does she do next?

CHAPTER 22

SLEEP. BLESSED SLEEP. That's what Ellen needs most right now.

As if she weren't exhausted enough from the stressful hell of the past few weeks, her pulse-pounding drive the wrong way down the 101 has left her drained, both physically and emotionally.

And now, the sound of that faraway police siren seems to be drawing closer.

Ellen holds her breath. She clenches her fists. She says a silent prayer.

Finally, the siren passes, fading into the quiet night.

Ellen exhales in relief, then starts to consider her next move. She *could* get back on the freeway—heading in the right direction this time—and keep going, out of SLO. But where? And what would that accomplish? If anything, it would look like she was running away, and that would give the press even more reason to hound her.

"Those bloodsucking creeps!" Ellen screams out loud inside her car.

A small army of them are certainly still camped outside her house, waiting to pounce. If she dared go home now, especially at this ungodly hour, after leading them on that high-speed chase? The scene would be sheer chaos. Not very conducive to a good night's sleep.

So if Ellen can't skip town but can't go home yet, either, what now?

She gets an idea and shifts her Camry back into drive.

A few turns later, she's cruising in the direction of the freeway again, more or less retracing her path, but on surface streets. Eventually she starts driving through a residential neighborhood, nestled in the foothills, where there isn't another car or person on the road at all. The solitude is calming but also eerie. Unsettling.

Ellen glances down at her dashboard clock: 3:51 a.m. With a shake of her head, she tries to remember the last time she was out and about this late. Even when she and Michael used to celebrate New Year's Eve together at the old Moonbeam Lounge downtown, their one big night a year to let loose and drink and dance and act like kids again, they were always back home and in bed by one o'clock at the very latest.

Tonight, Ellen has been *run out* of her home. And Michael's bed is a cot in the county jail. How quickly life can change.

After passing a block of modest adobe-style houses, Ellen pulls into the driveway of an old-fashioned motor inn, the El Toro Motel, the building small and quaint and painted a light cantaloupe. Seeing a flickering neon sign out front advertising VACANCY, Ellen parks her car in one of the many open spaces and heaves her tired body out.

She pushes open the lobby door. As it swings shut, a set of old sleigh bells attached to the knob jangles. Inside, the air is air-conditioned cool, but smells faintly of marijuana. Ellen immediately spots the likely source: a young man slouching behind the front desk, his nose buried in his smartphone, his eyes at half-mast and bloodshot.

Ellen has a hunch this twenty-something stoner— CARSON C., according to his name tag—isn't about to give her a world-class customer-service experience. But that's just fine by her. Better than fine, actually. Between his youth, his slovenliness, and his likely altered state, the chances of him *recognizing* her are slim to none. Which is something Ellen definitely doesn't want right now.

"Excuse me, Carson?" she asks, after standing there unseen by the man for nearly thirty whole seconds.

"Oh, sorry...can I, uh, help you?" he finally mumbles.

Ellen requests a room for the night. Carson tells her that checkout is at 10:00 a.m., meaning she'd have it for only about five and a half hours. Ellen thinks about that and changes her request.

"Two nights, then, please. Under the name Judith Hayes."

Using an alias gives Ellen a quick shiver of excitement, as if she were a spy or undercover agent. But that was the name of her maternal grandmother, a woman she loved dearly, and using it now also provides her a tiny bit of comfort.

"Sure thing, ma'am. I just, like, need a credit card?"

Ellen opens her purse and removes a thick wad of bills instead.

"How about cash?"

Key in hand, Ellen shuffles down the walkway to room 4.

Four—*oh, great,* Ellen thinks. That's the number of girls who have gone missing. The number her husband stands accused of kidnapping and murdering.

Ellen hesitates before unlocking her room. She debates whether to go back and ask Carson for a different one, one that won't remind her of—

No. Forget it. She's just seconds away from passing out anyway, so Ellen opens the door, locks the bolt behind her, and without even turning on the lights, literally collapses face-first onto the queen-size bed.

In her final few moments awake, an image of Detective McGrath flashes through Ellen's mind. He'll probably be waking up soon for work, she thinks. He'll be told about her daring late-night "escape" from her own home, and her reckless driving down the freeway, too. He might even guess her alias and figure out what motel she's staying at.

McGrath might then pay her private room a visit.

And maybe a part of Ellen wants him to.

CHAPTER 23

ELLEN WAKES UP IN the exact same position: face-down on the bed, arms slightly akimbo, feet and calves dangling off the edge. Only now, her sparse little motel room is flooded with morning sunlight.

Ellen peels herself off the itchy maroon bedspread and looks around, squinting, and fighting off the faintest feeling of nausea. Just like the outside of the motel, the walls are painted a pale orange. *The color of vomit,* Ellen can't help but think. And although San Luis Obispo is land-locked, the room is decorated with a maritime theme. A bland watercolor of an anonymous beach is over the bed. A cheap print of a nineteenth-century whaling vessel hangs next to the dusty TV, slightly askew.

Ellen stumbles into the bathroom and splashes her face with cool water. She gargles some, hoping to flush the sour taste from her mouth. In the process, she gets the briefest glimpse of her ghostly appearance in the mirror—and quickly looks away.

Debating what to do next, Ellen gives her motel room

a once-over. Other than a few creases in the bedcovers, it looks completely untouched, as if she'd never been there at all. As if all the pain and stress and anger she felt last night never even existed. As if it *were* all right to head back home—which is what Ellen decides to do.

Next to a decorative glass starfish paperweight on the nightstand sits an ancient clock radio. The time is 10:05 a.m. Which makes Ellen grimly chuckle. She paid for this room for a whole extra night and has ended up needing it for only an extra three hundred seconds.

Maybe I'll keep it anyway, she thinks. *Just in case.*

Ellen locks the door behind her, then gets into her Camry and pulls out of the El Toro's parking lot. Some twenty minutes later, she's rounding the corner onto her block. And the scene is an absolute zoo, the street and sidewalk in front of her home crammed with more reporters and news vans than ever before.

Just as Ellen starts considering making a U-turn and heading back to the motel, she sees a familiar white Impala parked in her driveway. And there's good old Detective McGrath again, leaning against the hood, talking on his cell phone. When he spots Ellen's approaching car, he quickly hangs up. Ellen knows she can't turn around now. And part of her doesn't want to anymore.

"Mrs. Pierson, where did you go last night?"

"Were you thinking about running away because you're guilty?"

The reporters' questions again come flying at her fast and hard the moment Ellen steps out of her vehicle. But just as fast, McGrath is next to her. He lays a comforting hand on her shoulder and draws her close to him, shielding Ellen from the verbal assault and speaking softly into her ear.

"Hey . . . you doing okay?" he asks.

"Yes, I suppose. I've been running errands all morning, just trying to—"

"Because I was having some trouble sleeping last night, not an uncommon problem for me, either, when I heard a call come over the radio. A car was spotted driving wildly down the 101, the wrong way. Female driver. The descriptions of both sounded familiar. But she somehow slipped away. Crazy, huh?"

Ellen nods solemnly, realizing now why McGrath is there. She braces herself for what will be coming next: handcuffs and further humiliation in front of the rabid press.

"If you're here to arrest me, Detective, just go ahead and—"

"Arrest you?" McGrath asks, the faintest twinkle in his deep-set eyes. "For what? I just swung by to make sure you are okay."

Ellen flushes with relief—and decides to extricate herself as quickly as possible.

"I'm fine, Detective. Thank you. No need to worry. Now, if you'll excuse me . . ."

Ellen shrugs off McGrath's touch and starts to hurry inside, averting her gaze.

She doesn't want the detective to know how she *really* feels.

CHAPTER 24

"WAIT," I CALL OUT to Ellen as she rushes past me toward her front door. "Just promise me you won't ever do anything that stupid again."

Ellen stops and spins around to face me but still won't look me in the eye.

"Why? Are you afraid I might die, and you'll lose all that precious evidence in *here*?" She taps the side of her head, a little tauntingly.

Despite the crowd of reporters at the end of the driveway, their cameras watching our every move, I feel the sudden urge to grab Ellen's shoulders and give them a violent shake. *Of course that's what I'm afraid of!* I want to shout. *What the hell are you hiding from me?*

But instead, I say gently, "I want you safe, Mrs. Pierson. For a lot of reasons. Is that so hard to understand?"

Ellen nods and finally looks me in the eye.

"I do understand," she says. "I'm just not sure if I believe you. Or if I trust you." She pauses, then asks, "I *want* to trust you, Detective McGrath, but should I?"

I've had similar doubts about Ellen's honesty since the moment we met. I'm usually damn good at reading people, too. But these past few weeks, the more I've gotten to know the intriguing, alluring Ellen Pierson—the low-key wife of one of the most despicable killers I've ever put away—the more mysterious she's become.

"For someone with those kinds of doubts," I say, "you seem pretty willing to keep talking to me."

Even though you never actually say a damn thing, I think.

Ellen smiles and tucks a few errant strands of hair behind her left ear.

"Maybe . . . maybe that's because I *like* talking to you."

I look back at all the reporters crowded up and down the sidewalk, jostling to get the best position, their cameras and microphones pointed at us like weapons.

"There's another pretrial hearing today in your husband's case. Starts in less than an hour, actually. I guess you're not going?"

Ellen bites her lip. And shakes her head.

"Just take care of yourself, Mrs. Pierson. Okay? No more late-night joyrides on the freeway. No more disappearing on me. I need you to be—"

Ellen takes a sudden step toward me, getting right up in my face.

I flinch, caught off guard—and reach for my sidearm. But Ellen is too fast.

She leans in and plants a kiss on my cheek.

I'm too startled to pull away. But I hear the reporters

going wild, hurling questions at us, their cameras *click-click-click*ing like a swarm of angry cicadas.

"I—I'm sorry, Detective," Ellen says, backing away now. "I don't know what came over me."

I'm feeling equally flustered. Maybe more so.

"Bye, Mrs. Pierson," I mutter, and get back in my car as quick as I can.

CHAPTER 25

THIS TIME, I REALLY stepped in it.

After leaving's Ellen's place, I decided to skip the hearing, drive around town for a little while, then head back to the station. I was feeling so . . . *thrown* by the whole episode. So confused. Pierson wasn't going to be in court today anyway—just his public defender, Kirkpatrick, and the state prosecutor squabbling over some pretrial motions. I could use that extra time to catch up with my partner, get ahead on some paperwork, and think.

But as soon as I step into the bullpen, I realize I've made a big mistake.

Nobody says a word, but I can feel the judgmental glares of every officer, sergeant, and fellow detective I pass boring right through me.

"What the hell were you thinking, man?" Gina demands before I even sit down at my desk. "You see the *Tribune* yet?"

With dread, I fire up the website of San Luis Obispo's local paper.

Sure enough, the home page's lead headline reads: SLO COP LOCKS UP SUSPECT, LOCKS LIPS WITH SUSPECT'S WIFE.

And below it, in full color, is a giant picture of me and Ellen caught in the act.

"She kissed *me,* okay?" I insist to my partner, who's more pissed off than I've ever seen her. Not that I can blame her. "And it was on the cheek, for godsakes. You can see it right there in the photo."

"Tell me *why,* Andy," Gina says. "Is there something going on between you two? Something I gotta know about? Are you sleeping with this woman?"

"Christ, no," I answer. "She's lonely is all. Scared. Confused. And I'm the only one in this town who's still willing to talk to her. Maybe Ellen's developing a...a little *thing* for me. I don't know. I can't help the powerful effect I have on women sometimes."

Gina smirks and tosses one of her empty Red Bulls into the trash.

"This could actually be a blessing in disguise," I continue. "Think about it. The more she trusts me, the more she might tell me. Might be the only chance of finding those girls alive that we've got."

Gina is about to respond when her cell phone rings. She checks the ID.

"Hmm. It's my guy at the courthouse. Hold that depressing thought."

Gina picks up. She listens. She shakes her head with quiet fury. She hangs up.

Then she shares the terrible news she's just learned.

Son of a bitch!

Now it's my turn to place a call. To Ellen Pierson.

The line rings and rings. It goes to her voicemail, which an electronic voice informs me is completely full. I angrily hang up and dial again. This time she answers.

"Detective McGrath, I'm glad you called. What happened earlier, I—"

"That's not what this is about," I snap, struggling to control my simmering rage.

I don't want to push Ellen away. I need her on my side right now more than ever.

"They just threw out all four murder charges against your husband."

"Wait . . . what?"

"Without a murder weapon, without any eyewits, without the girls' *bodies,* Judge Knier ruled that there's not enough evidence. Michael's only going be tried for Brittany Herbert's abduction and *attempted* murder. That's it."

I pause for a moment to let that sink in and to hear Ellen's response.

"Well . . . at least he'll go to prison for *something.* That's good, right?"

"No, Mrs. Pierson, it's *not* good!" I explode. "He's a cold-blooded killer. I want justice for Claire, Samantha, Maria, and Patty. I want your husband to pay!"

There's an even longer pause on the line now. I use it

to try to slow my sharp breathing and lower my soaring blood pressure.

After what feels like an eternity, Ellen finally speaks again.

"Come over again tonight," she says. "Anytime after sunset. Use the back door. Not the front. There's something I want to give you."

CHAPTER 26

ELLEN WOULD BE HARD-PRESSED to name her favorite butterfly. She admires every species and type. But there are some in her vast collection that she particularly cherishes. Like her rare Kaiser-i-Hind, native to India and Nepal, with its brilliant green-and-gold coloring. Or her South American glasswing, whose delicate wings are literally translucent, like tiny panes of glass.

But it's her European peacock that Ellen has always felt a special kinship with. Seen from below, its wings look as boring as tree bark: speckled, rusty brown. Yet viewed from above, they are a stunning pattern of red, yellow, and blue.

Which side is the "real" one? They both are. Which is what Ellen likes so much. It's all a matter of perspective. The butterfly possesses some strange contradictions.

Just like she does.

Ellen is currently using a pair of tweezers and a magnifying loupe to inspect this beloved specimen. Outside, the sun is going down; it's starting to get dark. So with her

free hand, she flips on the lamp beside her attic workstation to get a better view.

When suddenly, she hears a faint knocking.

It's coming from downstairs.

And not from the front door, but the back.

A shiver of anticipation buzzes through Ellen's body.
She carefully sets down her European peacock and shuts
its glass case. Then she goes to greet her visitor.

Detective McGrath is standing on the rear patio, fid-
geting slightly, backlit by the setting sun. The sky behind
him is a blend of lavender purple and bubble-gum pink.

Ellen takes a moment to compose herself. She smooths
down her hair and flattens the imaginary wrinkles in her
simple blouse. Then she opens the door.

"Well, I'm here," he says. "Wanna tell me what this is
all about? I really don't like surprises."

"Good evening, Detective," she says. "Thank you for
coming. Would you like to come inside?"

"I don't know, Ellen," he huffs. "Would I?"

Ellen smiles demurely, but on the inside she's burning
up. In all the weeks they've been getting to know each
other, McGrath has always called her Mrs. Pierson. Ellen
takes his casual use of her first name as a very good sign.

"I think you *do* want to come in," she replies. "Very much."

Growing hesitant, McGrath checks behind him and
looks around, making sure the coast is clear. Unless a reporter is hiding in her bushes, it seems that they're alone.

At last McGrath steps inside. He shuts the door behind him.

Then he turns back to face Ellen. Stares into her eyes.

And suddenly, they're kissing.

It's so much more this time than just a quick peck. It's deep. Raw. Electric.

Passionate.

It goes on for quite some time, their hands clawing at each other, their breath quickening—until it becomes too much. Certainly for McGrath. Maybe Ellen, too.

Just as suddenly, they both pull away, shocked and bashful.

"I—I'm sorry," McGrath says. "That was completely unprofessional."

"It's all right, Detective. I don't know what came over me, either."

McGrath rubs a shaking hand over his scruffy cheek.

"At this point," he says softly, "you can probably start calling me Andy."

"Okay, then...*Andy,*" Ellen replies a little playfully, enjoying how the name rolls off her tongue. "Here's what I wanted to give you, *Andy.*"

From her back pocket she removes a blank, sealed envelope and holds it out to him.

"What is it?" McGrath asks.

Ellen says nothing, so McGrath snaps on a pair of latex gloves and plucks it from her grasp. He can feel that there isn't a letter inside, but something else. Something small. Pointy. Heavy for its size. McGrath begins to tear the envelope open when Ellen touches his gloved hands.

"No," she says. "Later."

CHAPTER 27

"**DON'T PUT THAT SHIT** in my mouth—it'll kill me!"

"It's applesauce, Pop, not arsenic," I say, clenching my jaw so tight that I'm afraid my jugular is about to burst. "And I'm a homicide detective, remember? If and when the day comes that I decide to put you and Ma out of your misery, I know about a hundred better ways to do it than hiding poison in your dessert. Okay?"

My father's flash of anger slowly disappears and turns into dark laughter. He gives me a good-natured jab to the shoulder as I finish spooning the yellow mush into his toothless mouth.

"Now let's get you ready for bed, huh?"

I lead my old man up the stairs and into the bathroom. I help him change into his pajamas, wash his face, moisturize his skin, and take his evening pills. Then I lead him into his bedroom, where my mother—always much more of a morning person than my night-owl dad—has already been asleep for over an hour.

I pull back the covers on my father's side and start to guide his frail frame into bed, when he suddenly reaches out and grabs my arm.

"Thank you, son," he whispers. "Andy...what would we do without you?"

"Aw, Pop. Let's hope we never have to find out. For both our sakes. G'night."

I pad softly back down the stairs. In the kitchen, I load my parents' dinner plates into the dishwasher. In the living room, I straighten up the throw pillows on the couch.

In the entryway, I reach into my pocket and pull out the envelope Ellen gave me, which I tore open the second I got back to my car.

Inside was a single metal key attached to a fob with the words EL TORO ~ RM 4 printed on it in faded, old-fashioned lettering.

First I make out with her...then she slips me the key to her motel room?

Jesus, what the hell am I doing?

I hold the key in my hand, feeling the cold, hard metal against my palm—and remembering Ellen's warm, soft lips against my own.

There's a chance I'm misreading this whole situation. A small one, but still. Ellen could be trying to tell me that the El Toro played some role in Pierson's crimes. Maybe room 4 is where he took those girls and killed them. Maybe their bodies are buried under the floorboards. Maybe Pierson had an accomplice, and the guy is holed up there right now, waiting, armed and dangerous.

Oh, come on. Who the hell am I kidding?

This has nothing to do with the murders at all. It's strictly personal.

If I were smart—and if this were a more typical case—I'd ask the San Luis County SWAT team to set up a perimeter and breach the El Toro, just to be safe. At the very least, I'd tell my partner about the key. Log it into evidence.

What I wouldn't be doing is going to the motel alone and actually *using* it.

Which is what I'm seriously considering. I know I shouldn't... *but should I?*

My cell phone suddenly rings, startling me out of my deliberations. I check the ID. *Great.* I can't dodge this call any longer. I have to take it. So I do.

"Well, shit, man, forget you have a partner?" Gina says. I can hear her sarcasm has a slight edge to it tonight. "I've been calling you for the past three hours."

"Yeah, right, sorry," I say. "My phone died, then I had to give my folks dinner, then I—"

"Whatever, it's fine. Your visit with Pierson's wife—don't leave me hanging. What did she wanna give you? And I just ate, so if it was some kind of freaky sex act, keep it G-rated, please."

"Funny," I say—with a gulp.

I look down again at the old key in my hand. In all the years I've known my partner, I've never lied to her. Not once. Honestly, I trust this woman with my life.

But can I trust her with *this*?

"Nothing," I finally say. "Ellen was full of it. Maybe the charges being dropped against her husband rattled her. I don't know. She just wanted somebody to talk to."

"Hey, Andy, are you okay? You sound distracted or something."

"Me? I'm good, Gina. Just tired. Thanks. Let's talk in the morning."

I hang up, feeling like a total piece of shit. But I've made my decision.

Now I gotta live with the consequences.

CHAPTER 28

MY IMPALA'S HEADLIGHTS ILLUMINATE the El Toro's peach-orange facade as I pull into the parking lot. I take a spot on the far end of it, cut my engine, and pause to think.

I still have a chance here to back out. To go home.

To *not* sleep with the goddamn killer's wife!

Instead, as if my body is on autopilot, I get out of my car and march up to 4.

I knock, then wait for a reply. Which never comes. So I try to turn the key—but the lock sticks. Shit. Is this the right place? The right door? The right move?

I try the key again. This time, the lock clicks open.

Stepping into the dark little room, I can sense it's empty even before I flip on the lights. It's cozy in here, but creepy, too. The nautical artwork on the walls is plenty tacky. And the maroon bedspread is plenty ugly—and the color of dried blood.

As I wait for Ellen, my mind starts trying to work

backward, posing way more questions than I can answer. When did she book this place? Last night, when she went for that crazy drive down the freeway? Or earlier? And at what point did she decide to give me the key? I called the motel from the car, but the guy at the front desk told me no one by the name of Ellen Pierson had checked in recently at all. Makes sense she'd want to use a pseudonym. But what else is she hiding from me?

And where the hell *is* she, anyway? What kind of one-sided rendezvous is this?

I pull my cell from my pocket and start to dial Ellen's number—when I stop myself. Come on. It's not like she *forgot*. If she's coming tonight . . . she'll be here.

I wander around the room a bit, looking for any tiny details that could prove helpful, treating it like a possible crime scene, not a love nest. At least for now. This also helps occupy my mind and ease the butterflies in my stomach. But the room looks so untouched, I wonder if Ellen has even stepped foot in here before.

I adjust the crooked whaling-ship painting near the TV. Then I check my watch. It's nearly eleven; I've been waiting for almost half an hour. And I'm starting to get a little sleepy. So I sit down on the bed. Ellen could walk in any minute, and we'll probably end up on the bed anyway . . .

Jesus, this is so wrong!

A few more minutes pass. I lean back against the headboard, propping myself up with a few pillows. My eyelids are getting heavier, so I rest them for just a moment.

Next thing I know, I'm startled awake by my ringing

cell phone. I fumble to answer it—noticing some predawn sunlight peeking in through the curtains.

"Gina, hey," I say groggily. "Everything okay? What time is it? You're calling so early."

"It's me, Detective. I mean . . . *Andy.*"

Ellen's voice hits me like a shot of espresso. I'm instantly wide awake.

"Where are you?" she asks. "I need to see you. Right away."

I can't help but scoff, feeling stood up.

"I thought that was the plan last night," I answer.

"I'm sorry. I lost track of the time. I never—"

"And I think you know exactly where I am. Where I *still* am."

I can tell that Ellen is trying to stifle a big smile.

"You . . . you really waited for me? The whole night?"

I don't tell her that most of the night I was fast asleep.

"Look, it's probably for the best this way. What's up *now*?"

Ellen takes a deep breath. "I have something else I need to give you."

This freaking woman! Messing with my head. Toying with my heart.

"Tough shit, Ellen. You had your chance. I'm not falling for that again."

"Please, Andy," she begs. "This is different. I was up all night going through my husband's things. I think it might be important for your case. *Very* important. I swear."

I hate these kinds of games. And I'm quickly running out of patience.

But I need this woman. To put Pierson away.

And I *want* this woman. And Ellen knows it, too.

"Tell me what it is first. Then I'll decide."

"I would, Andy," Ellen replies. "But you wouldn't believe me."

CHAPTER 29

HERITAGE OAKS BANK: a squat, redbrick building in the middle of downtown San Luis Obispo. If Ellen's hunch is right, this unassuming spot might be where this whole case is finally blown wide open.

I swung by her house again after we hung up. Like she asked, I didn't bother getting out or even turning off my engine. She hopped right into my car and said, "Just drive," hoping to throw the press off our tail.

Once we were a few blocks away, she handed me what she'd found.

Another key.

"For crying out loud, Ellen!" I snapped. "I thought we were past this."

"Look closer," she said. "It's not a motel room. It's a safe-deposit box."

Ellen explained that right after they got married, she and Pierson rented a box together at Heritage Oaks to store their marriage license, various other documents, and a couple pieces of jewelry she'd received as wedding presents. A few years later, after they bought a locked filing cabinet for the house, she and her husband gave the box up.

At least, Pierson *told* her they gave it up.

Ellen was moving a pair of her husband's shoes that night when she heard something rattling around. She grabbed a screwdriver, pried off the sole, and hidden inside the hollowed-out heel was the old, familiar key.

I have no way of verifying a word of that story, of course. And after last night, I don't exactly trust Ellen much anymore. But an opportunity like this—I can't pass it up.

We're sitting in silence together, parked across the street, waiting for 9:00 a.m. to strike and the bank to open up. From the corner of my eye, I watch as Ellen takes a dainty sip of the steaming cup of coffee I bought her. Stood up or not, I'm still a gentleman.

"That looks like the manager," I say, noticing a comely middle-aged woman with jet-black hair unlock the front door and roll up the metal gate. "They're open. Let's go."

Ellen and I head into the bank so fast, the manager has barely had time to sit down at her desk. Noticing a name placard on it—ALEXANDRA GARCIA—I hold up my badge and call out: "Excuse me, Ms. Garcia? Urgent police business, please."

I bring her up to speed on our situation. But this lady is smart. The moment I mention Pierson's safe-deposit box, she shrugs apologetically and says, "I'm afraid you'll need a warrant to access it, Detective."

"Not if I've got the consent of one of the box's co-lessees," I reply, gesturing to Ellen. Reluctantly, Garcia looks up the agreement on her computer. Sure enough, it's still in both Michael Pierson's *and* Ellen Pierson's names. Bingo.

Garcia leads us into the main vault room, a claustrophobic space lined with metal boxes from floor to ceiling. She inserts her manager's key into one slot, I put Ellen's into the other, and the shoebox-sized steel container slides right out.

"I'll leave you two alone," she says, and does just that.

Snapping on a pair of latex evidence gloves, I consider asking Ellen to scram as well. But I can see she's just as eager to see what's inside as I am.

Carefully I lift up and remove the top.

Inside is an old cigar box, the kind I used to keep my baseball-card collection in when I was a kid. But the lid is sealed shut with duct tape. Great. Using a different key from my own keychain—the house key to my parents' place—I slice through the tape.

And I open the cigar box.

"Oh, my God!" Ellen gasps. "No, no...no!" She covers her face with her hands and crumples to the floor in sobs. "I didn't want to believe it. It can't be true!"

My reaction is far more controlled, but I'm just as stunned as she is.

Inside the box is a small stack of pictures. They look

like they were taken on a cell phone or digital camera but printed out on typing paper from a personal printer.

I sift through them, delicately, almost numbly.

The terrified, bloodied faces of those four missing girls—Claire, Samantha, Maria, and Patty—are staring back up at me.

CHAPTER 30

KEEP IT. MAYBE I'LL take another drive tonight.

Those are the words Ellen leaned over and sensually whispered to me as I dropped her at home and tried to give her back her motel-room key a few hours after the bombshell discovery at the bank.

As Gina and I continue dealing with the pictures' fallout all afternoon, they're the words that keep echoing inside my head. "Hey, Andy, focus here," my partner snaps at me as we comb through old security footage in the bank manager's office. Eventually we find a tape showing Pierson entering the vault and presumably accessing his safe-deposit box, just two days after Patty Blum, the most recent victim, went missing.

Oh, Ellen. How could you not have known you were sharing your bed with a monster? And are you really inviting *me* to share it again? Are you actually going to show up tonight? Am *I*? I swore I wouldn't go near this mess a second time, but—

"Sorry, uh, say that last part again?" I have to ask Dr. Hyong as he shares his lab's analysis of the photos of Patty and the other four young women. I want nothing more in the world than to find these girls and punish the bastard who did this...but all I can think about right now is the bastard's irresistible wife.

Hyong clears his throat. "What I said was, it's impossible from a few grainy photographs to know any of the victims' past or present conditions for certain. The images could have been altered. The victims *themselves* could have been altered—their appearances degraded, for instance, with makeup or fake blood to make us think they were killed and discourage us from actively searching for them. However..."

Hyong removes his tortoiseshell glasses and lets out a sad sigh.

"If the photos are real, I believe the four victims...are long since deceased."

That statement literally knocks the wind right out of me. It's all I can do to whisper "Thanks, Doc" as Gina and I leave his cluttered office.

"Just got a message from the District Attorney," my partner says, lowering her cell phone from her ear as we climb back into my Impala. "If there's any silver lining in all this, the DA is going to refile the abduction and murder charges against Pierson. The photos plus the bank security tape—they're confident they can make a case now."

"That's great news," I say. "Will Ellen have to testify?"

"Shit, I hope not. No way a jury buys a word she says. I haven't trusted that bitch since the moment we met her."

I feel the urge to push back. To defend Ellen. To explain to Gina that she has it all wrong. That the woman I've been getting to know all these weeks is kind and decent and gentle and good. Instead, I keep my mouth shut. At least for now.

After a few more hours back at the station, Gina decides to head home. "My mom's taking the twins," she explains, "and me and Zoe have date night. I'm not feeling too frisky after the day we just had, but hey."

If my partner knew I *also* might have a date tonight— and with whom—she'd blow a gasket. Disown me. And I can't say I'd blame her.

I hang around the station for another few hours, catching up on paperwork, dodging calls from the press asking me to comment. But mostly I stare at those grisly photos, which are now all over the news. I keep scanning them for clues. Praying that Dr. Hyong is wrong. Wishing I had the willpower to not do what I'm considering.

It's after nine o'clock when I finally leave the station. I swing by Noah's Bar & Grill, a quiet neighborhood spot with the best burgers in town. I wash one down with an ice-cold beer. Then a second beer. Then a third.

It's half past ten when I pay the bill. *Okay, decision time.* I sit behind the wheel for a good ten or fifteen agonizing minutes, twirling the cool metal motel key in my hand. My brain is screaming *Go home, you moron!* But I can't. I just can't.

Soon I'm pulling into the shadowy El Toro parking lot, scanning for Ellen's car—but I don't see it. I shut off my engine, get out, and approach room 4. The front window's curtains are drawn, but the inside looks completely dark. Before I can change my mind, I give the door a quick knock. I wait. I listen.

No response. I guess Ellen must not be here yet. It's only eleven, still fairly early. After glancing around to make sure the coast is clear, I unlock the door and enter, shutting it quickly behind me.

I flip on the lights—and there she is.

Ellen is lying on the bed, wearing nothing but a sheer black bra and red lace panties. The sight stops me in my tracks. I open my mouth to speak, but no words come out.

"Hello, Andy," she says. "I'm glad you came. You look a little nervous. Why?"

Gee, maybe because I'm alone in a motel room with the killer's half-naked wife?

"To be honest, I'm nervous, too," she continues. "Because the truth is . . . I'm falling in love with you, Andy. But I'm afraid. That you're just using me. The way my husband did."

Ellen looks so vulnerable right now. So innocent. And yes, so unbelievably sexy. Her pouty lips, her porcelain skin, her firm breasts. It's all making my head spin.

"Of course I'm not using you," I answer. "I would never. That's not who I am. I really care about you, Ellen. I think I . . . I think I'm falling in love with you, too."

Ellen smiles and slowly sits up. "Then what are you waiting for?"

I approach the bed—and we *pounce* on each other. Kissing ferociously. Pawing at each other's clothes. Releasing weeks of pent-up tension. Ellen is soon moaning and trembling in my arms, digging her nails into my back, drawing blood.

I know this is so, so wrong . . . *but it feels so, so good.*

CHAPTER 31

WE MAKE LOVE THAT night for hours. We're both so drained afterward, we can barely speak. We just lie there, holding each other, exhausted but exhilarated. Then we get dressed and, without exchanging a word, part ways.

It's almost 3:00 a.m. when I finally get back home. Nearly dawn. I stumble into my bedroom to try to steal a few winks of sleep before heading in to work.

But then my cell phone starts ringing. My head's barely touched the pillow, so I let it go to voicemail. It rings again. I roll over and check the ID. It's the San Luis Obispo area code—805—but I don't recognize the number. I decide I should probably answer it.

"Detective McGrath? This is Sergeant Matt Kerr with the SLO County Sheriff's Office. I'm calling regarding an inmate in our custody, Michael F. Pierson..."

The news makes me leap right out of bed.

No... I can't believe it... those fools—how could they let this happen?

After I hang up with the sergeant, feeling a little dazed and hoping it was just a bad dream, I dial Gina. But my partner says she just got a similar call from the jail. Next I phone the county lockup myself and confirm the news a second time.

So much for getting any sleep tonight.

I throw some clothes on and speed to the station. I request urgent copies of the correctional officers' incident reports and the deputy warden's preliminary assessment. When they arrive, I read the few dozen pages of documents as fast as I can. Soon my desk phone starts ringing with reporters asking for comment—until I literally yank it from the wall. When bleary-eyed, Red Bull–chugging Gina arrives an hour later, I tell her to hold down the fort for me here while I step out for a little while.

There's something I have to do.

I turn onto Ellen's street and see that the reporters camped outside her home have been whipped into a frenzy. I'm not surprised. As I pull into the driveway and get out, they swarm my car, shoving their cameras in my face, shouting questions like:

"Detective McGrath, how will this impact the search for the missing girls?"

"Do you believe it was triggered by the discovery of those photos?"

"Was justice done today—or now can it never be done?"

"Jesus Christ, you people are vultures!" I exclaim as I march up the path to Ellen's house. I pound the door, calling out her name. No answer. I keep knocking, louder, rattling the doorknob. Maybe she's not here. But finally, she opens it.

"Sorry, Andy," she says, quickly ushering me inside. She's wearing a simple tank top and baggy sweatpants, but still looks incredible. The tension between us is suddenly so charged, I half expect her to push me against the door and kiss me.

Instead, Ellen holds up a pair of tweezers and a magnifying loupe.

"I was in the attic, working on my butterfly collection."

"I wish *I* had a hobby like that to distract me at times like this," I answer. "I'm not sure if you heard the news, but—"

"Of course I did. In the middle of the night, while you and I were at that motel together . . . while I was *cheating* on him . . . Michael hanged himself inside his cell."

Ellen's bottom lip begins to quiver, and she starts fighting off tears.

"I know you used to love him," I say tenderly. "You have every right to be upset."

But Ellen shakes her head. "The case is closed now. Those girls are dead, and so is their killer. You don't need me anymore." Then she adds, softer, "I lost *two* men I cared about today, didn't I?"

It's breaking my heart how sad and helpless Ellen looks. I know the decent thing to do would be to take her in my arms and try to comfort her. Tell her it will all be okay. That maybe we *can* still be together.

But we both know that's a big, fat lie.

CHAPTER 32

ELLEN TURNS AWAY FROM McGrath. She has to. It's simply too painful to look him in the eye. She's hoping against hope that he'll step up and embrace her, or fight with her—fight *for* her—but she isn't surprised when all he says, weakly, is "Oh, Ellen."

She hears him place something small and metallic on the entry table as he leaves: her motel-room key, no doubt.

And just like that, the dreamy detective is gone.

From her house. From her life.

Forever, Ellen thinks.

She listens to the legion of reporters outside shout another round of questions at McGrath as he exits and heads to his car. But once he drives away and the journalists stop yelling, Ellen's home falls instantly, eerily quiet.

Ellen looks down at her hands, still holding the tweezers and magnifying loupe. Her husband is dead, and she has a million things to take care of. Forms to fill out, calls to place, arrangements to make. And yet, in this moment, there is nothing in the world Ellen wants to do except get back to her beautiful butterflies. Tinkering with her collection has always helped soothe her. And right now, a little comfort is what she craves most. So she heads back up to the attic to get to work.

Many hours later, in the middle of the night, Ellen wakes up slumped forward across her worktable. She was up until God-knows-when arranging a display box with some of her newest specimens and must have dozed off.

To her great horror, she sees she fell asleep directly on *top* of an uncovered case—crushing the butterflies' delicate bodies and wings.

"Oh, no...no, please..." Ellen mutters, frantically inspecting the damage in a state of disbelief. She might be able to fix a few of them with glue and patience, but most of the butterflies are mangled beyond repair.

"No, no!" she exclaims, louder now.

Ellen did not cry when she heard her husband had taken his life. Or when McGrath silently confirmed that their relationship was over.

But now the sobs come heavy and ugly.

When she finally calms down, Ellen blots her puffy eyes. She blows her runny nose. Then she stands and heads downstairs. She knows what she has to do.

Dreading it, she approaches her front bay window and pulls back the curtains just a hair to check the size of the mob of reporters camped outside.

Ellen is stunned. She can't believe it.

Every last one of them—they're gone!

True, it's almost one o'clock in the morning, but they've

been spending nights out front for weeks now. With Michael dead, apparently they've abandoned her, too.

Just like McGrath.

It feels a little strange to Ellen to be able to walk calmly out her front door and down her driveway without two dozen rabid journalists clamoring at her and recording her every move. She gets in her car, slowly pulls out, and heads down her quiet street, bound for her destination. She checks her mirrors multiple times as she drives. It feels even stranger not to be followed.

Ellen takes a spot in the El Toro Motel parking lot. Not one near room 4, but the closest available to the front desk. She leaves her engine running; she won't be long.

Pushing open the lobby door, she hears that jangle of the sleigh bells hung from the handle again, followed by "Hey there, Mrs. Hayes."

It's Carson, the stoner twenty-something who works the night shift, who knows Ellen only by her alias. "Is everything, like, cool with your room?" he asks.

"Yes, yes," Ellen assures him. "And I know I've prepaid for it for a few more days, but I won't be needing it any longer."

Before she can change her mind, she places her room key down on the desk.

"Uh, okay, sure," Carson replies. "You're all set, then, Mrs. H. Hope you'll stay with us again soon."

Ellen smiles, a little sadly.

"I'd like that. Very much. But, Carson? I wouldn't count on it."

CHAPTER 33

BACK IN HER CAR. Back on the road.

Ellen heads along Santa Rosa Street, then takes the on-ramp for the 101, the same freeway she sped down the wrong way just a few days ago, which feels like another *lifetime* ago.

Merging into the middle lane, she settles in for a long drive.

Again, this late at night, the freeway is nearly deserted, and the hum of the road is almost hypnotic. Most people driving at this hour on so little sleep might worry about nodding off, but Ellen is wide awake. Jittery with nerves. Jumpy with anticipation.

The minutes tick by, turning into hours. Ellen finally exits the freeway at about half past two. She's soon cruising through the sleepy town of Landor, California, such a dusty, tiny speck of a place that it makes San Luis Obispo look like San Francisco.

Ellen turns left off the main drag and onto Sheridan

Road, which leads out of the town proper and up into the adjacent hills. Knowing there will be no streetlights for miles, she flips on her high beams, but the winding road is still dark and treacherous.

After a good fifteen minutes of careful driving, Ellen makes another left turn, onto a hidden dirt path that leads even deeper into the rolling woods.

At last, she arrives—at an old cabin. An old abandoned *shack,* more accurately.

With so many dense trees and overgrown shrubs around it, it's extremely well camouflaged, practically invisible. Using her cell phone as a flashlight to help guide her way, Ellen gets out of her car and approaches.

But instead of going to the front door, she walks toward one of the trees, a leafy oak. On one of the lower branches hangs a plastic bird feeder, filled about a quarter of the way with stale seeds. Ellen unhooks it from the tree, unscrews the top, and dumps the birdseed into her open palm. She spreads her fingers and shakes, until all that remains in her hand is a rusty metal key.

Now Ellen goes to the front door. She unlocks and opens it. The hinges creak, like in a classic horror movie, but there aren't any cobwebs or cloth-draped furniture inside this cabin. The outside might look decrepit, but its interior is clean and cozy—if small and sparsely furnished.

Ellen turns on the lights, illuminating display case after display case of colorful butterflies, hung on virtually every square inch of wall. There are hundreds of specimens in total, outnumbering her home collection many times over.

And in the corner sits a small drafting desk, identical to the workstation in Ellen's attic. On it rests a glass display case that's still a work in progress, only partially filled with freshly pinned butterflies, all in perfect condition.

Ellen walks over and takes a seat, excited to get to work—when she hears something outside.

CHAPTER 34

THE CRUNCHING OF TIRES. The slamming of a car door.

Someone's here, now? Ellen thinks. *Impossible!*

She's in the middle of nowhere, a hundred miles from home, at three o'clock in the morning. She came here to be alone, to escape—and now she has a visitor?

Ellen returns to the front door and looks through the peephole.

Parked beside her Camry is a vehicle she's seen dozens of times: a white Impala. And walking toward the cabin— slowly, cautiously—is Detective McGrath.

Ellen's eyes widen in disbelief. She feels a flurry of conflicting emotions. Shock. Confusion. Anticipation. Arousal.

Flustered, Ellen hastily smooths the front of her blouse and runs some fingers through her hair, trying to make herself as presentable as possible while she waits for McGrath to knock.

But he doesn't.

Instead, McGrath suddenly kicks the door open and bursts inside, his Glock 22 service weapon aimed and ready.

"Andy!" Ellen exclaims with an almost giddy laugh. "My God, you scared me! What...what are you doing here?"

McGrath is just as surprised to see her standing there. He lowers his gun but doesn't yet put it away.

"What are *you* doing, Ellen? What the hell is this place?"

"An old hunting cabin. It's been in my family for generations."

"Who owns it?" McGrath asks. "Your house is the only property listed under your or your husband's name. We checked."

"Of course you did," Ellen says with a rueful smile. "Legally it belonged to my grandfather. After he died, it just kind of sat here. Michael and I rediscovered it a few years ago. We started coming up here sometimes to get away. It's peaceful. Quiet."

McGrath looks around at the cramped interior and floor-to-ceiling butterfly displays with apprehension. "Yeah," he says, "feels real relaxing."

"How did you find me?" Ellen asks. "I could have sworn I wasn't followed."

McGrath finally reholsters his sidearm and takes from his pocket a small electronic device about the size of a deck of playing cards.

"Last week...before our night at the motel, but after your crazy 3:00 a.m. wrong-way drag race down the 101...I came by your place and stuck a GPS tracker under the rear bumper of your car. I knew I couldn't risk losing you, Ellen."

Ellen absorbs that for a moment, trying to decide whether McGrath means it romantically as well as literally. He does.

"You were able to get a warrant to monitor the comings and goings of a suspect's spouse?"

McGrath slips the tracking device back in his pocket— and dodges the question.

"I don't regret anything I've done on this case, Ellen. Especially anything I've done with *you*. You're not like any woman I've ever met. If we'd crossed paths at a different time, different circumstances...maybe it would have been *us* spending weekends in this cabin."

Ellen nods, wistfully. It's a sweet sentiment, but painful, too.

"You're welcome to spend the night," Ellen offers. "On the couch, I mean. Unless—"

"That's all right," McGrath says, waving her off. "I wanna start heading back down the hill. Lousy cell service up here. I'm gonna ask Forensics to take a fine-tooth comb to this place, inside and out, first thing in the morning."

"You really think Michael might have brought those girls...*here*?" Ellen asks with a shiver.

"Honestly? Not a chance. He was smarter than that. But

maybe we'll find a print. A hair. A fiber. Anything we can use to find them. It's worth a shot."

With a resigned shrug, McGrath starts heading for the door.

Ellen, overwhelmed, takes a few steps backward toward her desk, bracing herself against it for support.

"Good night, Ellen," McGrath says. He holds up his cell phone. "Guess I'll see you in a few hours. I've got some calls to make."

"Sorry, Andy..."

McGrath has his hand on the doorknob when he hears the unmistakable *click* of a handgun's safety catch being flipped off.

He spins around.

He can't believe his eyes.

Ellen is aiming a compact .38-caliber handgun right at him.

"I can't let you do that."

CHAPTER 35

IN ALL MY YEARS with the SLOPD, I've had a gun pointed at me only once before, by a desperate coke dealer during a drug bust gone awry.

Tonight makes twice.

And it's by a woman I thought I loved.

Suddenly it all makes sense! I knew it all along—but I just couldn't see it.

Ellen is a hell of a lot more than just the killer's wife.

But there's no time for that now.

My heart is thundering. Adrenaline is coursing through my veins.

My life could be over in a few milliseconds—way too little time for me to draw my own gun, turn, and shoot first.

So I get a crazy idea.

I slap the light switch near the front door, plunging the little cabin into darkness. Then I quickly drop to the ground and roll out of the way.

Ellen yelps with shock and fires a shot—*blam!*—but it misses me by a mile.

"Damnit, Andy!" she exclaims as I frantically scramble behind the couch for cover. "Where are you?"

Ellen fires two more wild shots—*blam! blam!*—in my general direction. Again she misses me. But only by a hair.

Now it sounds like she's shuffling across the room toward the light switch herself. So I use those precious few seconds to quickly crawl around the couch and *behind* her. As soon as Ellen turns the lights back on...

I leap up and pounce.

I clasp my hands around the hot metal gun, squeezing Ellen's fingers tightly so she can't pull the trigger. Then we tumble to the floor together, our limbs intertwined.

"No, no, no!" she screams, again and again, kicking and flailing wildly as I wrestle with her for control of the weapon. Damn, she sure is feisty—and strong!

At last I manage to yank the pistol from Ellen's grip. Then I *smack* the hard steel clean across the side of her head. Ellen grunts in pain and goes limp.

I crab-walk backward a bit, then stand up, tucking her little pistol into my belt and drawing my own Glock.

"Don't move!" I shout. I keep my gun trained on Ellen as she groans and writhes. God only knows what this woman might do next, so I'm not taking any chances.

"What the hell did you do to those girls?" I demand, practically foaming at the mouth with fury.

Ellen doesn't respond.

Then she starts to laugh.

CHAPTER 36

"YOU DAMN *FOOL*, ANDY," she hisses, wiping a dollop of blood off her lip. "You know exactly what I did. What *we* did."

"You mean...?"

"That's right. Michael and I were *partners*. We picked those girls out together like we were ordering artwork from a catalog."

Ellen gestures to the hundreds of dead butterflies on the walls.

"I guess you could say we both liked collecting all *kinds* of beautiful things. This cabin is exactly where we kept them. Claire, Samantha, Maria, Patty—we did what we wanted to them, we took a few pictures, then we buried them out back, in the woods."

I'm too stunned to speak. My hands begin to tremble so much that I can barely hold my gun steady.

"Look at you," Ellen says, laughing even harder now. "You had it all wrong from the start. You thought you'd get close to me, use me, extract evidence from me, then dump me by the curb, didn't you?"

I don't answer...but what Ellen is saying, of course, is true. At least it *was*. Until I started getting to know her. Until I started *falling* for her.

"But I was the one using *you*, Detective," she snarls. "I loved my husband. We understood each other. That night he picked up Brittany, he knew you were following him. He let himself get caught to protect me." Then she adds, "He was a good man, Andy. He was ten times the one you'll ever be."

"He was a goddamn murderer!" I yell. "A monster. And a coward. And so are you!"

I feel a swell of emotions deep in my gut so powerful, I can barely describe it. Horror, disbelief, humiliation, rage. *That this bitch could have lied to me for so long...*

"I know you tried so hard, Andy," Ellen says, almost tauntingly now. "And you came so close, too. Patty was still alive just a few weeks ago. After Michael was arrested, I had to take care of her myself."

My jaw clenches like a vise. My eyes start stinging with tears. *It can't be...*

"Her body should still be pretty fresh. As for the other girls, they've probably all decomposed so much by now, not even their parents would be able to recog—"

Blam!

I'm almost as shocked by the gunshot as Ellen is.

And I'm the one who fired it.

The bullet strikes her in the throat. Her eyes bug out of

her pretty head. She starts to gag and choke on her own oozing blood.

But I just stand there, numb with shock at what I've done, watching as Ellen takes her last gasp of breath, then slumps backward against the wall.

Holy shit. I've just committed second-degree murder.

I've just killed the killer.

And yet, I feel an instant sense of tranquility come over me like a warm blanket.

I calmly reholster my handgun. I slowly push open the front door. I steadily walk back to my car. I carefully drive back down the dark, hilly road.

When I reach the main town again, I check my cell phone. Seeing I have a few bars of service, I pull over and call my partner. She answers groggily after the fifth ring.

"I solved the case, Gina," I say evenly. "I just closed it, too."

"Andy? What are you talking about? What time is it? Where are you?"

"Listen. Ellen's side of the family used to own a hunting cabin outside Santa Margarita. Dig up the address in county records, then send Hyong and his techs there right away. It's an unsecured murder scene."

"Hang on. It's a what?"

"The girls' bodies are in the backyard. Ellen's is inside, by the front door. I'll be back at my place when you're ready for me, after I pick up my parents and let them know I'll be going away for a while."

"Andy, you—you're not making any sense," Gina

stammers. "You found the girls? And . . . and Ellen's been killed, too?"

I don't blame my partner for not understanding.

Shit. I'm more confused than I've ever been in my life.

"See ya, Gina," I say.

I hang up my phone and turn it off. Then I pull back onto the road and start to head home.

As I do, I notice the sun is just starting to rise, painting the sky a vibrant orange and bloodred.

I imagine I see a swarm of butterflies, fluttering in the air.

THE
WITNESSES

JAMES PATTERSON

with BRENDAN DuBOIS

CHAPTER 1

IN A PERFECT WORLD, Ronald Temple wouldn't be sitting in his Barcalounger in the living room of his retirement home in Levittown, New York, with the side window open and a blanket across his legs, wishing a rifle was in his lap, ready to kill the terrorists living next door.

Yeah, he thinks, lowering his Zeiss 7x50 binoculars. In a perfect world, the Twin Towers would still be standing, scores of his friends would still be alive, and he wouldn't be slowly dying here in suburbia, lungs clogged with whatever crap he breathed in while working the pile for weeks after 9/11.

The light-blue house next door is normal, like the rest of the homes in his neighborhood, built in 1947 in an old potato field on Long Island. It was the beginning of the postwar rush to suburbia. Levittown is now a great place to go to school, raise families, or retire, like Ronald and his wife, Helen, are doing.

But their new neighbors?

Definitely not normal.

Ronald lifts up the binoculars again.

They had moved in just three days ago, when it was overcast, the dark-gray clouds threatening rain. A black GMC Yukon had pulled into the narrow driveway and a family had tumbled out, all dark-skinned, all in Western clothes they looked uncomfortable wearing. An adult male and an adult female—apparently the parents—and a boy and a girl. Ronald had been sitting in this same chair, his oxygen machine gently wheezing, tubes rubbing up against his raw nostrils, as he saw them hustle into the house.

And the woman and the young girl both had head coverings on.

It was a bit suspicious at first, so Ronald had watched the activities next door as much as possible, and he became more concerned with every passing minute and hour. No moving van had pulled in after that first day. Only a few suitcases and duffel bags had been brought into the house—quickly, from the Yukon. And the adults had not come over to introduce themselves to either him or his wife.

He moves the binoculars in a slow, scanning motion.

There.

He sees a large man walk past the kitchen window across the way.

That was the other thing that had gotten his attention three days ago.

Their driver.

Oh, yeah, their driver.

He had emerged first from the Yukon and Ronald could tell he was a professional: he wore a jacket to hide whatever hardware he was carrying, his eyes swept the yard and driveway, looking for threats, and he had kept his charges inside the Yukon while he had first gone into the house to check everything out.

Like the other four, he was dark-skinned. He was nearly bald. Although he wasn't too muscular—not an NFL lineman on steroids—he was bulky enough, similar to those Emergency Service Unit guys Ronald had met during his time in the NYPD.

A bodyguard, then?

Or maybe the terrorist cell leader?

Ronald sweeps the house again, back and forth, back and forth. He keeps up on newspapers, television, and internet news and knows this is the new way of terrorism and violence. People nowadays move into a quiet neighborhood, blend in, and then go out and strike.

The kids?

Camouflage.

The husband and wife?

Like that couple that had shot up that holiday party in San Bernardino, California, last year.

They blended in.

And the bulky guy . . . maybe he was their trainer, or maybe their leader?

He was probably ready to prime them to go out and kill.

Ronald lowers his binoculars, adjusts the oxygen hose around his head again. It was just too damn strange, too damn out of the ordinary. No moving vans, no friends stopping by; neither the husband nor the wife—if they were really married, who knew—left to go to work in the morning. No deliveries, no lawn mowing, nothing.

They are definitely hiding out.

Ronald wishes once more for the comfortable weight of an AR15 across his lap. To take down a cell like this one requires firepower, and lots of it. With a 20-round magazine and open iron sights—he sure as hell didn't need a telescopic sight at this range—he could take care of the three adults with no problem. If, for example, he saw them walking out to the Yukon, wearing coats, trying to hide weapons or a suicide bomber's belt, he could knock them all down with an AR15 before they even got into their SUV.

A series of cramps run up his thin legs, making him grimace with pain. And the kids? Leave 'em be . . . unless they picked up a weapon and decided to come over here and get revenge. Lots of kids that age were doing the same thing overseas, tossing grenades, grabbing AK-47s, setting up IEDs.

He picks up the binoculars once more.

In his twenty-one years on the New York police force, Ronald drew his service weapon only three times—twice at traffic stops and once while checking out a bodega robbery—but he knows that if he had to, he'd do what it took to get the job done, even today, as crippled as he is.

He removes one hand from the binoculars, checks the lumpy shape under his blanket, resting on his lap. It's his backup weapon from when he was on the job, a .38 Smith & Wesson Police Special.

Ronald nods with satisfaction. He'd had a chance once to be a hero on 9/11, and he blew it.

He's not going to let another chance slip by.

CHAPTER 2

LANCE SANDERSON WALKS INTO the kitchen of the rental home to get another cup of coffee. His wife, Teresa, is working at her laptop set on the round wooden dining table, and he gives her neck a quick rub as he goes by. Teresa has a nest of notebooks and papers and other reference books nearby as she types slowly and deliberately.

After pouring himself a cup, Lance asks, "Get you a refill?"

"Not right now, hon," she says. "Maybe later."

He stands at her side, takes a sip. Due to the last few weeks out in the harsh North African sun, his wife's skin has darkened, making her look even more radiant than usual. The sun has streaked her light brown hair, wavy and shoulder length, and has bronzed her legs and arms. Even after two kids, she's kept her body in good shape, with long legs and a cute round bottom. He remembers with pleasure the first time they made love, when both were in grad school. She had whispered, "My boobs aren't much, but they're designed for babies. The rest of me is yours . . . and wants a real man."

Lance rubs her neck again and she sighs softly, like a satisfied cat. "What's new?" he asks.

She doesn't look up from her keyboard as she continues writing. "The old perv next door is still staring over here with his binoculars."

"I told you to stop flashing him your butt," Lance says. "What do you expect?"

"Har-de-hah-hah," she says, which cheers up Lance. Nice to see her in a good mood after the past week. "If I did that, all he'd see is the desert sand I'm still picking out of my butt crack." She lifts her head from the keyboard and gives the kitchen a glance. "I miss home," she says. "I miss the ocean. I miss the fruit trees. I miss our backyard."

"Me, too."

She nods at the avocado-colored refrigerator and the bright-yellow kitchen countertop. "Just look at this dump. It looks like it was redecorated when we had a peanut farmer for president."

"Or a movie actor," he says. "How goes the guidebook?"

"Oh, that," she says, running a hand across her notes and the piles of books scattered across the table. "In these times, m'dear, it sure is hard to do research without having internet access."

Lance sips again from his coffee. "I know. Trying to do the same, cataloguing Carthaginian potsherds without knowing if you're repeating yourself or the work of others."

Then Lance feels a sudden chill, like a window has been

opened in the house, or an unexpected eclipse has blocked out the sun.

Close enough.

The man they know as Jason Tyler is in their kitchen. Lance tries not to step back in fear. At first glance, Jason isn't too large or hulking, but that's just the first glance. In the few days he and his family have gotten to know him, Lance has learned that Jason likes to wear comfortable sneakers, loose slacks, and short-sleeve shirts, like the ones he's wearing today: gray slacks and black shirt, shirt-tails hanging over his slim waist. It took Teresa one night in a hotel room in Marseilles to point out the obvious: "Honey, he dresses like that to hide his muscles and whatever weapons he's carrying."

The man is six feet, with broad shoulders and a head that is covered with just the bare stubble of black hair. His skin is dark, and it's funny, but if Jason turns one way in the light, he looks vaguely Asian, but from another angle, he can also look like he's from the Middle East.

A chameleon, Lance thinks, *a chameleon who is tougher than steel.*

Jason says, "You two all right in here?"

Lance says, "Doing okay."

Jason's eyes never stop. They're always moving, looking, evaluating. He nods just a bit. "I know you like to work here in the kitchen, ma'am, but I wish you would find another spot. That window makes you vulnerable."

"I like the light," Teresa says.

"It makes you vulnerable."

Lance sees his wife's hands tighten. "Are you ordering me?"

A slight pause. "No." Another pause. "I've checked in on Sandy. And Sam. Both seem to be doing well. I'm going out on the grounds for a few minutes. You know the drill."

Lance sighs. "Yes. Stay indoors. At all times."

And Jason leaves. Just like that. A big man, with those hidden muscles . . . Lance thinks he should move like an ox or a bull, trampling and bumping into things. But this man . . . he moves like a dark-colored jaguar, on the prowl, always hunting.

The kitchen's temperature seems to warm up about five degrees.

Teresa goes back to the keyboard, types two or three words, stops. Looks up at her husband.

"Lance."

"Right here."

"Do you trust what he says?" Teresa asks.

"About what?"

"That if we were to use the internet, we could be dead by the end of the day?"

He reaches out, rubs the back of her neck, and it's tense. No sweet sighs this time. "We have to trust him. We have to."

Lance feels out of time, out of place. How in the world did his family end up here?

"We're in too deep," Lance says. "We have no choice."

Teresa turns so she's looking directly at him. His hand falls away. Her pretty dark-brown eyes tear up.

"But what about our kids?" she asks. "What choice do they have?"

From the other side of the house, a boy's voice cries out. "Dad! I need you! Right now!"

His own eyes watering, Lance rushes out of the kitchen without saying a word.

CHAPTER 3

RONALD TEMPLE IS STARTLED by the noise and realizes he has drifted off. His hand automatically goes under the blanket to his .38 Smith & Wesson revolver as Helen comes in. He relaxes his hand when he sees his wife, thinks how close he came to doing something stupid. In his years on the job, he knew of at least two instances where fellow patrolmen were accidentally shot by their partners in a moment of panic or fear, and it feels good to bring his empty hand up.

In those two cases on the job, the shootings had been successfully covered up, but Ronald doubts he could get away with making up a story about some random gang-banger shooting his wife in their living room.

Helen manages to smile at him as she comes over. It's not that warm a day, but she's wearing a knee-length simple floral dress with a thin black belt around her thickening waist. Decades into their marriage there are wrinkles and more bulges than usual, and her black hair is secretly colored, but he knows he's lucked out with her, a now retired schoolteacher who most times has the knack of calming him down.

She kisses the top of his head and pats his thin shoulder. "How's the spying going?" she asks.

He resists snapping back at her, not wanting to hear what might come out of her mouth, even though she's got a cheery expression on her face. Helen is almost always cheerful, but she keeps a tight lid on her resentments and frustrations. He recalled with regret getting into a fight with her some years ago, after mention was made of their two sons, Tucker and Spencer. One worked as cop in the LAPD and the other was an Oregon State Trooper. Helen had said, "Of course our boys moved west. Do you think they wanted to listen to you bitch at them about how they're doing their jobs wrong, and how you would do it better?"

So Ronald smiles and says, "Just keeping watch, that's all. If more people kept watch, this would be a safer country."

Helen keeps a slim hand on his shoulder, rubs him for a few seconds. "You're right, but . . . really, Ronald. You really think that family next door means trouble?"

Ronald takes a breath, tries not to cough with all that 9/11 crap in his lungs. He was a security officer for an investment firm in the South Tower. Although he was home sick on 9/11, he spent weeks there later, working and doing penance.

"Look. They're not from around here. They keep to themselves. And I don't like that big guy walking around, like he's their private security or something. It just doesn't make sense."

His wife looks out to the house and he's irritated again—as a civilian, she can't see what he sees. All she sees is a simple house with simple people living inside. She can't see beyond that.

Helen says, "Really? You think terrorists are going to hide out here, in Levittown? And besides . . . they've got kids."

"Terrorists have used kids as a cover before," Ronald says impatiently. "And why not Levittown? It's got history, the first true suburbia in the country, it's as pure America as it gets. A perfect hideout, a perfect target. You know how terrorists like to hit at targets that make a lot of news. Why not here?"

His wife turns around, heads to the kitchen. "Then call the cops already, Ronald. If you feel that strongly about it, don't just sit here and fume. Do something about it."

Ronald feels the weight of the revolver in his lap. He is doing something about it, he thinks, and aloud he says, "The cops are too P C now. They won't do anything. Hell, they might even charge me with a hate crime or something."

Helen doesn't say anything in reply and he wonders if she didn't hear him, or is ignoring him. What the hell— what difference does it make?

Ronald picks up the binoculars, looks over at the house again. The man is talking to the woman, who appears to be working on a laptop.

But where's the big guy? The muscle? The cell leader?

He carefully scans the windows, the kitchen, the master bedroom, and the living room.

Nothing.

Where the hell is he?

No attached garage, and since he knows the house is practically identical to his own, there's no basement or attic, so—

A knock on the door.

He's seized with fear. "Don't answer it!"

But again, Helen either isn't listening or is ignoring him. She goes to the door and opens it up, and Ronald drops the binoculars in his blanket-covered lap.

It's the threatening guy from next door.

He stares at his wife.

Helen steps back.

He says one sentence, full of menace:

"You need to stop."

CHAPTER 4

LANCE MOVES QUICKLY THROUGH the house, again hearing Sam's plaintive yell—"Dad!"—and a moment later steps into his son's room. They've been here only a few days and already the ten-year-old boy's room is a cluttered mess. The bed is unmade, the temporary bookshelves are cluttered with rocks and books, and clothing is scattered across the floor like a whirlwind has just struck. Posters of San Francisco Giants players are taped up on the yellow walls.

Sam's face is red and he's sitting in an old school chair, in front of a small desk that's scattered with tiny white plastic bones. A cardboard box with a brightly colored image of a dinosaur—a T. rex?—is on the floor. He's wearing blue jeans, a black T-shirt, and white scuffed sneakers.

"What's up, sport?" Lance asks, going straight to his boy.

Sam jerks his chin to the left. "It's Sandy. She just came

in here and took my book about triceratops. Without even asking!"

Lance rubs the boy's light-brown hair. Sam looks a lot like his mother. "Okay. Anything else?"

"Yeah, can you get it back? And when are we leaving here? I'm bored."

"I'm bored, too. Let me go get your book."

Lance steps out and goes into the small bedroom next door, and what a difference. The bed is made. The small, open closet shows shoes lined up and clothes hung prop-erly. There is a small desk with a chair—identical to Sam's—but there's nothing on it. Homemade bookcases line the far wall as well, but they are filled with rows of books, all placed in alphabetical order by author. Sandy, two years older than her brother, is on her bed reading a book, her back and shoulders supported by two pillows.

The book has a dinosaur on the cover. Lance steps for-ward. "Sandy? Hon?"

She ignores him, flipping a page, reading some more. Her blond hair—lightened by the North African sun—has been styled into two braids.

"Sandy?"

"Let me finish this paragraph, please."

Lance waits. Then she looks up, face inquisitive, light-blue eyes bright and intelligent.

"Yes?"

Lance says, "Is that Sam's book?"

"Yes."

"He says you took it without permission."

"I didn't need permission," she says crisply. "The book wasn't being used. It was on the shelf. Sam is working on a dinosaur model. It has 102 parts. He can't work on a dinosaur model with that many parts and read this book at the same time."

"Still, you should have asked permission."

"But I needed the book."

"Why do you need the book?" Lance asks.

"Because I've read all of my books," she explains. "I needed something new to read, and if I were to ask my brother for permission, he might have said no, and then I would still have nothing to read. So I did the right thing and took the book to my room."

Perfectly logical, Lance thinks, *and perfectly Sandy.*

"But it's his book."

"He wasn't using it. I needed something to read."

Lance holds out his hand. "Give me the book, Sandy. You can borrow one of mine."

Her eyes widen with anticipation. "Really? Which one?"

"*Hannibal and His Times,*" Lance says.

His twelve-year-old daughter frowns. "By Lewis Chapman?"

"Yes."

"Dad, I read that last September. I read it from September 17th to September 19th."

Lance smiles. "That was the hardcover edition. The paperback edition is out, with a new afterword and a rewrite of several of the chapters. You could read it and compare and contrast."

Sandy seems to ponder that for a moment, nods, and gives the book on triceratops back to him. "Deal. How long before you can get me that book, Dad?"

"In about ten minutes, I suppose."

She checks her watch. "It's 2:05 p.m. I'll expect you back by 2:15."

Lance says, "Of course, hon."

Back in Sam's room, Lance gives his son his book back, and Sam smiles and says, "Thanks, Dad." He takes the book and tosses it up on the near bookshelf and misses. It falls to the floor.

"Dad?"

"Yes, Sam?"

Sam returns to his toy dinosaur bones. "Dad, don't forget your promise, about taking us to the Badlands later this summer. I want to help out on a dinosaur dig. You said you'd check with Professor Chang at school. You promised."

"I sure did," Lance says, recalling that promise, made back when things were so much simpler and safer. "And we'll see about that, okay?"

Sam's head is still bowed over the cluttered table. "See about what?"

Lance quickly turns away from his boy, unable to speak, his throat thick, his eyes watering, thinking only one thing:

We'll see if we're all still alive by the end of this week, never mind this summer.

CHAPTER 5

RONALD'S HAND SLIPS CLUMSILY under his blanket, grabbing the .38 revolver. Helen backs into the house, followed by the big guy from next door. *Damn it!* If he were the man he once was, he would have answered the door and gone face-to-face with this clown, and he would be standing in front of his wife, protecting her.

He slips off the oxygen tubes from his nose and heaves himself off the chair. Wrapping the blanket around himself and the hidden revolver, he strains to walk as fast as he can to his wife. "What the hell is going on here?" he shouts, hating how weak and hoarse his voice sounds. Being a cop and then a security officer means having a voice of command, and that command voice is gone.

The large man from next door has a voice that is strong and forceful. He says, "I apologize for bothering you, but I'm hoping you'll stop."

He's not too tall or too wide, and his dark clothes are loose, but Ronald senses his power and ability. He knows that man would be able to meet any challenge, whether it's intimidating a neighbor or a street gang.

"Stop what?" Ronald asks, standing next to Helen, holding the blanket around himself with one hand, his other hand hidden underneath, grasping the revolver. The damn thing feels as heavy as if it's made of lead. He feels guilty, on the spot, like a young boy called to the front of the class by the teacher.

His observing, his viewing, his . . . spying. Had he been noticed? Was this bulky guy going to threaten him and Helen?

The man smiles, but it doesn't comfort Ronald. The smile just shows perfect white teeth—no humor, no friendship. "If you could please stop parking your car on the street so close to our driveway," he says. "It makes it challenging to back out of our driveway without scraping our fender."

Helen clasps her hands together, steps forward, going into peacekeeper mode—like when they were raising their two hellion boys—and she says, "Absolutely. I'll go out in a few minutes and move it. Sorry to be a bother."

The smile widens, which makes the man look even fiercer. "No bother at all." And he shifts his gaze, looks straight over at Ronald. "You be careful, too, all right?"

The man turns and slips out. After Helen shuts the door, Ronald says, "Why did you say yes so quick? I wanted to ask him who he is, what he's doing here, how long they plan to stay. Damn it."

He struggles to turn around without tripping over the

blanket and goes back to his chair, where he settles back down, puts the oxygen tube back under his nose, and takes a deep breath through his nostrils. He tries not to let the tickling in his lungs explode into a full-scale coughing fit.

Helen comes over, hands still clasped, face nervous. "I just wanted him out of the house. Can you blame me?"

Ronald looks out the window. The big guy is at the house, going into the front door, but, damn, look at how his head moves. He's always scanning, always looking, always evaluating.

"Did you hear him?" Ronald asks, turning back to Helen. "'Be careful, too,' he said. Like he knows I've been watching. Like he knows I'm carrying. That guy . . . he's smart. And tough."

Helen stands by him, looks over the tidy grass and to the house. *My God,* Ronald thinks. For years they've seen tenants go in and out of that house, and, except for a couple of phone calls about noise complaints, it's been a peaceful place.

Now? That simple little house seems as dangerous as a crack den.

Or worse.

Ronald asks, "Did you see his eyes? Did you?"

"What about his eyes?" Helen asks.

Ronald settles back into his chair, breathes deeply through his nostrils, and shifts the revolver around so it's easily accessible. Memories come back to him, some of them dark indeed.

"Back when I was on the job, even before 9/11, we'd get

security alerts, and we'd be shown mugshots of various terrorists and shooters who could be a threat, who could be in the city."

The tickling in his lungs suddenly gets worse, and he coughs and coughs and coughs. Helen goes to a nearby little table, removes some tissues, and wipes his chin and lips, and he coughs some more.

Ronald finally catches his breath, but he can't stop wheezing. "All the mugshots of those men, they were white, black, brown, every skin color under the sun. But they all had one thing in common: the stone-cold look of a killer in their eyes."

He coughs one more time. "Just like him."

CHAPTER 6

MORE THAN 3,600 MILES from the suburb of Levittown, Gray Evans is sitting at an outdoor café in Paris, his long, muscular legs stretched out. Sipping another glass of *vin ordinaire*, he watches the world in this part of the City of Lights go by.

This arrondissement isn't the neighborhood near the Eiffel Tower, of green parks and the Quai d'Orsay, of pricey restaurants and American tourists strolling around on well-lit streets, of bateaux sliding along the Seine, carrying long rows of sightseers. Nope, this part of Paris is on the outskirts, with narrow streets, even narrower alleyways always stinking of urine, and angry-looking men walking in groups of five or six. At this time of night, not a woman is to be found here.

Based on how dumpy the little café looked, Gray had half-expected to be served *la viande de cheval*. Still, the place served a nice steak frites. And the wine was cheap and filling.

As he watches the people scurrying by on the narrow

street, punctuated by the burping sound of a Vespa scooter, he spots his contact. A swarthy-looking young man with thick black curly hair, wearing baggy jeans and a tan sport jacket. Gray sips again from the wineglass, checks his watch, and decides to amuse himself by watching how long it will take for his contact to meet him.

The young man walks up and down the far sidewalk, studiously ignoring Gray, and then makes a point of looking into a shop window, like he's seeing if he's being followed. Even the worst agent in France's counterterrorist unit—*Direction générale de la sécurité intérieure*, or DCRI for short—would have spotted this clown minutes ago, even if said DCRI agent was blind in one eye and confined to a wheelchair.

Gray checks his watch. Nearly ten minutes have passed and he's about to go across the road and grab the kid by the scruff of his neck to drag him over to his table, but then the young man makes his move.

He trots across the street like both ankles are sprained, and sinks into a chair across the small round table.

"*Bonsoir,*" he says, whispering, voice hoarse.

Gray nods. The young man smells of sweat and cooked onions. Gray reaches into a coat pocket, slips out the torn half of a ten-euro note, the one with a Romanesque arch on one side and a bridge on the other, and slides it across the table, past the plates and silverware.

The man has half of a ten-euro note as well, and his piece matches Gray's perfectly. He grins, like he's proud he's done so well undercover.

"My name is Yussuf," he says.

"Nice to meet you," Gray lies. "Would you like something to eat? Or drink?"

A quick shake of the head. "No. I have no time."

Gray smiles. "You're in one of the finest cities in the West, with food and drink envied around the world, and don't have the time?"

Yussuf shakes his head again and keeps on looking around the street and café, like he's expecting the entire force of the Paris Police Prefecture to rappel down these concrete and brick walls nearby and jump on his empty head.

"We have a job for you," he whispers.

"I'm sure you do," Gray says. "What is it?"

A hand goes back under Yussuf's stained coat and comes out with a slip of paper and a color photograph. Both are passed over and Gray looks down, without touching either the paper or the photograph.

Yussuf says, "We need for you to go to America and kill a target. In a place in the New York State. Called Levittown."

Gray memorizes the four faces in the color photograph.

"Why?" he asks.

The young man seems taken aback. "I thought . . . an understanding had been reached earlier."

Gray shrugs. "The agreement has been reached, yes. But I don't go in blind, ever. I need to know the why."

Yussuf reaches over the cluttered table and taps a face on the photo. "The target, here, it stole something from us."

"Don't you want it back?"

Yussuf draws his hand back. "It's gone beyond that . . . a decision has been made, and a lesson needs to be taught."

Gray says, "All right, I can understand that. Anything else?"

"The target . . . when you get there, may be with its family," Yussuf says. "You should take that into account."

Gray looks down at the photo again, of the four smiling faces—dad, mom, daughter, and son. "Do you want me to kill them all?"

Yussuf leans forward, lowers his voice even more. "Is that a problem?"

Two scooters race by on the narrow road, horns blaring, young men sitting on the little machines yelling at each other. When it's quiet, it's Gray's turn to lean forward.

"No," he says quietly. "Not a problem."

CHAPTER 7

JASON TYLER HAS GONE to more than half the continents of the world in service to his nation. He's jumped out of planes, swum rivers, has fired weapons and has been fired upon, and has negotiated and dealt with people from Afghan tribesmen to the elite members of the British Special Air Service. But none of it has prepared him for dealing with this angry young American mother.

"Look," Teresa Sanderson says, arms crossed, standing in the kitchen, "I just want to go for a walk in the neighborhood, all right? Clear my head, stretch my limbs, get a bit of fresh air before going to bed."

Jason says, "I'm sorry, ma'am. I can't allow that. You know the rules. All of you must stay in my presence at all times. The only way you're leaving this house is if your family joins you. And at this time of the night, nobody's leaving."

Teresa walks to the kitchen door, puts her hand on the handle, like she's daring him. "And what are you going to do if I open this door and walk out?"

"I'm going to do my job," he says, glancing away for just a moment. "My job . . . to defend all of you, to the maximum extent."

Teresa stares at Jason, and he stares back, and she says, "I'm sorry. I can't stand this anymore." She storms out of the kitchen and Jason hears the door to her and her husband's bedroom slam shut. Voices are raised. He shakes his head and goes down the hallway, heading to the kids' rooms.

A knock on the first door, and the little girl says, "You may enter."

He opens the door and takes one step into the clean and tidy room. He says, "You all right, Sandy?"

The young girl is in bed, blankets pulled up to her chest, a thick book in her slender hands. "I'm fine," she says, not lifting her gaze from the book. "Why shouldn't I be fine?"

"Ah . . ." Jason has spent a number of days alongside this pretty young girl and still can't figure her out. "Okay, just checking."

As he leaves, she says, "Oh, Mr. Tyler?"

"Yes, hon?"

"What's your birthday?"

"Ah . . . May thirtieth."

"And the year?"

He tells her the year. Young Sandy nods her head with satisfaction.

"You were born on a Monday," she says.

He's amazed. "That's right," he says.

She returns to her book. "Of course I'm right. I'm never wrong."

The young boy's mess of a room brings back fond memories of Jason's own, when he gave his single mom such a hard time growing up in Seattle. The boy looks up eagerly and says, "Yeah, I'm fine. Look, can I ask you something?"

"Sure."

"Are you a soldier?"

Jason isn't about to go into the details of being in the armed forces before working for one of the many intelligence services operating out there in the shadows, so he says, "Yeah, I am."

"You ever fire a gun?"

"Lots of times."

"Can I see your gun?"

Jason smiles. "Goodnight, kid."

Outside, the night air is warm and comfortable. Jason walks around the perimeter of the house, checking the windows, checking the doors. Sweet kids, sweet family. He hopes they will all be asleep in a while, because that will make his job easier. He doesn't need a full night's sleep—not for a while, and not for the duration of this op—but he will be happy when this job is done. He has survived and done well in circumstances that were much worse, in places that even the smartest American couldn't find on a map.

Jason looks next door, where the old man and woman live. Nosy neighbors. He hopes they won't be a problem.

He pauses at the rear, near the bedroom windows. More voices from the master bedroom.

Still, one big thing is bothering him, one very big thing.

He hates lying to that nice lady, even if she is pissed at him.

Because his classified orders are clear, quite clear.

If things go bad, and go bad quickly, he will have to do something that will make him hate himself for the rest of his life.

There's a crackling noise in the far shrubbery, border-ing another home. His hands move on their own, one taking out a 9mm Beretta pistol and the other a monocu-lar night vision scope. He starts scanning the rear yard, and there's something moving, and it's—

—a fat raccoon, waddling its way through a supposedly safe neighborhood in this supposedly safe country.

Jason lowers his weapon and his night vision scope, looks around at the calm and pleasant lights of suburbia.

"Christ," he says. "I wish I was back in Kabul."

CHAPTER 8

LANCE SANDERSON IS HANGING up his shirt and pants when his wife barrels into the bedroom. Without a word, she goes to the closet, pulls out a black duffel bag, and starts throwing clothes inside.

"Honey, what's going on?"

Teresa says nothing. She tugs clothes out of the closet so hard that the empty wire hangers clang into each other.

"Teresa . . ." He feels foolish standing there in the bedroom, just wearing his boxer shorts. But knowing his wife, he can't ignore what's going on.

"I'm tired of being on the run," she says, bringing the duffel bag over to the bed and dropping it down with a heavy *thump*. "I'm so damn tired of it. We're eating crappy food, we're scared all the time . . . hell, we don't even have the right clothes! Remember the first day we got here, it was about to rain, and I had to put scarves on Sandy and me? I can't stand it."

Lance takes a breath, steps forward. "But what can we do? What choice do we have?"

Teresa looks at him, her eyes sharp. "We have a choice right now. We leave. We be careful, keep a low profile, hook up with my cousin Leonard . . ."

"Your cousin Leonard would be out of his league," Lance says. "He's a good cop, a brave guy, but—"

Teresa interrupts him. "Maybe, but he's family. I can trust family. I don't know if I can trust . . . them."

"But . . . we have something important, or so they say," Lance says, wondering if he can possibly defuse this situation before the kids hear them. "We need to wait here before we pass on what we've got to the right people. And we can't do that if we're on the run on our own, keeping our heads down."

Teresa stops on her way back to the closet. "You believed them? Really? Look, you can tell me now, Lance . . . what really went on at the dig? What nearly killed us over there?"

"You know what happened," he says. "You were there."

"Not all of the time," she says. "I find it hard to believe their bullshit story about what we supposedly have . . . and you swallowed it, hook, line and proverbial sinker. Tell me what really went on. There was a dispute over the pay at the dig site, wasn't there? You pissed off the wrong people, right?"

Despising himself, Lance feels anger starting to build. "Every season, there's always a dispute about pay. It's nothing new. I've told you a million times: there's nothing to tell. You were there. And what went on . . . it had nothing to do with money."

Their eyes are locked on each other, and she goes back

to the closet. "Fine . . . so says you. You want to keep secrets like them? Go right ahead. After all, you've already given up your responsibility."

Lance asks, "What responsibility?"

"To be a man," Teresa snaps. "A husband. A father. To protect this family . . . and not to outsource it, like one of your diggers at a site."

Lance opens his mouth but finds there's nothing he can say. Her words are to the point, hurtful, and, worst of all, they're the truth. He knows what he is, an academic more at home at a dig site than in a conflict or a confrontation, and now he's let his family get bossed around and moved halfway across the world, like the weakling he is.

Teresa runs a hand across her face, and her eyes fill with tears. "Sorry, hon, that was a cheap shot. You don't deserve it."

Lance steps forward, eases her into a hug, and feels a rush of gratitude when she hugs him back hard. She whispers, "I'm so scared. I'm sorry . . . but I'm so scared. No matter what happened over there . . . I'm scared now."

He rubs her lower back. "We'll get out of this. I promise. We'll be safe."

Lance stands there for a minute, just holding his wife tight, and there's a slight knock on the door. Teresa kisses his neck and he gently breaks away, throws on a light-blue terrycloth robe, goes to answer the door.

Jason is there. "I'm going lights-out in a few minutes. Everything okay?"

Lance looks to Teresa. She bites her lower lip and gives

a slight nod. He turns back to Jason and says, "Everything's fine."

Jason nods and turns away. Lance closes the bedroom door and goes to the bed, takes the duffel bag off, and puts it on the floor.

Teresa says, "Did you see it?"

Lance has no idea what she means by her question, so he decides just to go ahead and plead ignorance. "I'm sorry, see what?"

"That man's face," Teresa says. "There's something going on. He looks . . ."

"Guilty," Lance says, finishing her phrase. "Yeah, he looks guilty. I've seen it, too. Like . . . he's keeping some secret from us."

"But what?"

Lance says, "Honey, I don't know. I just don't know."

CHAPTER 9

AT THE LITTLE STREETSIDE café in Paris, Gray Evans checks his watch. Time to wrap up this little meet and greet.

He asks Yussuf, "Did you support the team that came in here two Novembers ago?"

The other man grins. "No, but I knew most of them . . . and respected them for what they did. Brave martyrs they were."

Gray nods as if in sympathy, but in reality he thinks, *No, they were stupid fools*. It's one thing to strike at your enemies, but to get yourself killed in the process? What's the point? Gray knows he could never convince this man before him, a true believer.

Yussuf says, "So, it is agreed then?"

"Yes," Gray says.

The young man brings out a handheld device. "I shall arrange your payment." His dirty fingers manipulate the screen and he says, "It is done."

Gray has his own iPhone in his hands, sees a healthy

deposit has just been made in his Cayman Islands numbered account. "All right," he says. "We have a deal."

He puts the phone away and picks up a white napkin, starts absentmindedly rubbing the handles of his knife and fork. Yussuf ignores his movements and says, "Two things more, if I may."

"Go ahead," Gray says, feeling a soothing sensation come over him as he works on the silverware.

"You are an American. Why do you do this? In your country? To your own tribe?"

Gray finishes off his *vin ordinaire*, starts rubbing the glass as well with the cloth napkin. A small battered Renault taxi rolls by, its exhaust choking him for a moment.

"To be an American once meant something," Gray says softly. "You were part of a people and country that was respected and feared. When an American walked the street or a fighter plane took to the air, or a ship to sea, the world took notice. The world now mocks us, teases us. We've given up. We concern ourselves with silly things, like the style of a candidate's hair or which bathroom people should use. That's the way of losers. I don't associate with losers."

Yussuf says, "I see what you mean. And here is the other thing."

From his coat, he pulls out a small envelope. "I was told to give this to you and have you read it before I depart."

Gray opens the small envelope, reads the slip of paper contained within. He looks up at Yussuf and says, "Do you know what was in here?"

"No."

"Good."

With the cloth napkin, he picks up the sharp steak knife he had used earlier, quickly leans over the table, grabs Yussuf's hair with his free left hand, and shoves the knife into his right eye. Yussuf coughs, shudders, and collapses. Gray slips the knife out, gently pushes the body back so it's slumped against the chair, like Yussuf has eaten or drunk too much.

Gray gets up, retrieves Yussuf's phone, the family photo, the piece of paper with the word "Levittown" scribbled upon it, and the envelope with the small sheet of paper. He rereads its bold-faced writing and smiles to himself.

KILL YUSSUF FOR A BONUS.

CHAPTER 10

IN A CUBE-SHAPED glass-and-metal building in an obscure office park outside of Arlington, Virginia, an intelligence officer known by most as "the Big Man" looks up as his office door opens. A woman strides in without announcing herself and without having knocked. She's rail-thin, wearing a red dress and a white leather belt, and her blond hair is cut short and to the point. Her thin arms are weighted down by gold bangles and she says, "We have a problem with the Sanderson family."

The Big Man nods. "Go on."

The woman—known to most as "the Thin Woman"— says, "We got a text this a.m. from their minder. The family's getting restless, making threats to leave on their own. You know we can't let that happen."

"I know," the Big Man says. "But that's the choice they demanded in exchange for their cooperation. Low-key, not staying at a military base, keep it simple for their children's sake."

The Thin Woman says, "We could have a response team in place in their neighborhood."

He says, "That just adds another level of complexity. A unit like that can't be hidden, you have to notify local law enforcement, rumors and tales get spread around . . . no, they stay in place. Besides, we have more to worry about than just that."

"What is it?" she asks.

He opens up a red-bordered manila folder and says, "Our brothers and sisters at the NSA say they're picking up chatter about the Sanderson family from cells located in North Africa. No decrypt yet, but you can be sure they're not discussing sending the family a fruit basket. A hit squad is being dispatched to find them."

"Damn," the Thin Woman says. "Can we move the Sandersons?"

"Moving makes them more vulnerable."

She asks, "How much longer?"

"Two days, I hope," the Big Man says. "We need Clarkson to debrief them, and she's currently stuck at the Libyan/Egyptian border near Salloum. She's getting extracted as soon as we can make it happen."

"Why Clarkson?"

The Big Man grows irritated. His day has just started and already it's in the crapper. "You saw my memo. She's the only one with the necessary talents to do the debrief. So we have to wait until she gets stateside."

The Thin Woman shakes her head, goes to the door. "You're gambling with their lives."

The Big Man sighs. "That's what we do, every damn day of the week."

CHAPTER 11

AFTER BREAKFAST THE NEXT morning, Jason Tyler asks Teresa if she and the family would like to go for a shopping trip, and Lance is pleased by how quickly she accepts the offer. Their discussion from last night hasn't been mentioned since he and Teresa woke up, and that's fine with Lance.

Now they are at a Super Stop & Shop and Jason is parking the Yukon at a distance from the store, where no other vehicles are parked near them. Sam says, "Boy, why couldn't we park closer? There are lots of spaces up front."

Jason says, "It'll give you a chance to get some exercise."

He gets out of the car, and Lance studies him, now knowing better. He sees how the man works. He wants their Yukon isolated, so it's easy to find—not easy for anyone to sneak up on it.

Their bodyguard also insists that they depart the Yukon one at a time: Lance, Teresa, Sam, and, last, Sandy. Back at their rental home, Jason had insisted that they enter the

Yukon in the opposite order, Sandy going first and Lance bringing up the rear.

He shepherds them quickly across the parking lot and Lance feels relaxed amid the other shoppers out on this spring morning. It's pure America, with the shopping carts, aisle displays, and families of all ages and colors crowding around, and Lance looks to Jason to see if he's finally relaxed as well.

No, he's not. The man is with them, moving constantly, going forward, bringing up the rear, always looking around, always . . . guarding.

Always guarding. What a life that man must have.

They spend some time going slowly up and down the crowded aisles, and near the dairy coolers, Teresa abruptly stops and says, "Oh, dear, yogurt, that's worth stocking up on."

She moves around and starts handing containers to Lance, who in turn puts them in the cart, and he looks up and—

The kids are gone.

Jason is gone.

What the hell?

Teresa sees him stop and says, "What's the problem?"

"The kids have left. And so has Jason."

His wife looks around the bustling aisles and says, "You know those two. They probably decided to see if they could sneak away from Jason and us. I wouldn't worry."

Lance hears what she says, but, based on the look on her face and in her eyes, neither of them believes what she's saying.

CHAPTER 12

A FEW MINUTES LATER, he and Teresa are in the produce section of the supermarket. Teresa is doing her best to appear calm, and Lance is acting similarly placid. The to-and-fro of the safe shoppers, the long counters overflowing with fruit and vegetables . . . Lance finds it hard to believe that just a number of days ago, he and his family were in the middle of the Tunisian desert, living on canned goods and freeze-dried food.

A woman with dark-blue hair and yoga pants that are two sizes too small smashes into the side of Teresa's cart, shrugs, and walks off, and Teresa says, "This is an okay place, but, damn, I miss my Mollie Stone's from back home."

"Me, too," he says quietly, eyes shifting back and forth, "but my waistline isn't complaining about not getting those breakfast pastries. Hey, I saw you working this morning before we left. How's the guidebook coming along?"

Teresa starts examining yellow peaches with studied nonchalance, one at a time, constantly scanning the crowd for the kids. From long practice, Lance holds open a plastic bag. "How do you think?" she says. "No internet means no research. Without the great God of Google, it's like we've been tossed back in time thirty years . . . but at least I'm not pounding out my copy on a Remington typewriter. And your work?"

"Not good," he says. "After the time it took to get the permits and paperwork in place to get to the dig site, then leaving the dig nearly two months early . . . no matter the excuse, it's going to tick off Stanford pretty seriously when they get word. It'll knock my research back at least a year, if not longer."

Lance ties the plastic bag, gently places it in the shopping cart, and there's another bump as Teresa's cart hits the corner of a banana display. She mutters something and her face flushes, and Lance eyes the nearby vegetables and tries to lighten the mood.

He picks up a long, thick cucumber, shows it to his wife. "Hey, hon, does this remind you of anyone you know? Except for the color, I mean."

A wry smile that warms his heart. Teresa takes it from his hand, tosses it back, and puts a smaller pickling cucumber in his hand.

"I don't care if you've got your doctorate in archaeology, honey, you still don't know how to measure things."

He laughs and leans in for a kiss, but as he does so, Jason moves in unexpectedly, one hand on Sandy's shoulder, the other on Sam's. Sandy is reading a thick paperback almanac of current science facts, while her brother is holding a Batman comic book. Sam's not reading but squirming under the grasp of their bodyguard.

"Mom, Dad, do I have to listen to Jason?" he asks, voice loud. "He says I have to do what he tells me. Do I have to do that? Do I?"

Teresa stands still, both hands tight on the shopping cart handle. Lance notes the determined face of Jason and the angry face of his boy and thinks, *You have no idea, son.* Aloud he says, "Yes, at least for a while longer."

Sam squirms away. "How long is that? Huh? How long?"

Jason gives a not-so-gentle tap on Sam's shoulder. "Listen to your father."

Teresa reaches over, takes the almanac and comic book from her children's hands, puts them in the shopping cart, and continues her determined pushing and shopping.

Outside in the sunlit day, Lance moves along through the parking lot with his family and Jason. Sandy is reading her new almanac again and Sam is looking down at the ground, holding his Batman comic in his hands.

Jason opens the rear of the Yukon and helps Teresa put the groceries inside.

Lance is about to ask her what's for dinner when it happens.

On the other side of the parking lot comes a loud *bang!* Even though Lance sees every motion, every second, he still can't believe how fast Jason moves. The near rear door of the Yukon is thrown open and Sandy and Sam are literally tossed in. Lance races to the front passenger door, but by the time he opens it, his wife is already in the rear with the kids. The doors are shut and Jason has started up the Yukon, driving ahead with the driver's side door open.

Nervous, Lance asks, "What's going on—"

"Quiet!" Jason barks out, and from the rear, Teresa says, "It's okay, it's okay, it looks like a fender bender, that's all."

Lance swivels in his seat, looks back, sees a light-blue VW Beetle with its side caved in by a red Volvo station wagon backing out of its spot. He shakes his head. He can't believe the two things he has just seen.

One was how quick, efficient, and focused Jason was in getting all of them safely into the Yukon. It was parked such that they could easily leave the parking lot and get on the main road.

And the other . . . the other was his wife, Teresa.

How she was looking at Jason with thanks, admiration . . .

And something else?

Just to punctuate that thought, Teresa reaches forward, pats Jason on his big right shoulder.

"Thanks, Jason," she says. "Thanks for looking out for us."

Then she sits back without having said a word to her husband.

CHAPTER 13

NEW YORK STATE TROOPER Leonard Brooks reluctantly approaches the Second Precinct building of the Nassau County Police Department. The one-story brick station house, which provides coverage for Levittown, looks more like a bank branch.

Even though he's in full uniform, he's here on a personal mission, nothing to do with his work, and he's wondering what kind of reception he's going to get. After spending a couple of minutes in the lobby, he's escorted back into an office area and meets with Mark Crosby, a heavyset man with black hair who serves as both deputy commander and deputy inspector for the precinct.

Crosby leans over his clean desk and says, "All right, what can we do for you today, Trooper Brooks?"

His round campaign hat is in his lap, and he says, "It's delicate."

Crosby gives a knowing smile. "It always is. What do you have going on?"

"It's about my cousin," he says. "Teresa Sanderson. Her mother is concerned. She was overseas on a trip and wasn't due back for at least two months. But her mother got a disturbing phone call from her two weeks ago."

"How disturbing?"

"She told her mother that she was okay, and that she was stateside, and that she was staying in Levit . . . and then she was cut off."

"Levit? That's all?"

"That's all," Leonard says. "The phone call was disconnected, but her mother thinks she was going to say Levittown."

"Uh-huh," Crosby says, tapping fingers on his desk. "Does she have any friends or relatives here?"

"No."

"Do you know if she's ever traveled here before?"

"No."

"Any connections whatsoever?"

"Not that I'm aware of," Leonard says, knowing this conversation isn't going well. "All I'm asking is that if you could put the word out to your officers, keep a lookout for her, and—"

Crosby raises his hand. "Where's her home address?"

"Palo Alto, California."

"Have you contacted the police there?"

"Yes, but—"

Crosby shakes his head. "Troop L covers this part of the state. Are you in Troop L?"

"No, sir."

"Yet here you are," Crosby says. "Unofficially."

"Well, it's a favor, I guess, and—"

"What troop are you in, exactly?" Crosby asked, brows furrowed.

"Troop T, sir."

"Troop T! So you work on the Thruway, and you come here, looking for a favor like that? Christ, if you were in Troop L, maybe I could be convinced to work something out, but nope. Not going to go out on a limb for you and your cousin. I don't know you, I don't know what you're up to."

"But if I—"

"You're wasting my time, Trooper Brooks. And I don't have enough of it. I think it's time for you to head on back to the Thruway before I make a phone call to your superior and tell 'em you've gone rogue. I don't think you'll like that, am I right?"

Leonard gets up, knowing his appointment is over. "You're very right, Inspector Crosby. I appreciate your time."

Crosby stays seated behind his desk and holds both hands up. "Look. These things work out, okay? I'm sure your cousin and her kids are fine."

"I hope you're right."

Back outside in the bright sun, Leonard Brooks adjusts his campaign hat and thinks through the conversation as he approaches his dark-blue Dodge Charger State Police cruiser. He opens the door.

Fruitful, but probably not in the way the good inspector had intended.

How had the man known his cousin had children?

CHAPTER 14

HELEN IS TAKING AWAY an empty cup of tea from the nearby coffee table when Ronald Temple sees the black GMC Yukon pull into the driveway. The big guy gets out first and then opens the door. The adult male and female step out, followed by the young boy and the young girl. He escorts them into the house and a few minutes pass, and then the big guy comes back and takes several plastic bags of groceries into the house.

Helen comes back to wipe the table and Ronald says, "Do you see that? Do you? They all go as a group. Who in hell goes shopping as a group? And with a bodyguard as well?"

Helen rubs the table carefully with a soft cloth. "How do you know he's a bodyguard? Maybe he's just a friend. Or a relative. A brother of the man or woman."

Ronald picks up his binoculars, looks over at the house. He spots the woman putting groceries away in the refrigerator.

"I just know," he says, binoculars still up to his eyes. "When I was on the job, before going into security, you knew these things. Instinct. You could tell by the way somebody was walking that they were carrying a concealed weapon. That guy's carrying. I just know it."

Helen loses her patience before she leaves the living room. "Then for God's sake, call the police."

"Huh?" he asks, lowering the binoculars and turning his head.

"You heard me," she says, dishcloth still in her hand. "If you think that man over there is carrying a gun, and probably an illegal one, then call the police. Have them check it out . . . otherwise, Ronald, I'm getting tired of all of your conspiracy theories. Please."

Ronald feels his face warm. "Okay, that's what I'm going to do. Hand me the phone. I'll call the cops right now."

CHAPTER 15

LANCE HELPS TERESA PUT the groceries away. She frowns as she sits back at the round kitchen table with her books and laptop. "Once more, trying to write a book in the twenty-first century without using twenty-first-century technology."

He kisses the top of her head and says, "Just a couple more days. That's all."

She reaches up, squeezes his hand. "All right, professor, but if we get to day three and I'm still cut off from Google, you're going to be cut off from something more intimate. Got it?"

He kisses her once more. "Got it."

Lance takes a short walk down the near hallway and sees that Sandy is reading a thick textbook he lent her yesterday. Then he pokes his head into Sam's room. He's bent over a slowly developing dinosaur model.

Lance goes back into the hallway and nearly bumps into Jason.

"Professor," he says.

"Jason," he replies, remembering with a sour feeling a talk he'd had with Teresa last night. "Look . . . can we talk somewhere?"

Jason says, "Sure. Where?"

Good question. The only rooms not being used at the moment were the tiny bathroom, the small living room, and the master bedroom. "Come with me, will you?"

Lance walks into the master bedroom and Jason follows him. Lance says, "I want to help."

Jason pauses for a second and says, "You can help me by staying together with your family, under my watch, until Langley's ready to move you. That will be very helpful."

"You don't understand," Lance says. "I'm the head of the household. I'm responsible for them, I'm responsible for them being in trouble and for being here, undercover. I want to help defend them if . . . if things happen."

Jason's face is impassive. "You ever serve? You ever been a cop? You an NRA member?"

"No to all three, but that doesn't mean I can't—"

And Lance can't believe how quickly Jason moves, because in a second or two, a black pistol has been pulled from somewhere in his clothing and is now in his right hand.

Time stands still. The pistol is pointing right at Lance's chest.

And without warning, Jason abruptly tosses the pistol at Lance.

Lance fumbles and catches it, almost dropping it along

the way. The gun is cold and unfamiliar in his hand. It's bulky, ungainly, and it's the first time he's ever held a pistol in his life. The sense of power, the potential of being able to shoot, wound, and kill, practically emanates from the shape of the weapon.

"Shoot me," Jason says.

"What?"

"Shoot me." Jason steps forward: big, bulky, scary-looking. "You've got the pistol. I'm threatening you, your wife, your kids . . . react! Shoot me! Now!"

Lance starts fumbling with the pistol, and in a quick snap, Jason takes it back, twisting two of Lance's fingers. He cries out.

"I don't have the time or the inclination to train you in self-defense, Professor Sanderson," Jason says, his voice filled with contempt. "You're out of your league. So keep your family together and let me do my job."

Lance feels ashamed, flustered, and doesn't know what to say.

And then the doorbell rings.

The pistol in Jason's hand disappears back under his clothes.

"Lockdown, now," he says in a commanding voice, and goes out, heading to the children's rooms. "Move."

CHAPTER 16

FROM HIS COMFORTABLE BARCALOUNGER—
he has a brief, grim thought that he'll probably be buried
with this thing when the time comes—Ronald looks on
with satisfaction as a Nassau County police cruiser slowly
glides to a stop in front of the house next door.

"I'll be damned," he whispers, smiling. "They're actually going to do something."

He made the call about ten minutes ago. Due to the
bored response of the dispatcher—"Yeah, yeah" was her
favorite phrase—Ronald didn't think anything was going
to happen.

Sometimes it's nice to be proven wrong.

The cruiser door opens up and a female police officer
steps out. Ronald gets up from his chair, grimacing from
the pain in his legs. Taking his nostril tubes out, he slowly
walks to the door, blanket and revolver in his hand.

From the kitchen comes the noise of a television, volume turned up loud. Helen is watching one of her favorite

reality shows, about overdressed housewives yelling at each other. At the moment, they are baking a cake for an upcoming church function.

He goes to the front door and slowly opens it. Near the door is a small green oxygen tank with two wheels on its base and a handle—for use on those few occasions he steps outside. He drapes the hose around his head, turns the handle, and breathes in through his nostrils.

Despite all his ailments, he feels pretty good, watching the police officer approach the door, now partially hidden by a holly bush.

A thought from his past comes to him. This time . . . this time he won't screw up.

Tuesday, September 11, 2001.

He should have been at work that morning as a security officer for an investment firm, but the night before he had gotten hammered at Frank Watson's retirement bash. With a thudding hangover, he had called in sick, had switched off the phone, and had tumbled back to bed to sleep it off.

It was hours before he realized what had happened and days before he received the list of dead people from his firm. Then the whispers came to him, followed him, and never went away for more than a decade and a half:

If you had been there, you could have saved some of them. Instead, you stayed home and slept it off. Useless drunk. Those people depended on you and you let them down.

He opens the door wider, preparing himself to provide backup for that solitary cop next door.

This time he's ready.

If something happens—and a part of him hopes it does—he won't be a failure for a second time.

In a way, he almost wishes things would go wrong, so he could prove himself.

He takes the revolver out from behind the blanket and holds it at his side.

CHAPTER 17

OFFICER KAREN GLYNN OF the Nassau County Police Department wishes her shift was over so she could get home and do what she really wants to do, which is study up so she can apply to the New York City Police Department. Nothing against Nassau County and this dull suburb of Levittown, but she wants to do something serious as a cop, not track down stolen bicycles or take reports on vandalized mailboxes.

She pulls her white cruiser with its blue-and-orange stripes in front of the small blue house—the house that is supposedly harboring a man who might or might not be carrying a firearm, and who may or may not have a concealed pistol permit.

Biggest call of the week, she thinks, as she calls into dispatch that she's arrived. She opens the cruiser's door, walks up to the front of the house.

Clean and tidy, like every other house on this street, like practically every other house in this part of Nassau

County, and she rings the doorbell once, twice, and steps back as the door opens.

"Yes?" the man at the door asks. "Can I help you, officer?"

Karen steps back one more time, body on automatic, examining the bulky guy, and she goes into full alert. Even though he's well-dressed and his hands are empty, it's those eyes . . .

"Ah, yes," she says. "Officer Glynn, Nassau County Police Department. I'm investigating a . . . complaint."

"What kind of complaint, officer?"

She says, "Can I see some identification, please?"

A second or two passes, feeling like an hour. He smiles. "Of course." His right hand slowly goes to his pocket and her throat is dry, her hand is on her holster, and he comes back with a wallet, from which he pulls out a driver's license.

"Here," he says. "Will this do?"

She takes the license, gives it a very quick glance—Karen doesn't want to lose focus on this hulk in front of her—and returns it. "Thank you, Mr. Tyler. I see that license is from Virginia. Can I ask why you're here in Levittown?"

"Visiting," he says evenly.

"I see," she says. "Well, the department has received word that you've been seen walking off the premises, carrying a concealed weapon. Is that true?"

"Word from whom?"

"Is that true? That you're carrying a concealed weapon?"

Hesitation, then the slightest of nods. "That's true."

"Do you have a concealed carry permit, Mr. Tyler?"

"I do."

"May I see it, please?"

Another second that seems to drag on and on.

He looks at her.

"Yes," he says. "It's here in my wallet as well."

And another plastic-embossed card is removed and passed over, with the man's photo on it, and issued from Nassau County.

Karen gives it a glance, passes it back.

All in order.

Still . . .

Why is her heart racing so?

"May I come in?" she asks.

"Why?"

"Because I'd like to take a look around."

A slight smile that looks as dangerous as the bared teeth of a lunging German shepherd being held back only by a thin and fraying rope. "I don't think so."

"Why?"

"Because."

Karen is now convinced that even though this guy has all the right permits and identification, something strange is definitely going on, and she starts to—

He says, "Is this when you're going to say you're going to come in now, or go to a helpful judge to get a search warrant for some sort of malfeasance, imagined or otherwise?"

"I, uh—"

The man says, "Perhaps this might help."

The wallet is returned to his pants, and he reaches into another pocket, removes a business-sized envelope, folded in half, and removes a thick white piece of stationery, which Karen holds and reads and then reads one more time.

She nods. Mouth still very, very dry.

Passes the piece of paper back.

"Thanks . . . I, uh, I'll be heading out. Thanks for your cooperation."

"Glad to do it, Officer Glynn," he says, and he gently closes the door on her.

Karen turns and goes back to her cruiser, reviewing what she has just seen: a letter signed by both the governor and the president, asking the reader of said letter to give every courtesy and consideration to its bearer, one Jason Tyler of Arlington, Virginia.

Whatever the hell is going on here is way, way above her pay grade, and she wants none of it.

She stops at her cruiser and an old man approaches her, yelling.

Christ on a crutch, she thinks, *this day just keeps getting loopier by the second.*

CHAPTER 18

RONALD TEMPLE WAITS AND watches, waits and watches, and—

The police officer heads back toward her cruiser.

Alone.

Not calling for backup? Not dragging that big guy out to the cruiser in handcuffs?

Unbelievable!

He drops his blanket and revolver on the floor, grabs his oxygen tank handle, and starts out of the door.

The oxygen tank rattling behind him, he goes across the lawn, seeing the female officer reach her cruiser.

"Hey!" he calls out, ashamed at how weak his voice is. "Hey! Officer! Over here!"

She opens the door to her cruiser, hesitates just for a moment.

Long enough.

"Hey . . . what's going on here?" he asks, wheezing to a halt, the tank beside him. "Why are you leaving so soon?"

The police officer is cool, polite, and uncooperative, and Ronald remembers the times he behaved the same way when he was on the job.

"Are you the neighbor who made the complaint?" she asks.

"I did." His breathing is harsh, and he feels like a series of explosive coughs are about to rip from his lungs.

"It was unfounded."

"What?"

"Sir, it was unfounded."

He walks to her, stops as he forgets his wheeled oxygen tank. The tubes rip from his nose, the tank falling over. "What do you mean, unfounded? I saw it! Hey, I was on the job for twenty-plus years, back in Manhattan, and I know what the hell I'm talking about."

The female officer shakes her head again. "Sir, it was unfounded . . . and if you'll excuse me, I have to go back on patrol."

That's it. She's back in her cruiser. The engine starts right up, and in a few seconds, the cruiser makes a left-hand turn and is gone.

Ronald is alone on the empty street.

But he senses something.

He slowly moves, breathing hard, toward his oxygen tubes on the grass, his oxygen bottle on its side.

There.

The large man in the house . . . he's at the door.

It's open.

He's staring right at Ronald.

Right at him.

So now he knows who made the call.

Who told the police all about him.

The stare is quiet, unmoving, unyielding.

Ronald feels that old fear of being alone out on the street, no partner, no backup. He suddenly wishes the unhelpful officer from Nassau County was still here, with her cruiser and her radio.

It's been a very long time since Ronald has been this afraid.

CHAPTER 19

TERESA SANDERSON SITS ON the crowded bathroom floor with her legs pulled up to her and her arms wrapped around her knees, trying not to shiver with fear. Lance is next to her, arm around her shoulders. Her children are huddled in the bathtub, a heavy and bulky black Kevlar blanket draped over the two of them. Jason moved quickly, putting Sandy in first, then her brother on top of her, and putting the blanket in place. Another Kevlar blanket is attached to the locked bathroom door behind them.

The bathroom is a dump. Filthy tile, a dirty tub, a leaking faucet over an old porcelain sink, and a toilet that flushes itself every now and then, usually at three in the morning. Over the toilet is a small window, so dirty that the outside can't be clearly seen. There's a handmade crooked shelf that holds some cleaning supplies, most of them almost as old as Sam.

Lance notes Teresa's review of the dingy bathroom and gently leans into her.

"Honey?" he asks.

"Yes?"

"I love what you've done with the place." His smile warms her and she leans back into him.

Still . . .

How in God's name did she end up here, in danger, with her kids and her husband? What combination of forces and coincidences have conspired to do this to her and her family?

Risk.

Always a matter of risk, but long before, when Sam and Sandy were just barely toddlers, she wanted to go along with Lance as he dove into the past, unlocking the secrets of Carthage and its long-standing enemy, Rome. It all worked out from the start. She spent quality time with her husband, and her kids have grown up knowing there's more to the world than just a school playground and computer games.

She strains to listen to what's happening on the other side of the door. A murmur of voices, that's all.

Now?

Now she regrets it all, and though she hates to admit it, she regrets trusting Lance. Oh, he's a solid husband, smart, funny, and loyal, good in bed and good at taking care of the kids. But sometimes . . . sometimes he is caught in the past, thinking of battles involving Carthage and Rome instead of lifting his head and seeing the battles going on around them.

She shifts her weight, still listening.

Because this is a battle that has caught up to her and her family.

She thinks about their time in Tunisia, and with guilt flooding through her, she remembers one thing that she's been hiding from Lance and Jason and the other government people they've encountered since their abrupt departure.

About that day in the nearest city, Bizerte, when she was taking photographs in the marketplace.

Three hard-looking men were sitting at a café table, drinking coffee, and she loved the way the light was coming in past the overhanging tapestries. She took the photo, and the men—suddenly and scarily angry—leapt as one from the table and chased her through the crowds.

Who were they? Why didn't they want their photos taken?

Teresa knows . . . though she's too scared to admit it, even now.

She's never told Lance about what happened. She had planned to tell him the next day, but on that next day—

A knock on the bathroom door makes her jump.

"Sanderson family." It's the familiar voice of Jason. "Sanderson family, we are clear."

She untangles herself from Lance's grasp and gets up. Lance unlocks the bathroom door. Teresa goes over to the bathtub and pulls away the heavy Kevlar blanket, her heart breaking when she sees her boy and her girl scared and huddled in the bottom of the tub.

Jason comes in, going past Lance, helping out Sam and then Sandy. "You okay, kids?" he asks.

"I need to go back to my reading," Sandy announces. "I've wasted nine minutes in here."

Sam says, "And she farts. And won't say she's sorry."

Sam barrels out and his older sister follows him, and Jason says, "All clear."

Lance nods in satisfaction, but Teresa can't stand it. "All clear? For now . . . but for how long? Will we ever be safe, ever again, will we?"

The two men look away from her and say nothing.

And she wishes she was brave enough to tell them what she's thinking: that this is all her fault.

CHAPTER 20

TWO BLOCKS AWAY FROM Perry Street in downtown Trenton, New Jersey, Gray Evans locks his rental car in front of a boarded-up three-story brick building, one of at least six he sees up and down this side street. The streets are filthy, the streetlights are broken, and the sidewalks are cracked and have knee-high weeds growing out of them.

Gray glances up and down the street. A thin black dog trots along the other side of the street, disappears into a narrow alley. Gray takes a deep breath, smells the familiar scents he's encountered over the years in different parts of the world, and knows where he is: a place where people and the government have given up. Lead-tainted water, uncollected trash, decaying buildings. All the signs of a collapsing civilization.

He walks up a block, takes a right. Another series of three-story brick buildings, but the one at the end has lights on and is a bodega. Two bars are across the street, lights on, some men walking in, others stumbling out with drink-fueled vigor. Shouts, music, and more shouts punctuate the night.

At the center of the block is a secure metal-frame door with reinforced hinges and a keypad combination lock. He punches in eight numbers he's memorized, turns the knob, and enters a different world. The floor is covered in clean tile and the lights are all on. There's a narrow elevator in front of him—again, with a keypad lock. He punches in another set of numbers, the door glides open, he gets in, and the elevator gently takes him up to the third floor.

It opens up into a wide, open loft with recessed lighting. There's a grouping of comfortable leather furniture in front of him, a kitchen to the right with stainless steel appliances, and a wide work area in the distance consisting of a conference table, four large-screen monitors, banks of servers with blinking lights, and two computer workstations.

A man leaning on a cane approaches him, smiling, holding out his right hand. "Gray. On time, as always."

"That's how I roll, Abraham."

"Come on in."

Abraham leads him to the conference table. He has on leather moccasins, khaki slacks, and a Yankees T-shirt. He's in his early thirties, with trimmed black hair, a black goatee, and gold earrings in each ear.

He settles down and Gray sits across from him. Abraham says, "Refreshments?"

"Not now," Gray says.

"Suit yourself," Abraham says, sitting still, his cane tight in his left hand. "What do you need?"

Gray says, "Looking for the Sanderson family. Husband and wife, Lance and Teresa. Preteen daughter and son, Sandy and Sam. All from Palo Alto. Hubby is a professor at Stanford, wife is a freelance author, has written two travel guides. A couple of weeks ago they were in Tunisia. Now I think they're in Levittown."

"From Tunisia to Levittown, what a letdown," Abraham says.

"I guess."

"You want them found?"

"Very much so," Gray says.

"Usual fee?"

"Plus ten percent," Gray says. "Your skills . . . I think they deserve to be compensated."

"Glad to hear it."

"Plus I'm in a rush."

"You or your client?"

"What difference does it make?"

Abraham looks up at the open ceiling, where a red digital clock is suspended. "Let's say . . . twenty-four hours."

"Perfect."

Gray gets up and walks out.

He's never been one for extended good-byes.

Back to his rental car—Gray always purchases the extra insurance, just because of trips like these—he comes upon two local youths sitting on the hood. They're dressed in baggy pants with their underwear showing, wearing lots of gold chains—or bling, he can never keep up with the latest trends—and baseball caps worn at an angle.

"Yo," the one on the left says, not moving. "Nice rig."

"Glad you like it," he says. "It's a rental."

The other youth says, "Rental or no, you owe us a parking fee."

"I do?" Gray asks, stepping closer. "Funny, I don't see any signs."

The first one says, "It's understood, bro. This place and all. It's . . . understood. We watched your rig, nothing happened to it, we get compensated."

Gray says, "Appreciate the concern, fellas, but I respectfully decline."

The first one gets off the car. "Bad move, bro. We're not taking no for an answer."

Gray eyes them both and says, "All right, here's the deal. Tell me what happened here in December 1776 and I'll let you go."

The second laughs. "You'll let us go?"

They both advance on him. The first one says, "Who the hell you think you are?"

Gray waits until the last moment, relaxed. Unless these two are well trained and exceptional, and know how to work as a team, they are quite vulnerable.

They just don't know it yet.

He spins and kicks hard at the right knee of the closest one, making him cry out and fall to the ground. His friend attempts to run away and Gray snags the waistband of his exposed underwear, gives it a severe tug—crushing whatever might be in the way—and spins him back so he falls against the hood of his rental.

The two youths are on the ground, moaning and clasping at their injured parts. Gray leans over and says, "Tell you who I am. I'm the guy who knows Washington and his troops saved the revolution here in Trenton, for the eventual benefit of you two dopes."

More moans and they scramble away in fear as Gray gets closer and says, "Guys?"

Neither one of them attempts to speak. Gray says, "Guys . . . I really need to go. Mind getting out of the way?"

And in seconds they're gone.

Gray gets into his rental and heads out.

It's been a full day.

CHAPTER 21

AFTER A THREE-HOUR RUN north from Levittown, New York State Trooper Leonard Brooks arrives in Latham—just north of Albany, New York—and parks his cruiser at the office building that houses the New York State Intelligence Center. Having called ahead, he gets a friendlier reception here than he had in Nassau County, and he is quickly ushered into a plain-looking office where he meets with Beth Draper, an intelligence analyst for the State Police.

She stands up from her desk, which is piled high with forms and folders, and comes around to give him a hug and a kiss on the cheek. "Brooksie, good to see you again."

"The same."

He sits down, feeling warm, thinking, *Oh, yes, much nicer reception than Levittown.* He and Beth dated for a year or so right after both of them graduated from the New York State Police Academy in Albany.

She went into intelligence and he went into patrol. They

see each other every few months or so and are now less than lovers and more than just friends.

Beth sits down, runs both hands through her long blond hair. She's wearing a plain white blouse and black slacks that fail to conceal her pretty curves. "Okay, it's past quitting time. Tell me what you need."

He spends the next few minutes explaining his search for his cousin, the lack of response from authorities in Palo Alto and Levittown, and how messages to Teresa's cell phone, home phone, and email have all gone unanswered.

"Damn," she says. "Don't like the sound of that."

"Neither do I."

"What do you think?" she asks. "She have enemies? Her husband?"

"She's a freelance writer. He's an archaeologist. Not the enemy-making type."

"You'd be surprised. You said they were in North Africa recently?"

"Tunisia."

"The whole family?"

"Teresa . . . she's one of those granola types. Wants to expose her kids to the bigger world. And her husband . . . he's sort of an expert on Carthage."

"Car what?"

"Carthage. North African empire that were rivals of Rome until Rome crushed them. You've heard of Rome, haven't you?"

She smiles, a perfect little smile of white teeth that still stirs him. "Sure. Rome. About ninety minutes away. Where the Erie Canal was started. Please stop busting my chops, Brooksie."

"Chop-busting done."

Beth sighs, scribbles a few things on a piece of scrap paper. "I'll do what I can, I'll start sniffing around . . . but you should prepare yourself."

His hands feel chilled, like a block of ice was suddenly nearby. "What are you saying?"

"What you already know, in your heart of hearts," Beth says, still writing. "Phone call unexpectedly broken off. No information from any authorities. Friends and relatives don't know where they are. Phone, cell phone, and email all unanswered."

She looks up, pretty face solemn. "You remember the Petrov family, two years ago? On the run from the Russian mob? Hiding out?"

Leonard feels much cooler. "Yes."

Beth says, "It took one slipup . . . a postcard to a relative, saying all was well. And that's all." Beth pauses. "I hear that when the house was finally cleared by the F B I, they had to bulldoze it down to the foundation. Because they couldn't get all the bloodstains out of the floors and walls."

CHAPTER 22

SAM SANDERSON OPENS THE door to his bedroom, checks out the hallway. All quiet. Lights off. Of course it would be quiet . . . this crappy place doesn't even have a television!

He closes the door, pops himself down on his unmade bed. He's got books, he's got dinosaur models . . . and he's bored.

God, he's so bored.

No television!

And there's no computer!

Oh, Mom has a laptop, but something inside the computer has been switched off, meaning it can't be used to access the internet.

So Sam can't do research on which new dinosaur models he wants to order, he can't check out the dinosaur forums he loves to poke around on, and he can't email . . . About a half-dozen of his buds back in California must be wondering why he hasn't answered them.

Great. When he finally gets back to Palo Alto, his friends will think he's been a jerk because he hasn't answered their emails.

Plus . . . he reaches into his jeans pocket, tugs out a piece of metal and plastic, rolls it around in his fingers. This is something he picked up back at that desert place, something he hasn't shown Dad. It's not one of those broken bowl pieces, for sure . . . it looks too new. So what is it?

He puts it back in his pocket. If he had a computer that really worked, he could find out . . .

Sam bounces off the bed, opens the door one more time. Still dark, still quiet. He wonders where Jason is hiding. Ever since they left Tunisia, that scary bad guy has been hanging with them, day after day. Sam knows something bad happened back in Tunisia, but why should he have to pay for it?

He can't go anywhere alone, he can't go play in the yard by himself, and no computer . . .

Man, he's bored!

He closes the door and tries to tiptoe back to his bed.

Bored or not, he has a plan.

This crappy house has a house to the left and one to the right. The one to the left has some snoopy old guy who keeps on peeking in at them with binoculars. But the other house . . . there's a guy and girl who live there together, and the funny thing is, they both work at night.

Which means that, right now, their house is empty.

The house he can see through his bedroom window.

And he knows they use a computer . . . because he can see them working on it in their living room.

Sam knows something else, too.

The other day the two of them came back from some errand, and he saw the woman dig and dig through her purse, and then the guy laughed at her and removed a brick from the steps, took out a key, and unlocked the front door.

So the house over there is empty.

The house that has a computer.

And he knows where the key to the door is hidden.

Sam goes to the window, unlocks it, and slides the window open, and then the screen. It makes a squeaky noise.

He waits.

And waits.

No one seems to have heard him.

Good!

He clambers outside and steps on the grass and then starts to the empty house.

If he's very, very lucky, he'll be on the computer in just a few minutes, and no one will ever, ever know.

CHAPTER 23

LANCE SANDERSON TOSSES AND turns, Teresa deeply asleep next to him.

He admires his wife in so many ways, including how she can instantly drop off to sleep. She'll be reading a magazine or a book and will then put her reading material down, give Lance a quick kiss, and say, "Night, honey. I'm off to sleep."

And within a minute, she will be deep asleep.

Oh, to have that power!

He stares up at the ceiling. Memories come back to him, the memory of that last full day in Tunisia, when everything went wrong.

The dig site is three years old, about fifty or so kilometers from the famed ruins of Carthage, which are situated near Tunis, the capital of Tunisia. It is in a remote section of a desert near the P11 highway, and Lance and his graduate students, along with local laborers, are excavating an estate that may or may not have belonged to a prominent

Carthaginian official before the Romans sacked the city in 146 BC.

On this day the sun is overhead and very bright. His two graduate students from Stanford, young men who still have the vigor and enthusiasm he remembers from his own grad school days, have gone off on a day's worth of errands to the nearby port city of Bizerte. Teresa and Sam are under a flapping canvas tarpaulin, cataloguing and photographing some of the artifacts—coins, broken pottery, cooking vessels—that he and his crew have recovered. Teresa has been quiet this morning, only saying she has something to discuss with him later at the morning break, and he puts it out of his mind. Poor honey is probably still upset at the stench coming from their shared chemical toilets.

And Sandy? Lance smiles to himself. Sandy is Sandy, sitting in a corner on a folding camp chair, reading and reading, ignoring her surroundings, only bestirring herself to find something new to read.

The surroundings are familiar to Lance after years of work, digging and cataloguing: carefully dug square pits, grid lines set up with strings and white tape. Some of the laborers are bent over at work, with Karim, the cheerful site supervisor, overlooking it all. A couple of bored militiamen carrying AK-47s sit under their own small tents and sip tea all day long.

There was the briefest tussle earlier over the pay, but that was quickly settled via the most common North African economic practice—haggling.

Lance takes a long swig of water from his canteen, starts walking down to the excavation site to see how the latest dig area is proceeding. A wall was found two days ago.

And he looks up to the tent and—

Sam and Teresa are bent over a long wooden table, both examining a piece of pottery that may or may not be from Greece, and—

Where's Sandy?

Where's his little girl?

He whips his head around. The dig site is mostly flat, except for a line of hills about a hundred meters away. A dirt road to the main collection of tents leads off to a poorly paved road that leads to the government highway, and—

If Sandy is anywhere near here, he would be able to pick her out immediately.

But she's missing.

"Sandy!" he yells.

He starts running to the tent, as Teresa looks up, her face frozen in fear.

"Sandy!"

And a scream wakes him up.

He's in Levittown.

Teresa is sitting up next to him.

The screaming goes on and on.

Teresa leaps out of bed, saying, "Oh, God, it's Sandy!"

Lance races out of the bedroom, right behind his wife.

CHAPTER 24

SAM SANDERSON FEELS LIKE a ninja or a secret agent, sneaking across the side lawn, going up to the other house. The grass is wet from the evening dew and he scampers up to the front door. It's easy to see because of the streetlights and lights from the other houses in this boring place.

He goes up to the brick steps, tugs at one of the bricks, then another, and, yes, the third brick is the one! It comes free, and he pokes his hand in and comes up with a key, attached to a small piece of string.

There.

He goes up to the door, looks around, opens up the storm door, puts the key in the lock, and . . .

Yep.

He's inside!

He steps in, trying to be quiet, and he remembers to close the door behind him. For just a moment he feels scared, guilty, but it passes. The neighbors are gone, everything's quiet back at the other house, and he just wants to get in long enough to go online for a while.

Sam walks into a place that smells new and clean, unlike the dump they're living in. He doesn't mind camping out, like they were doing in Tunisia, but that place back there . . . ugh.

He goes through a wide and clean kitchen, and there, on a table in a little nook, is a laptop hooked up to a large-screen display. A couple of night-lights are on, and the light over the stove is lit up as well, meaning it's clear going.

He sits in the big chair, scoots forward, and smiles. The computer is a MacBook Pro. Just like the one he has back home in California. Sweet!

Sam powers it up and the screen flickers to life, starting with the Apple logo, and then the desktop comes into view, and, along with everything else, there's the little icon for Safari, the Apple web browser.

Double-click there, and Google comes up, and maybe he should figure out what that piece of metal and plastic is that's in his pocket, but, no, that's for later. He types in his Gmail account, and signs in, and . . .

Score!

Look at that.

He's in.

Wow.

It's been a long, long time . . .

He starts tapping, answering one email and then

another, and then there's one from his best bud, Toby, and he writes to him, *Toby, you won't believe what's going on and it's been some scary shit, and believe it or not, I flew on my first helicopter ride and*

Sam stops typing.

He feels like something weird is going on.

Was that a noise out there?

Or a light?

He finishes the email, sends it, shuts down the computer, and starts out of the house.

Darn it, he wanted to spend at least an hour here, but now . . .

He's scared now.

Scared of being caught.

Suppose the man or the woman who lives here, suppose one of them got sick?

And they came back home right now? With him in the house?

How could he explain that?

Sam stops at the door, peers out.

The driveway's still empty.

Good.

Maybe . . .

Well, he could go back. He was just scared. That's all.

A wuss.

But still . . .

Maybe he could come back tomorrow night, now that he's done it once already.

He steps out, locks the door, puts the key back under the loose brick, and, again, like a ninja or a secret agent, he races across the lawn, back to where he's supposed to be.

A shadow comes toward him and he screams and is tossed to the ground.

CHAPTER 25

IT'S A RACE DOWN the hallway outside of their bedrooms and Teresa wins it, bursting into Sandy's bedroom. She's standing at the foot of the bed, screaming, wearing a long Winnie-the-Pooh nightshirt and in bare feet, and Teresa scoops up her daughter and Lance says, "What's wrong? What's wrong? Did you have a bad dream?"

His wife picks up on what he's just said, and she kisses the top of her head, stroke's Sandy's hair, and says, "It's okay, honey, it's okay. Was it a bad dream? Was it a bad dream?"

Sandy squirms free from her mother's grasp. She's panting so hard that she's almost hyperventilating, and she says, "The bad man got Sam! The bad man got Sam! The bad man got Sam!"

Lance goes out of Sandy's room, opens the door to Sam's.

It's empty.

"Sam!" he yells. "Sam!"

The bedroom window is open. Lance strides forward, leans his hands on the sill, pokes his head out. "Sam, you out there?"

Teresa comes in, holding Sandy by her shoulders as she stands before her mother. The young girl has stopped screaming. Her face is red and is set. "Is he here? Is he?"

"No."

Lance goes out of Sam's room, goes into the kitchen, the small living room, and—

No Sam.

"Sam!"

He checks the bathroom.

Empty.

Teresa comes up, still holding Sandy.

"Where is he?"

"I don't know."

"And . . . where's Jason?"

Lance is stunned. How in God's name had he missed *that*?

"Jason! Where are you?"

Teresa's eyes well up. "Lance . . . what's going on? Where are they?"

A loud slamming noise startles them all, and Lance steps back as the rear door to the little house flies open. Jason strides in, face screwed up with fury, dragging young Sam in by his T-shirt collar.

CHAPTER 26

GRAY EVANS IS STRETCHED out on a hotel bed, relaxed, comfortable, with a woman named Vanessa resting next to him on a pillow, looking at him, her finely manicured nails tracing circles on his chest.

"You doing okay?" she asks.

"Fine."

"You interested in more?"

"How much time do I have left?"

She raises herself up, revealing an impressive set of curves, pulls a length of red hair from her face, and checks out the clock radio.

"Another fifteen minutes. If you want."

She settles back down, and Gray remembers that old, old joke from way back: you don't pay a prostitute to stay, you pay her to leave when you're done.

Still . . . it's nice to have some female company for a while, to refresh and recharge his batteries before he resumes his job.

His iPhone starts ringing.

Vanessa says, "You want me to answer it?"

Gray gives her his best smile. "You want some broken fingers?"

He rolls off the bed, grabs his iPhone, goes into the bathroom. He looks back and says, "Stay on the bed, all right? That's what I'm paying you for, to do what I want . . . and I want you to stay on the bed."

She stretches and smiles and says not a word.

Inside the bathroom he turns on the faucet to help mask his voice, answers the phone, and it's Abraham, his researcher.

"Got a hit about ten minutes ago."

"Fantastic," Gray says. "Tell me more."

Abraham chuckles. "Over the open air? For real? I don't think so."

"Okay, I'll come over right now."

"Please . . . I'm going back to bed," Abraham says. "Come over tomorrow after 9 a.m. and I'll give you the information."

"Solid?"

"As a rock."

Gray says, "Why don't I come over now?"

Abraham chuckles again. "I don't meet clients at night. You know that."

"Okay. I'll see you at 9:01 tomorrow."

"That's a date."

Gray hears the call disconnect and says to the dead air,

"Oh, one more thing. Can you tell me where you got the hit from?"

No answer, of course, but he moves to the bathroom door and swings it open. He startles Vanessa, who's been standing right there, a hotel robe wrapped around her. Vanessa's eyes are wide and she looks like a little girl being caught doing something naughty by her teacher.

Gray smiles, steps by her, and goes to the hotel room door.

Makes sure it's locked.

Vanessa moves away from him, sits on the bed.

"Look—" she starts.

Gray puts a finger to his lips, shushing her. He switches on the television, finds an HBO movie, and boosts up the volume.

"Honey," he says, and then says the last words she will ever hear. "All I told you to do was to stay on the bed."

CHAPTER 27

LANCE CATCHES HIS BREATH. "Okay, what the hell is going on here?"

Jason propels Lance's son—his son!—forward into the kitchen and says, "I was outside, maintaining a surveillance position. Approximately fourteen minutes ago, I saw your son depart his bedroom via an open window."

Lance feels like his legs have just morphed into solid stone. "Sam, is that true?"

"Dad, he hurt me! He hurt my shoulder!"

Lance says, "Sam, did you sneak out? Did you?"

Sam is defiant. "I'm bored! I wanted to go outside. Is that a crime?"

"No," Lance says. "But we have to . . . we have to do things to stay safe."

Teresa has her arms around Sandy, whose face is cool and impassive. She says, "Your father is right, Sam. We have to . . . we have to stay together, to be safe."

Sam's face is still screwed up in young defiance, and Jason says, "There's more."

"More?" Lance asks. "What the hell do you mean by that?"

Jason is standing still and collected, like a military professional making a report. "Sir, after your son left the house, I observed him going to the Barnes' house."

Teresa says, "Who are the Barnes?"

Lance says, "The young couple that lives next door. Not the dirty old man."

"Dad—"

Lance says, "Go on, Jason."

"Sir, I observed your son go to the front steps of the Barnes' house. Apparently there is a house key hidden in the brick steps leading in. After retrieving the key, he gained entrance to the house."

Teresa put a hand to her mouth. "Sam!"

Lance says, "Hold on, you mean—"

Jason goes on, speaking over Lance. "After entering the house, I lost sight of your son. But I did see movement within, and I saw a computer being turned on. The glow and light were unmistakable. And I saw the outline of your son sitting in front of the computer. I then approached the house and the computer screen went dark, and your son exited."

The kitchen falls quiet. Lance stares at his boy, who blinks his eyes and looks away. Teresa is just quietly shaking her head. Jason catches Lance's eyes.

"Sir?"

Sandy speaks to her younger brother. "Sam, you've been naughty. I've told you to stop being naughty." And she falls quiet.

Lance says, "Sam . . . you know the rules. We . . . we can't go online. That's why Mom's laptop has been disabled. It's too dangerous."

Sam says, "I didn't do it."

Teresa says, "But Jason says he saw you."

Sam steps over and joins his mother and sister, looks back at Jason. "Yeah . . . I was there . . . but . . . I turned on the computer . . . and I waited . . . and I got scared. I remembered the rules. So I turned it off and ran outside."

Lance sees something strange going on with Jason's face, like he's wrestling with some struggle he can't vocalize.

He says, "Sam? Are you telling the truth?"

Sam says, "Yes! You know I am . . . you can trust me . . ."

Lance's heart aches. His boy . . . versus what Jason saw. *What to do?*

Lance says, "Sam? Did you go online? Did you put us in danger?"

Jason still looks . . . guilty. The man looks guilty.

Sam says, "Dad . . . I didn't. Honest."

Another few seconds pass.

Lance says, "All right, I trust you, Sam. C'mon, let's get you to bed."

Teresa pats Sandy on her shoulders. "Yes . . . all of us, let's go to bed. And, Jason . . . thank you. Thank you for keeping us safe. Sam . . ." She tugs at his near ear, making him squirm. "I swear to God, you do anything like that, ever again, I'll break you. Got it?"

One last look at Jason. The man should be happy at being complimented by Teresa, but no.

He doesn't look happy at all.

CHAPTER 28

TWO HUNDRED SIXTY-FIVE MILES to the south-west of Levittown, New York, in a quiet office building in a crowded suburban office park, a government employee named Williams yawns as he monitors newsfeeds from various cable networks from across the globe. One of the open secrets of the intelligence agencies in the United States is that they get the bulk of their emerging information the same way everyone else does: from television.

Williams yawns again. He has the overnight shift and hates it. He wants to make a difference, wants to fight extremism, and so far, all he's done is ruin his sleep patterns and watch too much television.

Damn, it's like he's back in college . . .

Except in college he had a better room.

This room is square, functional, with flickering overhead lights, and it's stuffy, like the air in here hasn't been refreshed since this new, disturbed millennium began years back.

His phone rings, and he sees it's the internal line, one that can only be accessed from within the building.

He picks it up. "Williams."

"This is Cauchon." A female voice. "Domestic observation."

"Go," Williams says, picking up a pen.

"We have a breach of internet protocol, for an individual named Sanderson, Samuel. Occurred thirty-seven minutes ago. He's under covert protection in Levittown, New York. Make the necessary notifications."

"Got it," Williams says.

He goes to his keyboard, goes through the department's intranet system, finds the covert protection order for SANDERSON, SAMUEL—a ten-year-old boy!—and notes who he needs to contact.

The guy known as "the Big Man."

He gains a secure outside line for his telephone system, calls the Big Man at home.

No answer.

He tries the Big Man's office.

No answer.

He calls the Big Man's personal handheld device, issued by the same group Williams works for.

It rings, rings, and then it's picked up.

"Sir, this is—"

The voice is a recording. "You know who this is. Leave the message. Off."

Williams clears his voice. "Sir, this is James Williams, calling from Department G-17. We have a breach of internet protocol for a . . . Sanderson, a Samuel Sanderson. This is your official notification."

He hangs up the phone, goes back to the protocol section. If he doesn't hear back from the Big Man within the hour, he is to dispatch a federal police unit to the Big Man's house and physically make the notification.

Then Williams looks up at the monitors.

CNN, MSNBC, and now Fox and some of the international cable stations are all broadcasting the same scene: a billowing cloud of black smoke and flames coming out from an Underground station in London.

Williams starts making other, more urgent notifications.

Within minutes, he has forgotten all about the ten-year-old boy and the Big Man.

CHAPTER 29

LANCE PUTS SAM TO bed and closes and locks the window.

"Sam."

"Yes, Dad," he says, quiet and subdued.

"You . . . I know it's boring. It's boring for all of us. But you've got to listen to us, including Jason. You've got to do what you're told."

"Yes, Dad."

Lance goes to the door, turns off the light. "And this light remains off. Until it's time to get up."

"Yes, Dad."

"And tomorrow . . . sorry, you're confined to your room."

In the kitchen, Jason is making a cup of coffee, and there's an aura, a sense of danger in his tense shoulders as Lance passes him by. He knocks on the door to Sandy's room and she says, "Come in," and he goes in.

She's reading another one of his books and says, "I plan to read for another twelve minutes. Then I will shut the light off and go to sleep."

"That's good to know," he says. "You doing all right?"

Sandy says, "I do have a question, Dad."

"Okay."

His young daughter says, "When we left Tunisia, we were in a helicopter. Why didn't it crash?"

Lance is puzzled. "Sorry, honey, I don't understand the question."

She says, "I understand why aircraft fly. The theory of lift over the wings. That makes sense. But I don't understand helicopters. They don't make sense. They should crash."

Lance says, "We'll talk about it tomorrow, okay? I'll see what I can find."

"Okay, Dad."

He closes her door and stands for a moment in the hallway, remembering.

With Karim at his side, and with the other local workers fanning out, he and Teresa race around the dig site, frantically looking for their daughter, after he orders Sam to stay put.

Lance goes up along the hills on the near side of the camp, and Karim says, "Look! Look!"

Fresh, small footprints in the dirt.

And a few minutes later, he and Karim find Sandy, happily sitting in front of a small open cave that is well hidden from view. Behind her, there are wooden and black plastic crates, piled up high on each other, and in a corner of the cave, one of the crates is open.

Revealing a tangled collection of RPG-7s, rocket-propelled grenade launchers.

"Sandy?" Lance asks, coming forward. "What are you doing?"

"I ran out of things to read back at camp," she says. "I'm reading now."

In a metal box near her that's been broken open, there are magazines, newspapers, and books, all in Arabic or French. Lance squats down, examines what she's reading, a thick pile of papers, printed on one side and loosely bound in a black binder.

Lance takes the binder out of her hand, his breathing quickening. "Honey, we've got to go."

"But I haven't finished reading."

He grabs his daughter, picks her up. Karim looks past them, at the boxes of weapons piled higher and deeper into the cave.

Karim's eyes are wide with fright. "Oh, Lance, this is bad. Very, very bad."

Lance starts out of the cave entrance, carrying Sandy, his breathing now labored and harsh.

"Oh, yes, very bad," Lance says. "Very bad."

CHAPTER 30

LANCE IS FINALLY IN bed with Teresa, who nuzzles his neck, and he says, "Sandy . . . she asked me something odd."

"Oh, what's that?" she asks. "Did she ask you to explain the four laws of thermodynamics again?"

He joins in laughing with Teresa at the memory.

"She asked me about the helicopter that got us out that day," Lance says. "Why it didn't crash."

"Really?"

"Yeah, really. It's like bees . . . for a long time, scientists couldn't figure out how the little buggers fly. Sandy picked up on the same thing for helicopters . . . how they can fly."

Teresa nuzzles him again. "Just be thankful that one could fly that day."

Lance is drifting off, comfortable with the sensation of Teresa in his arms, in knowing Sam is safe, Sandy is safe, remembering that last grim day in Tunisia . . .

He remembers running back in the heat, holding Sandy

close to his chest, Karim shouting into his cell phone, now back at the dig site, more shouts and yells, and the men guarding them, they . . .

They toss their AK-47s to the ground, start running away, going to the two sole pickup trucks, starting them up and driving away, tails of dust marking their retreat. Lance is dumbfounded. The trucks belong to Stanford. They've just been stolen!

Karim is still yelling into his cell phone, his free arm up in the air, like this movement can strengthen the cell phone signal, can signal his message.

Teresa takes Sandy from his arms just outside of the tents and says, "Where did you find her? Is she okay?"

Lance's chest is tight and it's hard to catch his breath. "Sandy . . . she's fine. We . . . found her . . . in a cave, just over those hills."

Teresa grabs Sandy and checks her over, and yells, "Sam! Over here! Right now!"

Lance whirls around. One by one the men who had worked with them are running away as well, dropping their hand tools, their shovels. Only Karim is still here, still shouting.

"Lance!" Teresa says, frantic. "What's wrong? Where is everyone?"

Lance pulls Sam to his side, and he says, "Sandy . . . she found a cave. Full of guns, bombs, rockets. It's an arms cache . . . probably belonging to terrorists . . ."

Teresa looks wildly around their now deserted dig site. "Lance . . . what do we do? Where do we go?"

Even in this hot Tunisian sun, Lance feels frozen in place. He has always depended on the generosity and friendship of the locals whom he and the university have hired, and he has always convinced himself that he could bring his family here and work in a bubble of safety and protection.

What a fool he's been.

"Karim," he shouts. "Karim, what's going on?"

Karim turns away, still yelling, and Lance feels alone, abandoned, even with his family nearby.

And he wonders . . . who the hell is Karim talking to? Is he actually looking for help? Or something else? Is Karim upset, insulted over the pay dispute?

"Look!" Teresa screams.

She's pointing up at the hillside, where two and then three black-clad men appear, carrying AK-47s.

The stuttering gunfire stuns Lance, and he pulls his family down, turning over one of the tables piled high with recently excavated precious artifacts, hearing them smash and crash to the ground and not caring one bit.

Sandy and Sam are huddled under Teresa's arms, and Lance has a flash of memory, of learning how the Romans sacked Carthage and its surrounding lands back in 146 BC and how women and children were put to the sword and slaughtered.

More men are up on the hillside, and some are running toward them.

"Lance!" Teresa yells. "We have to do something!"

Never in his life has he felt this helpless, and he starts to debate with himself: Should he send his family running while he and Karim give themselves up, or should he and Karim try to get the weapons abandoned by their supposed guards and put up a desperate fight, or—

Karim yells in triumph. "See! See!"

Lance turns and looks to the east. Two helicopters are descending on the dig site, low and fast. Both are painted the same, with contrasting brown-and-tan schemes, but one looks to be a transport helicopter, and the other—

The other approaches the hill, starts firing its machine guns. Teresa screams, and Sam and Sandy hold their little hands against their ears. The transport helicopter swoops down beyond the tents, tearing one up with its rotor wash, throwing up clouds of dust and dirt, and Karim says, "Go, we go!"

Lance pushes, pulls, and drags Teresa and Sam and Sandy along, not caring about the artifacts, the records, their belongings, knowing only that the rattling machine with the spinning blades ahead of them is their lifeboat, their rescue.

Two soldiers with big helmets lean out of the side door, frantically waving their hands. Karim jumps in first, turns, and helps Sam and Sandy board, and as Lance is dragged in, there's a change in the pitch of the engine, and the helicopter lifts off.

Teresa is hugging him, crying, and she shouts. "Thank God we're safe! We're safe!"

Lance rolls over, and through the dust and dirt, he sees their dig site, sees two pickup trucks approaching, big black flags flapping at the rear . . .

And then he's awake in the uncomfortable bed in Levittown, thinking now what he thought back there, in that Tunisian Air Force helicopter, as they left that arms cache and their dig site behind.

They'll never be safe, ever again.

CHAPTER 31

AT 9:03 A.M. THE NEXT day, Gray Evans is back at the third-floor offices of his information contact, Abraham, sitting in one of the comfortable chairs around the conference table and reflecting on what he saw walking up to this building.

Which was nothing. His two parking attendants from the other day were gone.

What a city, what a world. Maybe his little interaction has put the two of them on the road to a fruitful life, but Gray wouldn't bet on it.

Hand clasping his cane tight, Abraham sits across from him and says, "Well, sometimes it comes down to skill, and sometimes it's luck. Last night it was luck."

"Glad that Lady Luck is smiling on you," Gray says, sipping on a cup of coffee Abraham has provided. "Did she flash her boobies at you, too?"

"Better than that," Abraham says with a smile. "Once I got started, I set up a nice little sniffing program that goes through every crack and crevice of the internet, looking for the family and where they might be. Relatives, places of employment, friends, former friends . . . a nice program that I devised myself, and then . . . well, it's like making this huge extravagant dinner from scratch and having everyone compliment you later on the Sara Lee cake you bought for dessert."

"Tasty," Gray says. "Go on."

Abraham smiles. "It was the boy, the ten-year-old kid. He popped up online last night for exactly twelve minutes, checking his Gmail account, before he logged off." Abraham shakes his head. "Kids nowadays, they don't know it, but they're living in a science fiction world. Most of them carry around a device that can access the complete stored knowledge of the human race, and they use it to send fart and booger jokes to each other."

Gray is getting impatient. "Yeah, kids nowadays . . . so where is the little punk?"

Abraham slides over a sheet of paper. "Here are the particulars. The ISP the kid was using came back to a David and Susan Barne of Levittown . . . but I don't think that's where the Sanderson family is staying."

"Why not?"

"Two reasons. Because the Barnes have no connection whatsoever to the Sandersons, and because the house right next door is owned by something called the Hampton Realty Trust."

"Which is what?"

Gray sees that Abraham once again has the happy and

serene smile of a man who knows it all and who loves rubbing that in someone else's face. Gray allows him that little victory, because it'll be the last smile he ever flashes.

"Because Hampton Realty Trust is a front organization," Abraham says. "There's a shell corporation behind that, and another one behind that . . . all very hush-hush and well concealed . . . except to me. The home's real owners reside in Langley, Virginia."

"The CIA," Gray says.

"Bingo," Abraham says. One hand still grasping his cane, Abraham reaches over and taps a line on the sheet of paper. "And check this little bit of information out. The wife and mother, Teresa Sanderson, she has a family connection with law enforcement. You might want to keep that in mind before you proceed."

Gray looks again at the information Abraham has provided, nods his head, and folds the sheet of paper and places it in his coat pocket.

"Great work, Abraham," he says. "The very best. Which is why this is going to pain me so much."

And he pulls out his 9mm Smith & Wesson pistol.

CHAPTER 32

LEONARD BROOKS IS DREAMING about his response to his first fatal motor vehicle accident as a New York State Trooper—a stolen Toyota Camry had struck a bridge abutment on the Thruway outside of Buffalo and had ejected two high school boys through the windshield— when his bedroom phone rings.

He wakes up, glad for the interruption. The dream was going into some strange, dark places, which Leonard assumed was a side effect of the stress he's been under while trying to locate his cousin. The dream started with the actual memory—the local fire department pumper truck eventually came by to wash down the blood and brain matter from the abutment's concrete—but then it took a dark turn: Leonard found himself standing in a drainage ditch, the bloody water swirling around his ankles.

He grabs the phone and murmurs a greeting.

A very chipper and alert Beth Draper is on the other end. "Gosh, aren't we the Gloomy Gus this morning."

"Just got off shift," he says, rubbing at his eyes. He hates the night shifts the most, for a variety of reasons. The main one is his neighbors, obsessed landscapers who are always outside after the sun rises with their leaf blowers and lawn mowers.

But so far, it's been quiet, except for this phone call. He rubs at his grainy eyes again and says, "What do you have?"

"What makes you think I have anything?" Beth asks. "Maybe I'm calling you because I'm going to be in your neck of the woods and I want to offer you the chance to wine, dine, and bed me . . . and not necessarily in that order."

"Beth . . ."

She laughs. "All right, couldn't help myself." And then the tone of her voice changes to the experienced intelligence official she is. "Your cousin, she has a son, right?"

"Yeah," Leonard says. "Samuel. Eight or nine. Too smart for his own good."

"Well, the lad is ten, and last night he was online for a few minutes, checking his Gmail account."

Leonard is now wide awake. He swings his legs around and sits up, and fumbles on the nightstand for a pen and a scrap of paper.

"Go on," he says.

"Your smart young fella accessed a computer belonging to a David and Susan Barne of Levittown."

"Perfect," he says, now with pen in hand. "Where is it?"

She gives him an address, which he scribbles down, and she says, "Before you race over, hotshot, here's the deal. I don't think he's there."

"What?"

"Hold on, hold on," she says. "It's like this. I didn't see any blatant connection between your cousin and the Barne family, and I did a little digging, and found out that the neighboring house belongs to a realty company . . . which has some spooky connections."

"How spooky?"

"I can't tell, not right now," Beth admits. "It's pretty well protected, but it's government-connected, that's for sure, and I don't mean the embarrassing government we have up in Albany."

"The feds."

"Yeah." Beth gives him that address, and he scribbles that down as well, and she says, "My guess is that the place is a safe house of some kind. You still sure your cousin and her hubby don't have enemies?"

"Positive," Leonard says. "She writes books, he digs in the dirt. How can you get enemies from that?"

Beth says, "You'd be surprised, my friend. In today's world, it's very easy to get on someone's list of enemies."

Despite the growing anticipation that he now knows where his cousin is located, he yawns and says, "Excuse me for that, okay."

"Sure."

There's a noise outside, like someone's knocking at the

door. He says, "All right, safe house. Got it. You've done good, Beth."

"Of course I have," she says. "But a safe house . . . it's only safe depending who's there, and who might be out there looking to do them harm. I found out where they live. That doesn't mean that bad guys won't do the same. And soon."

CHAPTER 33

GRAY EVANS IS STUNNED when Abraham suddenly laughs at the barrel of the pistol he is pointing at the man's heart.

Abraham says, "For real? You threaten me with that gun after all the times you've hired me?"

Gray supposes he should shoot and get it over with, but something is going on with Abraham and he wants to know more.

Gray says, "Nothing personal. After a while you need to clean up your business dealings, your patterns, and start new somewhere else. Otherwise you leave behind a traceable trail."

Abraham shakes his head. "You think I've survived all this time without taking precautions?"

His info man now really has his attention.

"Precautions," Gray says. "Go on."

Abraham holds up his cane. "See how tight I always hold this? It's a dead man's switch. You do me harm or kill me, and I drop the cane. And when I do that, this entire floor goes up in one hell of a bang."

Gray stares at Abraham, who doesn't flinch, doesn't move. Abraham adds, "Based on this neighborhood, that might even jump-start a revamp of the entire block, which means a lot of these people won't be able to afford their housing. You really want to do that, Gray?"

Gray laughs, puts his pistol away. "Only joking. That's all."

"Sure," Abraham says. "And your sense of humor just doubled your invoice."

CHAPTER 34

THE INTELLIGENCE OFFICER KNOWN as the Big Man moves as fast as his bulk allows him down the corridor leading to his office, because the morning news of the latest terrorist attack in the London subway has forced him into work two hours ahead of schedule.

Just outside his office, an IT worker—and who cares what her name is—is standing there in response to the call he made downstairs. The Big Man passes over his handheld device and says, "It crapped out on me last night. Get me a new one, transfer the information, and let me know immediately if there were any calls I missed."

"Very good, sir," she says, and she moves quickly past him as he unlocks his door and goes inside.

Not much time and a lot of work to do, and the only thing he does is grab a fresh legal pad. He leaves, heading to an urgent staff meeting to deal with what's going on in London.

He locks his office door behind him and is about six

feet down the hallway when he thinks he hears his office phone ringing.

Should he go back?

No, he thinks.

It can wait.

It has to wait.

London is burning.

He keeps moving.

CHAPTER 35

IN A NEW RENTAL vehicle, Gray Evans slowly drives along a quiet street in Levittown. By God, there it is, the little house that holds his target.

Quiet, with a fence out at the rear and no easy means of escape.

Right in front of him.

The trunk of his rental car has enough firepower to outfit a Georgia county sheriff's department, and he's tempted—oh, is he tempted—to park the car, pop open the trunk, and go in: a blitz attack.

No delay, no waiting around, just go right in and start blasting.

Very tempting.

He slows down . . . it's a small house, one-story, and, based on what he knows about Levittown, it's probable this house doesn't have a basement or an attic.

Could be pretty easy.

Could be.

He speeds up.

He hasn't stayed alive this long by relying on "could be."

An hour later he leaves the town offices of Hempstead, New York, which govern the hamlet of Levittown. He's spent some time with the easygoing and friendly town officials, who have passed on the tax records for the property where the Sandersons are living.

The best part of this research is that the tax records present the house as a typical one-story Cape Cod, with no basement and no attic. It has only seven rooms: three bedrooms, two bathrooms, kitchen, and living room.

Thanks to these very courteous small-town officials, he now has a detailed floor plan of how best to kill the person he needs to kill.

Still . . . even with all this information, he needs to tilt the playing field more in his favor.

How best to get in and do his job?

He has an idea. He checks his watch, thinks he needs to call a new intel source—though Abraham is breathing, he might as well be dead to him—to confirm the information on Teresa's law enforcement connection.

If all goes well, within the hour, his target—and, if need be, the entire Sanderson family—will be dead.

CHAPTER 36

THE BIG MAN UNLOCKS the door to his office and walks in. He's exhausted, thirsty, and hungry, and the day ahead of him stretches like one long session on a chain gang. He's unable to move, unable to do anything besides react to what's going on across the Atlantic.

"Sir?" A tapping noise at the side of his open door. The IT tech from the morning comes in and says, "Here's your new phone, sir. All information, passwords, connections, and files successfully transferred."

He holds his thick hand out, gives her a quick "thank you"—even if he doesn't know her name, there's no need to be rude—and she leaves as he powers up the phone. He starts sliding through the screens, checking and seeing—

What the hell?

Pressing the phone against his ear, he listens to the message again and drops his new piece of equipment on his desk. Then he picks up his secure interior line and dials four digits. When the man on the other line picks up he says, "Did I or did I not receive a notification from a James Williams, from Department G-17, last night?"

"Ah, sir, it appears—"

"There was no follow-up!" the Big Man yells. "None!"

"Ah—"

"Why wasn't I promptly informed?"

"Sir, a call was made to your office this morning and—"

"That's not confirmation!" he yells. "You and your section have just killed four innocents . . ." My God, what a screw-up! He goes on, "And by the end of the day, you and Williams will be in custody, pending an internal review."

The Big Man slams the phone down, takes a breath, picks it up again, and dials another number.

"Domestic Operations." A female voice.

He checks the nearest clock for the time. Do they have enough of it?

"We have an emerging situation in Levittown, New York," he says, checking a file and then rapidly giving the woman the address. "I need a response team."

"When?"

He takes another breath, knowing this isn't going to end well.

"As of last night," he finally says.

CHAPTER 37

LANCE HASN'T SLEPT WELL. After a quiet and strained breakfast, it seems like everyone in the household is off in their own little world. Lance helps Teresa with the dishes and checks in on Sam, who's back at work at the small desk, putting together his dinosaur model, hunched over in concentration, looking like one of those old medieval engravings of a monk working on an illuminated manuscript.

Lance asks, "How's it going?"

Sam says, "About halfway done."

His boy doesn't lift his head, and Lance is sure the kiddo is still ashamed over last night's events, and so he leaves him alone and checks on Sam's sister.

Sandy is on her immaculately made bed and he says, "How are you doing, honey?"

She turns a page, and he recognizes the book he gave her about Hannibal. "I'll be finishing this book at about 2:00 p.m. today, Dad." Another page flip. "And there are no other books to read."

"I'm sure I can find one."

"No, you're wrong," she says crisply. "I've checked every room in the house, the bags, and the shelves. This is the last book."

"Then we'll have to get you a new one," he says.

"Good," she says. "I've talked to Jason. You need to talk to him. He says we can only go shopping for new books if all of us go together. So we need to go together, but we can't, because you told Sam he had to stay in his room."

Lance says, "We'll take care of it, sweetheart."

"Good," Sandy says, and for a moment, Lance has the ugly thought that his young daughter has just dismissed him. *She doesn't mean it,* he tells himself.

He goes to the kitchen for a post-breakfast cup of coffee and surprises Teresa, who seems to have been looking through some of her photographs from Tunisia. He hasn't yet seen the one that's up on her computer. It seems to have been taken in a marketplace somewhere back there.

Teresa jumps and closes the photo program. Quickly she says, "How are the super kids?"

"One's being quiet for a nice change, the other one's concerned she's about to run out of books."

Teresa says nothing, goes back to her laptop. When he's finished with his coffee, he steals another glance at her laptop.

No photo program.

No Word document.

Nothing to do with her book.

His wife is quietly playing solitaire, like she's . . .

Killing time.

*

Jason is at the rear door where he dragged Sam in last night, looking out at the backyard. There's shrubbery and an old wooden fence. Shouts and cries can be heard from young children playing on the other side of the fence, and Jason's head moves with every sound.

To be this alert all the time . . . Lance is impressed by the skill, the dedication, the strength this man has.

"Can I get you something, Jason? Cup of coffee? Orange juice?"

"No, sir, I'm fine."

"Glad to hear it," Lance says. He stands there uncomfortably, like he's been called to the principal's office, and he says, "You know . . . when we got here, we were told it'd be less than a week before we'd leave."

"That's right, sir."

Lance says, "So we might leave today."

"You might."

"Then . . . I want to thank you for everything. I . . . we'll never forget what you've done for us."

Jason slowly turns and says, "I haven't done a damn thing for you."

The man's face is troubled, like he's under some extra, awful burden. Like he's got more on his shoulders than just the job of protecting the four of them.

Jason clears his throat. "I need to tell you something. I shouldn't . . . but I will."

The sound of the doorbell ringing startles Lance, making him spill some hot coffee on his hand.

Jason brushes by him. "Lockdown. Now."

CHAPTER 38

JASON IS PLEASANTLY SURPRISED at how quickly the Sanderson family moves under his direction. No fuss, no raised voices, moving like boots nearing the end of basic training. In the tiny bathroom he scoops up Sandy—"You be a good girl, all right?"—and puts her in the bathtub, and Sam jumps right in without being asked. He moves the kids around so Sandy is lying down, with her brother nestled on top.

Sam looks up, eyes wide with fear. "I . . ."

"Quiet," Jason says. "Protect your older sister, okay?"

Sam nods silently. The last he sees of the boy is when he picks up the heavy Kevlar blanket to drape it over his huddled form.

The mother and father are seated on the floor, legs pulled up so he can walk by. Considerate. As he moves past them, something odd happens.

Teresa, the wife, holds her hand up.

What?

It comes to him what she's looking for, and he gives the hand a quick squeeze and steps out into the hallway, closing the bathroom door behind him. There's a little *click* as it's locked.

Good. First time they did this, as a drill, the father had forgotten to lock the door.

Nice to see everyone doing well today.

The doorbell rings again and Jason quickly moves to the front door, gives a quick look through a side window, sees it's a cop standing there.

Cops again, he thinks. He wishes there were that many cops in his neighborhood when he was growing up in Seattle.

He opens the door, sees the man's wearing a New York State Trooper uniform, and immediately knows why the guy is here: Teresa has a relative in the force.

"Yes?" he asks. "Can I help you?"

The trooper, in his immaculate gray uniform, campaign hat, bright-purple necktie, and shiny badge pinned to his shirt, looks friendly and apologetic. "This is going to sound strange, but could you bear with me for a moment, sir? I'm looking for my cousin, Teresa Sanderson, and her family."

Jason is running through what to say to this friendly young man before shooing him away, when the phone belted to his side starts to screech at him.

He glances down for a second.

It's a second long enough.

The trooper has a pistol in his hands and with two loud, bright hammer blows, Jason is shot twice in the chest.

CHAPTER 39

LANCE HAS HIS ARM around Teresa. The sound of the two gunshots seems to echo in the tiny bathroom, and Teresa screams, and from the bathtub, Sam starts yelling— his voice muffled by the Kevlar—"It's my fault, it's my fault, I used the computer, it's my fault!"

He starts crying and Sandy shrieks, and Lance goes over to the bathtub, lifts the Kevlar blanket, looks at the scared faces of his children, "It's okay, it's okay, you just stay there, okay?"

Lance drops the blanket, sees that Teresa's face is pale with shock, her hands tightly clasped, and says, "What about—"

Suddenly, he shuts up. Neither one of them has a cell phone, because both were confiscated two weeks ago when Teresa was in the middle of calling her mother.

He looks to Teresa, then looks up at the tiny window over the toilet.

Trapped.

There's a knock at the door.

Teresa yelps and crawls over to him, curled next to him by the bathtub. Their son and daughter are wailing from underneath the protective blanket.

"Guys?" A new voice from outside. "There's been an incident. It's safe now. Come on out. I'm a state trooper, just like Leonard. More police will be here any minute."

Teresa grabs Lance's upper arm, whispers, "That's not the phrase to get us to open the door . . . what does it mean?"

Lance says, "It means Jason's dead."

CHAPTER 40

AFTER HE GETS NO response from the family locked inside the bathroom, Gray Evans tries the handle once again.

Still locked.

Okay, not a problem.

So far, the procedure's going fine, and Gray sees no reason why it shouldn't keep on going so. Hell, even an hour ago, his second intel choice, Neil, was quick and efficient over the phone, getting him the name and address of a local off-duty state trooper. Gray killed the man with a quick bullet to the head and haphazardly got dressed in his uniform, clipping its accessories in their most likely places.

And now it's simple—the entire family in one room.

Gray stands back, takes position, starts to aim his pistol at the doorknob, and then it begins to turn.

"Okay, we're coming out." A shaky male voice comes from inside.

Perfect. How sweetly perfect.

The door opens a crack just as Gray hears the creak and scrape of a window opening . . .

The door opens a little more. A woman is standing on the toilet, shoving a small figure through the tiny window, its legs going through—

"Hey!" he yells, bringing up his pistol, wondering where the father is, and—

A man comes from behind the door.

With something in his hand.

Gray turns and—

Yells as the man sprays him in the face and eyes with something harsh and burning.

CHAPTER 41

RONALD TEMPLE IS LIGHTLY dozing in his Barcalounger when the sound of two gunshots wakes him up. His consciousness goes from zero to sixty in one second. He's served on the job with officers who freaked out when they heard a truck backfire or a manhole cover slam shut, but Ronald has always known better: someone has just fired two shots next door.

He scrambles up in the chair, blanket sliding off, .38 revolver in his lap, as he shakily picks up the phone, dials 911.

When the male operator answers and goes through the usual bored answering shtick—"911, what is the nature and location of your emergency?"—Ronald carefully says, "Shots fired," rattles off the address next door, and drops the phone.

He doesn't have time to answer questions or fill out the operator's checklist, so he grabs the revolver and heaves himself off the chair.

Thank God Helen is out shopping. He doesn't want her here, where she'd be both in danger and telling him not to do what he's about to do.

Ronald tears the oxygen hose away and makes his way to the entryway with his lungs burning.

His hands are shaking.

Damn it, like a rookie alone on his first night shift!

He puts the revolver down, goes to the portable oxygen tank, cranks it up, drapes the tubes around his head, and opens the door.

Picks up the revolver.

This time he won't screw up.

This time he won't be hiding home, drunk.

Ronald goes to the house, revolver still shaking in one hand, his other hand dragging his green oxygen tank behind him.

This time he will do what has to be done.

CHAPTER 42

EYES BURNING—BRINGING BACK a memory of being exposed to tear gas during basic training—Gray swears, stumbles back, and fires off two shots at the door as it slams in front of him.

Damn it!

He wipes at his eyes, swearing again. Whatever the son of a bitch sprayed at him is burning and clouding up his eyes. He can feel them swelling.

Time to move.

He moves away from the bathroom, going through the kitchen and living room, bouncing off a chair, until he ends up at the front door. The big guy he had shot earlier is still on the floor, and Gray wants to make sure his rear is secure, so he fires another shot at the guy's head before springing out the door.

Gray is out the door and—

Thump!

Can you believe the luck?

He's bumped into the two kids, who have fallen to the lawn, crying.

But his eyes are burning and he can't tell which is which.

No matter.

He grabs one and then the other, starts running a hand over their heads and—

"Stop right there!" a man shouts.

CHAPTER 43

RONALD TEMPLE IS ON the lawn of his odd neighbors, revolver in both of his shaking hands, aiming it straight at the man standing in front of him, who looks nice and sharp in a New York State Trooper's uniform. The officer has his arms around the young boy and girl who live here. Ronald's lungs are burning and his legs are so weak he feels like his knees are about to give way.

But he stands his ground.

There have been three more gunshots since the first two woke him up, and he won't back away.

"Who are you?" he demands, straining to make his voice sound strong.

This is all wrong. His earlier plan was to attack his neighbors if they turned out to be terrorists, but what's with the gunshots and this guy standing in front of him?

The man—whose eyes are red and swollen—curses and says, "Who the hell do you think I am? Put that gun away!"

"Not until I know what's going on," Ronald says. The

boy is crying, snot dribbling from his nose. The young girl is . . . just staring, face frozen.

"What's going on? I'm a damn state trooper, and I'm ordering you to put that gun away. There's backup coming."

Ronald swallows, his throat sand-dry. "Let the kids go. Or else."

"Or else what?"

"You know what else," Ronald says, again hating how weak his voice is.

"Yeah?" the man says, not moving at all, the kids still in his grasp. "Sorry, old man, I don't think you're going to do a damn thing."

CHAPTER 44

JASON TYLER REGAINS CONSCIOUSNESS.

His right ear is ringing like a bell.

His lower chest and belly . . . feel cold, numb—like he's been hit twice by a sledgehammer.

You've been shot.

Twice.

Because you screwed up.

A memory surfaces from when he was a kid, watching some nature documentary that showed a rattlesnake attack. It attacked so fast, the human eye couldn't see it . . . and the camera had to slow down to show the coiled rattlesnake extend in one long, looping motion, mouth open, fangs displayed.

That trooper.

One hell of a rattlesnake.

Okay.

Situation . . .

We are seriously screwed.

Jason knows from experience that he has just a few minutes before the shock wears off and the real pain kicks in, so it's time to get to work.

He reaches down to his side, retrieves his government-issued phone. There's a side switch that he presses . . . but he misses it. He tries twice more and then . . .

Success.

All right, then.

Panic button pressed.

Meaning the cavalry—well armed and well equipped—should be here in a few minutes.

But . . .

Jason rolls over so he's on his hands and knees.

Look at all the damn blood.

He groans and stands up.

The mission . . .

Have to do the mission.

The cavalry is on its way, but it'll get here way too late.

He weaves, finds his weapon under his shirt.

Get to work.

Have to protect . . .

Have to do the job.

Jason weaves again, going to the door.

It seems like it's a mile away.

CHAPTER 45

GRAY WIPES AT HIS eyes. His full vision is almost back.

He stares in disbelief at the old man standing in front of him, skinny as a cornstalk, wearing baggy slacks and a flannel shirt, damn oxygen tank at his side, tubes running out of his big nose, pointing a revolver at him.

"Drop your weapon!" he yells. "I'm a state trooper! Drop it!"

The old man coughs and says, "No . . . no, you're not!"

The kids are squirming under his grasp and Gray says, "What do you mean I'm not a trooper, you sonavabitch?"

The old man pulls the hammer back on the revolver, cocking it.

"You have a badge on your uniform shirt," he says, now gasping, like his lungs are collapsing. "New York State Troopers don't wear badges on their shirts."

With his moving hands, Gray finds the long hair of the girl.

Finally!

He pushes the boy away, removes his weapon, and starts to pull the trigger, holding the girl in place with his other hand.

CHAPTER 46

RONALD HAD SEEN MANY amazing things while on the job and working security, but he can't believe how fast the fake trooper moves when he pushes the boy away, swivels the girl around, brings up his pistol, pushes the muzzle against the back of the girl's head.

Pulling the trigger on his .38 revolver is a heavy tug for Ronald, and, God, he's not quick enough, he won't make it, he's going to fail again and—

A gunshot erupts, loud and hammering.

He gasps, stumbling back.

The fake trooper grunts, sways, and the little girl breaks away from his grasp.

Ronald starts to squeeze the trigger again but the man before him slowly turns and collapses on the lawn.

God . . .

From inside the house comes the big guy—the bodyguard, the one he thought was a terrorist cell leader—staggering, an arm tight around his bloody belly, the other hand holding a pistol.

Ronald goes to him, dragging the oxygen tank behind him, clattering. The young boy and girl are standing by the front of the house.

The wounded man comes closer.

He sees Ronald standing there.

Ronald says, "Hold on . . . the police are coming. They'll be here any second."

The man stops, weaves.

He opens his mouth and blood trickles out.

Ronald says, "Hold on, don't say anything, you should just sit down . . ."

The man spits out the blood. "The girl . . . the young girl . . . is she safe?"

Ronald can't believe the question. All that's going on and he asks about the girl?

"Answer me!" the man says, voice stronger. "The girl . . . is she safe?"

Ronald checks her one more time, standing there with her brother, arms around each other.

"Yes," Ronald says. "She's safe. She's fine."

"Thanks," he says. Then he smiles and collapses to the ground.

CHAPTER 47

AFTER SHE HEARS MORE gunshots, Teresa pushes her husband aside and lurches to the front door.

Oh, God, look at that blood on the floor.

Lance is saying something about staying here and staying safe, and Teresa refuses to listen to a single word.

Her children are out there.

And she won't stay inside.

If there are men out there waiting to kill her because of the photos she took back at that Tunisian marketplace, well, she will die protecting her children and take her punishment.

She unlocks the door, pulls it open, and races out. Outside into the fresh air and sunlight and grass and with Lance right at her heels—

There they are—Sandy and Sam!

She gathers them in her arms, squeezes them, squeezes them, squeezes them, and says, "Oh, my babies, are you all right? Are you all right?"

Sam is sobbing but Sandy says, "We're not hurt, Mom, but please . . ."

"What?"

"Stop squeezing me so hard. It's hurting."

Teresa bursts out in a sob and turns around, hearing sirens in the distance. A man in a state trooper's uniform is on his back, mouth open, not moving. Lance goes to him, kicks a nearby pistol away across the lawn. Their nosy neighbor is standing there, shocked, a revolver in a shaking hand, oxygen tank by his side, tubes running from his nose.

He tries to say something, but he coughs and coughs and nearly doubles over from the hacking.

From inside her family's embrace, Teresa turns to the man and says, "What is it?"

"That man," the older man says. "He . . . he died saving your daughter."

Teresa sobs, turning her head away from the two dead men on the lawn. A helicopter flies overhead, the sirens are louder, and Teresa says, "Lance . . . it makes sense. God, now it makes sense."

Lance says, "What in hell makes sense in all of this?"

"You know how I said Jason looked guilty all the time?" Teresa asks.

"I remember," Lance says. "I saw it too. There was something going on with him."

Cruisers roar down the road, screech to a halt. Another helicopter swoops overhead. Teresa squeezes her children tight again. She refuses to let go of them.

"He was guilty all right," Teresa says, feeling tears roll

down her cheeks. "Guilty because his job wasn't to protect us. It was to protect Sandy, first and foremost. You saw how he always put Sandy first in the bathtub, covering her with her brother? How he always was closest to her? How Sandy was first in the Yukon, last one out? That's why . . ."

Lance is stunned.

Teresa . . . she's right.

He looks to his special daughter, who's calmly looking out at the chaos of police cars, ambulances, and other vehicles quickly filling up the road.

Their Sandy . . . He is so proud of who she is, so scared of what awaits her.

CHAPTER 48

LEONARD BROOKS IS VIOLATING about a half-dozen procedures and protocols, racing toward the address in Levittown where his cousin and her family are located, but he doesn't care.

The sirens are wailing, the lights are flashing, and with every twist and turn in this crowded suburb, he nearly scrapes or rams into a parked car. The radio traffic is one long, anguished chatter: an off-duty trooper has been shot in his home . . . shots fired at a Levittown residence . . . possible state trooper down . . . more shots . . . officer needs assistance, officer needs assistance . . .

The tires screech in protest as he slides through another curve, and up ahead . . .

There.

A confused scrum of police vehicles from what looks to be about a half-dozen jurisdictions are parked in a jagged mess up ahead. He pulls over, grabs his campaign hat, bails out of the cruiser, and starts running.

Civilians are standing on their little front lawns, peering at all the activity, tossing questions at him as he goes by.

"What's going on?"

"Who got shot?"

"Is this an act of terrorism?"

A police line with yellow tape has been set up, and he is waved through as he ducks under and gets closer, just in time to see Teresa, her husband, Lance, and the two kids—Sam and Sandy—being escorted into an armored SUV. Serious-looking men and women in full SWAT battle-rattle surround them.

"Hey, Teresa!" Leonard yells, and, by God, with all the confusion, sirens sounding, and steady roar of helicopters overhead, she hears him.

She turns and waves with a free hand, and he waves back, and then that's it.

The family is shoved into the SUV. It backs out of the driveway, escorted by three cruisers, and roars away from the crime scene.

And what a crime scene. Two bodies are on the grass, covered in yellow cloth. Forensics markers are being set up, and measurements and photographs are being taken. There are lots of men and women in civvies, with weapons and handheld radios in their hands, definitely not looking like civilians right now.

A SWAT team guy has his helmet off, and his close-cropped white hair is smeared with sweat. He's carrying an M4 rifle as he strolls over.

"Hey," he says.

"How's it going," Leonard says, taking in the scene. There's an old man with an oxygen tank, sitting in a folding lawn chair, gesturing to the house as two women stand next to him, taking notes.

"About as close a run-in as I've ever seen," the SWAT officer says. "That one"—and he points to the ground—"is dressed up in a trooper's uniform, exactly like yours."

"He's not a trooper," Leonard says. "One of my guys—not in my troop—got shot an hour ago, and his uniform was stolen."

"Jesus," the SWAT man says. "Well, the other one"—he points to the second shape—"was some sort of bodyguard for this family. Then the goddamn O.K. Corral broke out here about a half hour ago, gunfire left and right, if you can believe it in this little town."

"I can believe it," Leonard says. "The family?"

The SWAT man hesitates. "I saw you call out to the mom. You know her?"

"She's my cousin."

"No shit . . . well, so you know, they're all safe."

Leonard looks around at the vehicles, the armed men, the two helicopters hovering overhead.

"Yes," he says. "But for how long?"

CHAPTER 49

THE BIG MAN IS in his office, watching the continuing coverage of that morning's terrorist attack in London, when the Thin Woman comes in without knocking.

She stands in front of his desk and says, "Under control, but by the thinnest of margins. Cover story will be a drug deal gone bad, something like that, with a heroic state police trooper killed in battle. We might have to give their neighbor—a retired N Y P D cop—a clandestine medal to keep his mouth shut about what happened in his neighborhood. I think he'll be happy with that."

The Big Man says, "Wasn't the murdered state trooper at home on his day off?"

"He died for his state and country," the Thin Woman says. "What else do people need to know? How do we stand on Clarkson?"

The Big Man says, "She's on her way back to the states, should be landing at Andrews in about six hours. Then the real work will begin."

The Thin Woman shakes her head. "Hard to believe we've been waiting so long for her."

"We needed an ISIS expert, a cryptography expert, and someone who knows how to work with a child with Asperger's who's memorized reams of encrypted intelligence documents," he points out. "We got Clarkson. Be thankful we do, and that the little girl is still alive."

"What about the Sanderson family, then?" the Thin Woman asks.

"When the job is done, they'll be given compensation, new IDs, and a new life somewhere."

The Thin Woman pauses before turning to leave. "They didn't volunteer for this."

The Big Man gestures up to a television screen, showing smoke billowing out of a Tube station in London. "Who does?"

CHAPTER 50

THREE MONTHS AFTER LEAVING Levittown, Lance Sanderson returns to his family's new home, a little beach house on a remote stretch of Florida's Gulf Coast. He parks the old Chevy pickup in the crushed-shell driveway—imagine him, driving a pickup truck!—and grabs a small leather bag before going around back.

It's a gorgeous day on the Gulf, with sailboats and fishing boats out there, people playing and working, and birds weaving overhead. At least one of those birds is man-made, because one of the promises given when they moved here was that they would be watched, 24/7, by an unmanned drone.

Lance walks out back and his safe family is sitting underneath a striped awning over the rear deck. Since they're near the beach now, Sam is fascinated with seashells, and he's sitting in just a bathing suit, examining his latest haul at a round glass-covered table. One of the first days they had been here, Sam had shown him a bit of metal and plastic and had asked, "Dad, what's this? Is it important?" And Lance had laughed and passed it back. "An old transistor, from an old radio. Not important at all."

But for some reason that hadn't disappointed Sam . . . in fact, it had seemed to cheer him up.

Sam's sister is also dressed in her bathing suit, and since she's near the ocean, now she's fascinated with navies and warships. She's been working her way through the fifteen-volume *History of United States Naval Operations in World War II*, written by the historian Samuel Eliot Morison.

Both of his kids ignore him as he walks onto the deck. Typical . . . and considering what they've all been through, it feels so good that it nearly brings him to tears.

Teresa is working on her laptop, wearing a one-piece black bathing suit and a wide straw hat. Lance gives her a kiss as he sits down next to her. Teresa's lips taste of salt water and tanning lotion, and Lance hopes he might have some time with his love this afternoon while the kids are otherwise engaged.

Teresa says, "How were things at the range?"

"Getting better," he says, putting the leather bag with his licensed Glock pistol on the deck. Even with their movements tracked by a drone, he will never, ever solely depend on anyone else to protect his family. "I managed to get more and more of my shots dead center. How are the kids?"

She says, "Kids are fine."

"And you?"

"You know, I'm beginning to like writing children's

books, even if it is under a pen name," Teresa says. "You can make things up, and you can't do that writing a guidebook."

Lance stretches his legs out. "Good. Looks like I'm traveling next week. Consulting gig at Air Force Special Operations up at Hurlburt. Telling them what I know about that stretch of Tunisia. And you . . . ?"

Teresa smiles. "And what?"

"Don't be a tease," Lance says. "What did the doctor say?"

Teresa shifts in her chair, revealing a slight swell in her belly. "Three months along for sure, everything's healthy . . . and, hate to spoil the surprise, but the kids are getting a new brother."

Lances leans over, kisses and embraces his wife. Their son and daughter continue to ignore them. "You know what we're going to name him . . ."

"No debate here, hon," she says.

Lance gently strokes his wife's belly and whispers into it, "Little Jason, one of these days, we'll tell you about the hero you were named after . . ."

He chokes up. "Until then, you'll always be safe with us. Forever."

ABOUT THE AUTHORS

JAMES PATTERSON is one of the best-known and biggest-selling writers of all time. His books have sold in excess of 375 million copies worldwide. He is the author of some of the most popular series of the past two decades – the Alex Cross, Women's Murder Club, Detective Michael Bennett and Private novels – and he has written many other number one bestsellers including romance novels and stand-alone thrillers.

James is passionate about encouraging children to read. Inspired by his own son who was a reluctant reader, he also writes a range of books for young readers including the Middle School, I Funny, Treasure Hunters, Dog Diaries and Max Einstein series. James has donated millions in grants to independent bookshops and has been the most borrowed author of adult fiction in UK libraries for the past eleven years in a row. He lives in Florida with his wife and son.

SUSAN DiLALLO is a lyricist, librettist, and humour columnist. A former advertising creative director, she lives in New York City.

MAX DiLALLO is a novelist, playwright, and screenwriter. He lives in Los Angeles.

BRENDAN DuBOIS of New Hampshire is the award-winning author of twenty novels and more than 150 short stories, and his works have appeared in nearly a dozen countries. He is also a *Jeopardy!* game show champion.

Are you a fan of James Patterson's fast-paced, gripping thrillers?

If so, you'll love . . .

TEXAS RANGER

Officer Rory Yates has paid the price for his ambition.
He rose quickly through the ranks of the Texas Ranger
division, but his commitment to the badge cost
him his marriage. And when his ex-wife is brutally
murdered, Rory's life descends into chaos as he
is named a suspect in the case.

To clear his name, his only choice is to find the killer
himself. His job, his pride and his reputation are on
the line. Yates follows the Ranger creed – never to
surrender. That code just might bring him out alive.

Discover this stand-alone thriller with an extract

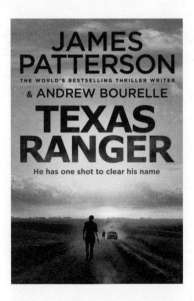

Out now in Arrow paperback

CHAPTER 1

I PUSH MY boot against the gas pedal, and the needle on the speedometer surges past one hundred miles an hour. The Ford's lights are flashing and sirens are howling, but I'm going so fast that I'm on top of the pickup in front of me before the driver even knows I'm there. I make a move to pass him, pulling into the oncoming lane, but there's a semi headed toward me like a freight train. I don't back down. I jam on the gas and yank my F-150 back into my lane, missing the semi and the pickup by inches. Horns blare and brakes screech behind me. I'm sure the two drivers are having heart attacks.

Right now, I can't let myself care. My heart is thumping like a bass drum. But I keep my hands steady.

I grab my radio and call the local dispatcher.

"This is Rory Yates of the Texas Ranger Division," I say. "I need backup."

I give the dispatcher my badge number and the address where I'm headed. She says she has no patrol cars in the vicinity. The closest one is twenty minutes out.

That's bad news because I'll be there in two.

The whole reason I've been working down in McAllen, a border town on the southern tip of Texas, is that I had to rush into another situation with no backup. When it's your word against a dead man's, there's always a lot of controversy and scrutiny—and media attention.

My division chief sent me to a hotbed of drug and human trafficking.

If this situation also goes south without any witnesses to corroborate my story, that won't help my chances of returning to my old post.

But I can't wait. There's a woman who might be dead by the time backup arrives.

Hell, she might be dead before I even get there.

I slow at an approaching intersection and take the turn as fast as the Ford's tires will let me. The rubber squeals against the pavement. As soon as I'm around the corner, my foot is back on the gas.

I check my cell phone again and study the message my informant sent me, the text that set me off on this high-speed race.

Four words: he knows about you.

The text message is from the girlfriend of an ex-con who's been working with Mexican coyotes, moving illegal immigrants over the border. The boyfriend, whose name is Kevin Jones but who goes by Rip, keeps those illegals locked in a storage shed somewhere until their families fork over more money. Sometimes the families can't come up with the money fast enough, and the illegals die of starvation, dehydration, heatstroke, or a combination of all three. Then Rip dumps the bodies in the Rio Grande.

I know all this. But I don't know where the storage building is.

That's where the informant comes in. Her name is Chelsea, and her daughter is in a state home. I promised her that if she helped the Texas Rangers, we'd get her visitation rights restored. And it was the truth. With her past, Chelsea will probably never get custody of her daughter again, but at least there's a good chance she'll get to see the girl again.

Chelsea said she could find out the secret location of Rip's storage building, except now it seems like it's Rip who found out Chelsea's secret.

And though Chelsea is an ex–meth user with terrible taste in men, she's not a bad person. She loves her daughter.

If Chelsea's dead, the blood is on my hands.

When I'm close, I kill the lights and the siren, and I roll into Chelsea's gravel driveway as quietly as I can. She lives in a manufactured home with chipped paint and a yard full of overgrown weeds.

Chelsea's car is parked there, and so is Rip's jacked-up four-by-four.

I am about to step out of the car when my phone buzzes again. I go cold, thinking it's a message from Chelsea. Worst-case scenarios roll through my head. I imagine Rip sending something from Chelsea's phone: a photo of her dead body lying in the mud on the bank of the Rio Grande.

But when I grab my phone, there's no message.

I hear the buzzing again and realize the call is coming from my other phone, my personal cell with a number that only my friends and family have.

There's an incoming call from Anne, my ex-wife.

When she calls, I usually drop whatever I'm doing to answer. True, she's not my wife anymore, but the two of us are still close friends. This time, Anne's going to have to wait.

I step out of the car and take a deep breath, inhaling South Texas air as humid as a greenhouse.

I unbuckle the strap on my hip holster, freeing my SIG Sauer for quick access, and approach the front door.

I hear Chelsea crying inside.

I try to see through the front window, but the house is too dark and the sunlight outside is too bright.

"Come on in, Ranger," a voice calls from inside. "But keep those hands where I can see them, or I'm gonna blow this lying bitch's brains out."

CHAPTER 2

I OPEN THE door and step inside. The room is dark, but I can make out the TV—a muted Dr. Phil talking to a guest—and then a chair, a couch, and the two people sitting in them.

Chelsea is frozen on the couch, plastered up against the armrest, as far away from Rip as she can get while staying seated. Rip is in a recliner, holding a long-barreled shotgun with one muscular arm. The barrel is aimed at Chelsea, dead center of her chest, and at the range of only a few feet, it wouldn't matter if it was loaded with bird shot or double-ought buck: the shot would open her up like a sardine can.

There's blood on Chelsea's lip, and one of her eyes is swelling and beginning to turn blue. She can't seem to stop crying, and she looks at me with pleading, apologetic eyes.

She shouldn't be apologizing to me. I should be apologizing to her.

"Don't do anything stupid," I say to Rip, holding my hands away from my body.

"Chelsea's the one that's gone and done something stupid," Rip says. "She caused this shitstorm of a mess, telling you a bunch of lies about me."

Rip's file said he was six four, but he looks even bigger than that because he's so broad and burly, built like an NFL tight end. He's wearing a wifebeater that has long since faded from white to the color of urine, and his exposed arms are muscular and veiny, painted here and there with amateur jailhouse tattoos. The shotgun he's holding—a single-shot 12-gauge with an extra-long barrel—would probably be hard for a normal person to keep steady with two hands, yet he's doing just fine with only one.

My strategy is simple: keep Rip from doing anything crazy until backup arrives.

There's a pile of paperback books next to Rip's chair, each one torn in half as if it were an envelope full of junk mail.

"Is that where you get your nickname?" I ask, nodding at the stack of torn-in-half books.

Rip tries to hold back a grin. "It's what I do when I get antsy," he says. "I'll rip anything I get my hands on: books, magazines, aluminum siding. I ain't never ripped the arms off a Texas Ranger before, but I bet I could."

I try to imagine how strong someone must be to tear a four-hundred-page book as if it were only a few sheets of paper. I feel a wrench of pity for Chelsea—she's lucky to be conscious.

I gesture toward Chelsea and her battered face. "Is that what you do when you run out of things to rip? Punch women?"

Rip fixes me with cold black eyes.

As earnestly as I can, I say, "How do you think this is going to play out, Rip? My backup will be here any minute. And you've only got one shot in that gun of yours. If you pull the trigger, you'll be dead one second later."

Rip grins, showing a gold cap on one of his teeth.

"If I pull this trigger," he says, "then you won't do anything. You'll be shooting an unarmed man. I know who you are. I heard about what happened in Waco. You don't want to get in any more trouble."

"I could always tell the police that I tried to shoot you before you pulled the trigger," I say, trying to match Rip's defiant grin with my own. "In Waco, there were no witnesses, but we've got one here. Your best bet here is keeping Chelsea alive."

Rip's grin falters.

"I'll ask you again," I say. "How do you see this playing out?"

In the distance, I can just make out the sound of a siren. It is a long way off. Sound carries far on the flat plains of Texas.

"This is what's going to happen," Rip says. "When the cops get here, you're going to tell them this was all a big misunderstanding."

Rip gestures with the gun to Chelsea.

"Chelsea's gonna tell the cops she made up every damn thing she said. She would do anything to get her daughter back, so what she done was lie to y'all. Ain't that right, Chelsea?"

Chelsea bows her head, saying nothing. Her listless hair hangs over her eyes.

"How about I make an alternate proposal?" I say. "You put the gun down. I cuff you and take you in. Then you tell me every damn thing you know about these coyotes you're working for. I'll get the DA to recommend leniency because you've been so cooperative. Don't that sound reasonable?"

Rip looks contemplative. He doesn't seem like he's seriously considering my offer, more like he's thinking about his next move. I don't think I'm going to be able to stall him until the backup gets here. The sirens hardly sound any closer.

"You don't get it, do you?" Rip says.

"Enlighten me."

"There's six illegals in a storage building only I know about," Rip says. "You take me in—or shoot me—and they die. They ain't got no food. No water. There's a tin roof on that building, and sitting in there is like sitting in an oven. You think I'm just bargaining with Chelsea's life? I ain't. It's those other six lives that are depending on what happens here."

I stare at him, saying nothing, thinking. The sirens sound like they're five minutes away. Not close enough.

I need a new tactic.

"Looks like we got ourselves a stalemate," Rip says, grinning with genuine pleasure.

"I don't see it that way."

"Yeah?" Rip says. "How come?"

"Because I'm calling the shots here," I say. "And I'm giving you until the count of three to drop that gun."

'Clinton's insider secrets and Patterson's storytelling genius make this the political thriller of the decade.'

Lee Child

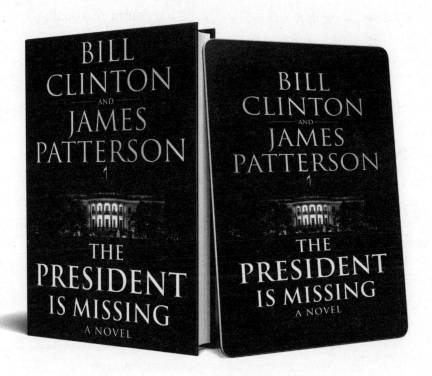

'A bullet train of a thriller. *The Day of the Jackal* for the twenty-first century.'

A.J. Finn author of *The Woman in the Window*

'Relentless in its plotting and honest in its examination of issues that strike close to our hearts.'

Jeffery Deaver

Also by James Patterson

COLLECTIONS

Triple Threat (*with Max DiLallo and Andrew Bourelle*) •
Kill or Be Killed (*with Maxine Paetro, Rees Jones, Shan
Serafin and Emily Raymond*) • The Moores are Missing
(*with Loren D. Estleman, Sam Hawken and Ed Chatterton*) •
The Family Lawyer (*with Robert Rotstein, Christopher
Charles and Rachel Howzell Hall*) • Murder in Paradise
(*with Doug Allyn, Connor Hyde and Duane Swierczynski*)

ALEX CROSS NOVELS

Along Came a Spider • Kiss the Girls • Jack and Jill •
Cat and Mouse • Pop Goes the Weasel • Roses are Red •
Violets are Blue • Four Blind Mice • The Big Bad Wolf •
London Bridges • Mary, Mary • Cross • Double Cross •
Cross Country • Alex Cross's Trial (*with Richard DiLallo*) •
I, Alex Cross • Cross Fire • Kill Alex Cross • Merry
Christmas, Alex Cross • Alex Cross, Run • Cross My
Heart • Hope to Die • Cross Justice • Cross the Line •
The People vs. Alex Cross • Target: Alex Cross

THE WOMEN'S MURDER CLUB SERIES

1st to Die • 2nd Chance (*with Andrew Gross*) • 3rd Degree
(*with Andrew Gross*) • 4th of July (*with Maxine Paetro*) •
The 5th Horseman (*with Maxine Paetro*) • The 6th Target
(*with Maxine Paetro*) • 7th Heaven (*with Maxine Paetro*) •
8th Confession (*with Maxine Paetro*) • 9th Judgement (*with
Maxine Paetro*) • 10th Anniversary (*with Maxine Paetro*) •
11th Hour (*with Maxine Paetro*) • 12th of Never (*with Maxine
Paetro*) • Unlucky 13 (*with Maxine Paetro*) • 14th Deadly Sin
(*with Maxine Paetro*) • 15th Affair (*with Maxine Paetro*) •
16th Seduction (*with Maxine Paetro*) • 17th Suspect
(*with Maxine Paetro*)

STAND-ALONE THRILLERS

The Thomas Berryman Number • Hide and Seek • Black Market • The Midnight Club • Sail (*with Howard Roughan*) • Swimsuit (*with Maxine Paetro*) • Don't Blink (*with Howard Roughan*) • Postcard Killers (*with Liza Marklund*) • Toys (*with Neil McMahon*) • Now You See Her (*with Michael Ledwidge*) • Kill Me If You Can (*with Marshall Karp*) • Guilty Wives (*with David Ellis*) • Zoo (*with Michael Ledwidge*) • Second Honeymoon (*with Howard Roughan*) • Mistress (*with David Ellis*) • Invisible (*with David Ellis*) • Truth or Die (*with Howard Roughan*) • Murder House (*with David Ellis*) • Woman of God (*with Maxine Paetro*) • Humans, Bow Down (*with Emily Raymond*) • The Black Book (*with David Ellis*) • Murder Games (*with Howard Roughan*) • The Store (*with Richard DiLallo*) • The President is Missing (*with Bill Clinton*) • Revenge (*with Andrew Holmes*) • Juror No. 3 (*with Nancy Allen*) • The First Lady (*with Brendan DuBois*)

DETECTIVE MICHAEL BENNETT SERIES

Step on a Crack (*with Michael Ledwidge*) • Run for Your Life (*with Michael Ledwidge*) • Worst Case (*with Michael Ledwidge*) • Tick Tock (*with Michael Ledwidge*) • I, Michael Bennett (*with Michael Ledwidge*) • Gone (*with Michael Ledwidge*) • Burn (*with Michael Ledwidge*) • Alert (*with Michael Ledwidge*) • Bullseye (*with Michael Ledwidge*) • Haunted (*with James O. Born*) • Ambush (*with James O. Born*)

PRIVATE NOVELS

Private (*with Maxine Paetro*) • Private London (*with Mark Pearson*) • Private Games (*with Mark Sullivan*) • Private: No. 1 Suspect (*with Maxine Paetro*) • Private Berlin (*with Mark Sullivan*) • Private Down Under (*with Michael White*) • Private L.A. (*with Mark Sullivan*) • Private India (*with Ashwin Sanghi*) • Private Vegas (*with Maxine Paetro*) • Private Sydney (*with Kathryn Fox*) • Private Paris (*with Mark Sullivan*) • The Games (*with Mark Sullivan*) • Private Delhi (*with Ashwin Sanghi*) • Private Princess (*with Rees Jones*)

NYPD RED SERIES

NYPD Red (*with Marshall Karp*) • NYPD Red 2 (*with Marshall Karp*) • NYPD Red 3 (*with Marshall Karp*) • NYPD Red 4 (*with Marshall Karp*) • NYPD Red 5 (*with Marshall Karp*)

DETECTIVE HARRIET BLUE SERIES

Never Never (*with Candice Fox*) • Fifty Fifty (*with Candice Fox*) •
Liar Liar (*with Candice Fox*)

NON-FICTION

Torn Apart (*with Hal and Cory Friedman*) • The Murder of
King Tut (*with Martin Dugard*) • All-American Murder (*with
Alex Abramovich and Mike Harvkey*)

MURDER IS FOREVER TRUE CRIME

Murder, Interrupted (*with Alex Abramovich and Christopher Charles*) •
Home Sweet Murder (*with Andrew Bourelle and Scott Slaven*) •
Murder Beyond the Grave (*with Andrew Bourelle and
Christopher Charles*)

For more information about James Patterson's novels, visit
www.jamespatterson.co.uk